SEMINARY SKETCHES

SEMINARY SKETCHES

by N. G. Pomyalovsky

TRANSLATED, WITH AN INTRODUCTION
AND NOTES, BY ALFRED KUHN

CORNELL UNIVERSITY PRESS
ITHACA AND LONDON

LIBRARY
University of Texas
At San Antonio

Cornell University Press gratefully acknowledges a grant from the Andrew F. Mellon Foundation that aided in bringing this book to publication.

First published 1973 by Cornell University Press.
Published in the United Kingdom by Cornell University Press Ltd., 2-4 Brook Street, London W1Y 1AA.

International Standard Book Number 0-8014-0765-6
Library of Congress Catalog Card Number 72-12284

Printed in the United States of America by Vail-Ballou Press, Inc.

Librarians: Library of Congress cataloging information appears on the last page of the book.

Contents

Preface

The English title of Pomyalovsky's *Seminary Sketches* (*Očerki bursy*) should not mislead Western readers into thinking that he is describing a genuine seminary. In the West, young men begin training for the priesthood after high school or college, but in nineteenth-century Russia boys began preparing for the priesthood in grade school. *Bursa,* the noun I translate as seminary, originally designated the student dormitory at ecclesiastical boarding schools on the primary and secondary level, but with time it became synonymous with the schools themselves, hence I translate it as seminary. Pomyalovsky's seminarians are living at an elementary boarding school operated by the Church for boys from the lower classes and particularly for sons of clergymen. After eight years of elementary education in such a boarding school, students could enter a seminary in the strict sense of the word, the religious equivalent of the secular gymnasium, and from there they could continue to the highest level of the Church's educational system, the theological academy. Although he had planned to do so, Pomyalovsky never takes his seminarians as far as a genuine seminary in the Western sense of the term.

In nineteenth-century Russia, elementary education normally lasted eight years. The first four years, divided into a lower and upper form, were spent in what was called a parish school since it was usually connected to a parish church in a small village. The second four years, also divided into a lower and upper form, were spent in a district school, so called because of its location in a provincial center. In larger towns and cities, parish and district schools were frequently located in the same building, as they are in *Seminary Sketches*. The first three sketches are set in the upper form of the district school, which I translate as the fourth form; it is equivalent to our seventh or eighth grade. The fourth sketch is set in the upper form of the parish school, which I call the second form, and in the lower form of the district school, which I call the third form; these forms are equivalent to fourth and fifth grade. The last sketch describes the second and fourth forms. Each form had its own separate classroom, but all the students lived together in the same dormitory and played together in the courtyard, hence the mixing of little boys and grown men in the sketches.

For this translation I used the text found in N. G. Pomyalovsky, *Polnoe sobranie sočinenij* (Moscow, 1935). This edition restores passages originally deleted by the censor. The most important of these are inclosed in brackets in the text. Pomyalovsky's own footnotes are indicated by asterisks and are placed at the bottom of the page. My explanatory notes can be found at the back of the book; they are numbered consecutively for each sketch.

I am very grateful to several individuals who have helped me at various stages in the preparation of this translation. Robert Hunter made a number of improvements, stylistic and linguistic, in one of the early drafts. Alexander Golubov's thorough knowledge of the Russian language and of the Orthodox Church is reflected throughout the text and notes. Although the size of my debt to Antonia Glasse cannot be reduced by a brief acknowledgment, her unusually conscientious examination of the text, a tedious job at best, saved me from many errors. The staff of Cornell University Press could not have been more helpful or considerate in preparing this manuscript for publication. It goes without saying that I am the only person responsible for whatever errors or shortcomings still remain.

ALFRED KUHN

Rochester, New York

Introduction

Nikolay Pomyalovsky was the most gifted of several writers in the 1860s and 1870s who are usually called "plebeian novelists" in order to distinguish them from gentry writers like Turgenev and Tolstoy. These men—Kushchevsky, Levitov, Reshetnikov, Nikolay Uspensky, Sleptsov—led the most cheerless lives imaginable. Except for Kushchevsky and Sleptsov, they were born into families of rural clergymen and educated in schools like the one described by Pomyalovsky in *Seminary Sketches*. When they broke with their class and its values by abandoning careers in the Church, they became spiritually and emotionally unstrung. Without the security of a traditional role in society and with little to put in its place except writing and radical politics, they succumbed, one after another, to poverty, disease, despair, alcohol, and premature death. They described, for the most part, people at the very bottom of the social ladder: peasants, workers, tramps, seminarians. Their somber, unsentimental realism, marked by a rough colloquial style and a ruthless honesty, reflected the heightened social awareness and sense of public responsibility that animated many Russian writers in the wake of the Great Reforms of the 1860s. When the social relevance of their writings faded, so did their reputations. By the end of the century they were mostly forgotten, only to be revived by the Soviets, who use their lurid accounts of past horrors as grist for propaganda mills.

These writers are nearly unknown in the West. When we think of Russian literature, we think of its greatest writers. If a writer does not measure up to their high standards, we leave his books untranslated and unread. This situation is unfortunate, particularly in the case of Pomyalovsky, who was a writer of undeniable accomplishment and originality. Turgenev and Tolstoy portray a sophisticated, upper-class milieu where the emphasis is on fine feelings and profound thought. Gogol and Dostoevsky explore the fantastic and perverse dimensions of everyday reality, and their characters, even those or humble background, live in an atmosphere of the abnormal and the extraordinary. Pomyalovsky takes his readers into a world altogether different from Turgenev's or Dostoevsky's, into the dismal, dreary lives of ordinary people in the lower and middle classes. Perhaps because he was untouched by Western culture, he did not feel compelled to defend or idealize the Russian soul, and his writing allows us to make the refreshing discovery that not all Russians were obsessed with the timeless mysteries of life and death. He had a tough, independent mind, a thorough knowledge of the seamy sides of Russian life, and plenty of talent—a rare combination among Russian writers of the last century. All in all, he was a writer of uncommon promise, one of those few men who, as Dmitry Mirsky remarked several decades ago, "had he been granted a longer life, might have turned the course of Russian civilization into more creative and less Chekhovian ways." Besides being unfair to Chekhov (but not to his characters), Mirsky probably overrates Pomyalovsky's potential influence.

Still, he reminds us that Russia produced many writers like Pomyalovsky who deserve our attention even though they do not stand in the very first rank.

Pomyalovsky was born on April 11, 1835. His father was a deacon in the cemetery church in Malaya Okhta, a village on the bank of the Neva River across from St. Petersburg. The third of eight children, he had a happy and relatively secure childhood. The family would gather in the evening to read the lives of the saints. During the day Pomyalovsky would romp through the countryside around Malaya Okhta, which, despite its proximity to the capital, differed little from a primitive provincial backwater. These early years also had a gloomier side: the funerals, burials, and wakes presided over by his father. Here, perhaps, we can see the origin of what Pomyalovsky was later to call his "cemetery" outlook on life. It was expected and inevitable that he would follow in his father's footsteps. In 1843 he entered the parish school located in the Alexander Nevsky monastery in St. Petersburg where, as Blagoveshchensky, his first biographer, put it, "he stepped into a rut from which he tried to escape for the rest of his life."

A religious education meant something quite different in Russia from what it meant in the West. Boys went to ecclesiastical schools not out of a religious vocation, but because they had no alternative. Sons of clergymen were not allowed to attend secular schools, and boys from other walks of life usually were not allowed to study in seminaries. When a young man completed his studies for the priesthood, which did not happen often, he had to marry before being ordained in the "white clergy," the parish priests, as opposed to the "black clergy," the celibate monastics, and it was rare for him to marry someone not from a cleric's family. Even if he left school before being ordained, he often had to marry the daughter of a deceased deacon or sexton in order to qualify for her father's vacant position. The Russian clergy was thus a self-perpetuating caste isolated from other social classes, insulated against change by its own hereditary structure, and distinguished by a narrow, oppressively patriarchal outlook on life.

The lower orders of the clergy—deacons, psalmodists, sextons—were the poorest and least educated clerics, little respected and notorious for their drunkenness and despotic family ways. The village priest lived on a slightly higher level. His income derived from a plot of parish land that he was expected to till, and from offerings for religious services. His earnings were barely adequate to support a family, so he often tried to add to his income by engaging in rather dubious business enterprises. His official duties were both civil and ecclesiastical. Besides conducting services, he kept records of vital statistics for the State and was obliged to report periodically on the social and political atmosphere in his area. He played an important role in the life of his village, but not necessarily for spiritual reasons. He knew more than did his peasant parishioners, who came to him for advice about farming, law, medicine, and other matters. Priest, farmer, businessman, bureaucrat, husband, informer—these were some of his functions. Priests in cities and larger towns were usually better off and better educated than their provincial colleagues. Chernyshevsky and Dobrolyubov, the two most influential radical journalists in the 1860s, grew up in a church milieu much more enlightened and comfortable than the one in which Pomyalovsky, a village deacon's son, was raised. Their fathers were prosperous and cultivated men who occupied prominent positions in their communities. They were exceptions, however, and in general the lot of a Russian clergyman was anything but happy. Few would have chosen it freely. A bleak future awaited young Pomyalovsky when he passed through the gates of the Alexander Nevsky monastery to begin his education for the priesthood.

Church schools in Russia were nightmarish places, and the Alexander Nevsky seminary was certainly no exception, even though it was considered a showcase of Russian ecclesiastical education. One can only wonder what other schools were like, for Pomyalovsky's sketches do not exaggerate the horrible conditions in his own school. Students were badly housed, badly clothed, badly fed, and badly taught. Older students delighted in taunting, humiliating, and beating up younger ones, and they did not spare the eight-year-old Pomyalovsky. Teachers were savage disciplinarians, and the smallest transgression resulted in a vicious flogging. According to his own estimate, he was flogged over four hundred times before he was graduated, thus vying with Anthony Trollope for the singular honor of being flogged more times in school than any human being alive. Students lived in constant terror of their classmates and teachers, and this atmosphere left a lasting mark on Pomyalovsky's personality. He withdrew into himself and became sullenly suspicious of everyone. His only comrades were other unfortunate lads who had neither the wit nor the strength to defend themselves. One of his most endearing traits was his sympathy for such downtrodden, helpless outcasts of life. In later years he felt more at ease with beggars, drunks, and prostitutes in Petersburg's slums than he did with his literary acquaintances. But in school he was basically a loner, and he remained so for the rest of his life.

In 1845, Pomyalovsky began the four-year course of the district school, which was also located within the walls of the

Alexander Nevsky monastery. As might be expected, the curriculum was emphatically religious—the Bible, Church history, catechism, the liturgy—but seminarians also studied the three R's, geography, and classical languages. Pomyalovsky was a bright lad, but a wretched student. Since it was a sign of integrity to break the rules and avoid studying, he idled about and misbehaved. Floggings were no deterrent. On the contrary, they provoked a rebellious bitterness and a desire for revenge, but they did not induce Pomyalovsky to study his lessons. When poor grades forced him to repeat two years of the district school, he finally settled down to a satisfactory, if undistinguished, completion of assignments. In 1851 he passed into the Alexander Nevsky seminary, the religious equivalent of a gymnasium, where he spent the next six years.

Although the seminary was located in Petersburg, it might as well have been in Siberia. Students were completely isolated from the city's cultural life, and the academic climate in the seminary was stifling. During class, students smoked, played cards, talked among themselves, or simply went to sleep. The following remark by the seminary inspector illustrates the attitude seminarians faced day after day, year after year: "If you are standing up, and a superior tells you that you are sitting down, you are sitting down and not standing up." Pomyalovsky had the reputation of a dolt and a troublemaker, and teachers left him to himself. Athletic games and drinking occupied most of his free time. He liked to read, but since only textbooks and edifying religious tracts were available, he had to rely upon a haphazard collection of songbooks, dream books, and cheap novels. Introspective, observant, and thoughtful, he also tried his hand at writing.

His most celebrated composition was a short essay demonstrating that animals, too, have souls. This heretical view astounded his classmates. They were certain his essay marked a revolutionary turning-point in the history of philosophy. He also wrote allegories, a play, the beginning of a novel, and short fiction, little of which has survived. When seminary officials authorized a weekly student literary magazine, he became its editor and chief contributor. His first piece of fiction appeared there, a short story about a seminarian who secretly marries his pregnant sweetheart. Pomyalovsky hoped to make the magazine the champion of seminarians throughout Russia, but the school withdrew its support and it soon folded. He was heart-sick. "What will I do with my time?" he asked a friend. "Study hermeneutics or something. No thanks. I'd rather drink." And he went off on a spree. In 1857 he was finally graduated, thirty-sixth in a class of fifty-two, and moved in with his mother in Malaya Okhta.

In nineteenth-century Russia a surprisingly large number of radicals (in varying degrees) and revolutionaries were former seminarians. All the leading radical journalists of the 1860s—Chernyshevsky, Dobrolyubov, Antonovich, Eliseyev—were educated in seminaries, as were many young terrorists during the 1870s and 1880s. There are several reasons why erstwhile seminarians were attracted to the radical cause. Radical propaganda flourished in seminaries. It had the allure of illicitness, and when a seminarian put down his Bible and picked up Herzen's *The Bell* or Belinsky's "Letter to Gogol," he did so with the knowledge of doing something forbidden and even dangerous. In essay after essay Chernyshevsky and Dobrolyubov vigorously attacked the very evils that seminarians experienced every day of their lives, and their violent tirades against the liberal gentry surely warmed many a plebeian heart. Seminarians thus looked upon radical journalists as defenders of their rights and human dignity.

The brutal seminaries also did their part by turning students against the Church and what it defended, the State. When they left school, seminarians took with them a deep hatred for their religious training, and many refused to become priests or to go on to the theological academy. Their education, however, had prepared them for one station in life, and society was stingy with alternatives. The most gifted became journalists and writers, others attended lectures in universities or joined radical groups then proliferating in the larger cities, but many simply wandered about Russia with absolutely no stake in a society that offered them nothing. They had shed their religious faith and deserted their caste, but they still felt a compelling need to believe in something and to belong somewhere. Radical ideology filled the spiritual void in a way that conservative or liberal thought could not, for it promised to rid Russia of the injustice and misery they had witnessed from childhood on. Radical activity was a corporate affair, whether in a university, on an editorial board, or underground, and it thus provided a group where the plebeian outsider could belong and feel at home. Demanding an ascetic devotion not unlike that usually asked of priests, the radical cause gave them a new mission to perform, and the mission gave meaning to their empty, lonely lives. It would be a mistake to say that Pomyalovsky fully subscribed to the revolutionary ideals of Chernyshevsky or Dobrolyubov, but he did sympathize with their passionate support of the underprivileged and with their bitter criticism of social conditions.

For two years after leaving the seminary, Pomyalovsky earned his keep by serving at funerals, singing in choirs, and giving occasional private lessons, but he was not inclined to seek a permanent position in the church. Ashamed of his inferior education, he had no confidence in himself and did not know what to do with his life. When he looked into the future, he saw two possibilities: he would either scale the heights, or he would sink to the bottom. "It is so depressing," he wrote at this time, "not to know who I am, an intelligent man or an utter fool, a deacon or a government clerk, or simply a working man, or more simply, a little great man. . . . Sometimes I think if I were an angel, I could satisfy my longings. Sometimes I think if I were a cat or a rat, I would not strive for anything. And sometimes, leaving higher matters aside, I drown my spiritual emptiness in a glass of vodka." To lend meaning to his life he undertook the education of his younger brother, and for eighteen months he spent as many as six hours a day at this "good work," as he called it. "I've been ruined," he said, "but I won't let my brother be ruined, and I won't let him go to the seminary. I'll tell him everything I've learned and, maybe, I'll make him into a man."

His teaching and an intensive study of pedagogical literature revived an interest in writing. At the end of 1858 he finished "Vukol," a short story about a young boy who is tyrannized by his uncle, and submitted it under a pseudonym to the respected *Journal for Education*. Much to his surprise, the story was published in January, 1859. He also wrote two other stories about children, "Danilushka" and "Rote-learning." "Danilushka" is a warm, autobiographical evocation of childhood happiness, of fun-filled days and peaceful evenings in the family of a provincial sexton. It ends, however, on an ominous note, with Danilushka leaving home to enter the seminary. "Rote-learning" describes Pomyalovsky's early experiences in the seminary. Dissatisfied with the story but needing the money, he allowed it to be published in the *Journal for Education* in 1860. None of these pieces show Pomyalovsky at his best, but the subtle portrait of his father in "Danilushka" reveals a fine understanding of how certain patriarchal prejudices turned a gentle parent into a moody and confused disciplinarian.

In the spring of 1859, at the urgings of relatives and friends, he began attending lectures at St. Petersburg University. Restrictions besetting secular higher education had been removed shortly after Alexander II came to the throne in 1855, with the result that increasing numbers of young men from plebeian backgrounds began making their way into the universities, where they tried to forge new lives for themselves. A spirit of freedom was pervasive, and St. Petersburg University in particular became the scene of much unrest. Students met there to discuss the latest radical theories and to demonstrate their opposition to the ways of the past. For Pomyalovsky, the contrast with the seminary was overwhelming, and it precipitated a profound and prolonged spiritual crisis. The writings of Dobrolyubov and Chernyshevsky had weakened the deep religiosity of his youth, but now he went without food or sleep for days at a time, elated and frightened by what he saw at the university. "Is it possible," he asked himself, "that all I have studied and racked my brains over, that all this is nonsense? Until now I did not know this. Must I start over again and begin learning the alphabet?" As his close friend Nikolay Blagoveshchensky indicated, it was not easy to abandon old values and begin anew: "Others go through this intellectual transformation with ease, but it is a painful struggle for a seminarian who has absorbed the old philosophical concepts into his flesh and blood, all the more so since he has nothing to put in the place of his shaken beliefs. And what about the awareness of a youth lost? And regret for years pointlessly wasted? . . . Oh, this is a painful affair! But Pomyalovsky looked straight into his soul and mercilessly tore out his former ideas one by one. And what daring, terrifying experiments he endured to test himself and make certain that his *past* had lost its power." The struggle lasted more than a year. When it ended, Pomyalovsky turned his energies to his three favorite activities: teaching, writing, and drinking.

His spiritual crisis occurred at the height of the vibrant, optimistic mood that swept the country during the early years of Alexander's reign. The promise of reforms and the possibility of contributing to them gave all but diehard reactionaries a new sense of vitality and social awareness. And so, in November 1860, Pomyalovsky began teaching at the largest of St. Petersburg's Sunday schools. These schools, staffed by well-meaning volunteers, were designed to spread literacy among the working classes, parents and children alike. He took a special interest in the slower, less gifted students, devising original and effective ways of teaching them to read and write. He was carried away by great expectations of unifying all Sunday schools under a common administration, of launching a journal dealing with their problems, of publishing a series of books aimed at the lower classes, a kind of folk library of useful knowledge. His dreams came to nothing, and he turned to the bottle. On one occasion he drank up money belonging to the school, and only a friend's loan rescued him from disgrace and possible imprisonment.

In February, 1861, he published his first novel, *Bourgeois Happiness*. It appeared in *The Contemporary*, Russia's most distinguished literary review and an outspoken advocate of radical beliefs. He made friends with its editor, Nikolay Nekrasov, and with its guiding spirit, Nikolay Chernyshevsky. Success led to a round of parties, delirium tremens, and a month in the hospital. While recuperating, he began a second novel, *Molotov*, which Nekrasov published in the fall of 1861. This novel secured his reputation and opened the door to the literary world of St. Petersburg. He became very busy, frequenting salons, haggling with various editors, giving public readings, and taking part in a radical literary group known as The Chess Club. He met almost everyone who mattered, including Turgenev and Dostoevsky, and he naively expected that he was joining a close-knit, harmonious family of writers and intellectuals. He hoped to publish an exhaustive description of St. Petersburg in which each writer would contribute a piece based on his special knowledge. Nothing came of it. He joined a cooperative journal run by writers themselves. It folded after one issue. Petty ambitions, backbiting, and vicious polemics quickly scattered his illusions about solidarity and fellowship. Like many plebeians who came to prominence in the 1860s, Pomyalovsky detected, or thought he did, a snobbish condescension on the part of the old-guard, gentry writers. He reacted by hitting the bottle and intentionally embarrassing respectable friends with his drunken antics. He broke the windows in the home of a reactionary editor he detested. When Dostoevsky invited him to a supper party, Pomyalovsky downed glass after glass of vodka, only to pass out on the floor just as supper was served. At the funeral of a noted publisher, Ivan Panaev, he walked up to the altar, grabbed a candle, and let its wax drip down the priest's robes in full view of everyone in church. "I'm sick and tired of tidied-up humanity," he said, "I want to know life in all its aspects, I want to see the ulcers of our society, and our downtrodden folk who are worn out with hunger and whom no one even looks at." He began dropping out of sight for weeks at a time, living among the beggars, prostitutes, and criminals of the Petersburg slums. Not infrequently his binges ended in a jail cell or on a hospital bed.

In *Bourgeois Happiness*, Pomyalovsky intended to show "a

plebeian's relationship to the gentry," and it is, in fact, one of the first Russian novels with a plebeian hero. Yegor Molotov, a carpenter's son with a university degree, is employed as a secretary to a prosperous, liberal landowner named Obrosimov. Molotov feels he is part of the family, although his actual position is that of an errand boy. When he overhears Obrosimov's wife say he has poor manners, dresses incorrectly, and eats too much of their food, he realizes he has been duped by these "dirty little aristocrats." He quits his job and goes into government service.

The romance between Molotov and a pretty neighbor named Elena is right out of Turgenev. Unfortunately, Pomyalovsky did not write as well, and his imitation of Turgenev's lyrical prose is flat and colorless. The counterfeit quality of the writing is particularly evident when the 25-year-old Pomyalovsky, copying Turgenev's melancholy asides, refers to himself as an old man with an aged heart. On the other hand, Molotov is an interesting variation of Turgenev's stock-in-trade: a weak male incapable of loving a strong female. Molotov is not weak, only passive and shy. He likes Elena, but he does not love her. It is as simple and commonplace as that. Similarly, Elena is not an exalted heroine ready to sacrifice everything for love. Molotov's rejection is a painful disappointment for her but not, as it is for Turgenev's heroines, the end of the world.

Gorky's remark that Pomyalovsky created Chekhovian types before Chekhov contains a useful, if partial, truth about *Bourgeois Happiness*. As Chekhov was to do later in the century, Pomyalovsky focused on the quiet suffering of ordinary human beings who live out their lives without realizing their potential for satisfying work and personal happiness. Lonely and bored, Elena wants to escape from a vulgar provincial world, but her vague longings for something different remain just that. Molotov, too, suffers from the disharmony between his hopes for happiness and the realities of his life. His origins separate him from the gentry, his education isolates him from his own class, and his idealism, a consequence of his education, makes government service seem unrewarding and pointless. There is no happiness here, Pomyalovsky concludes, because happiness is always out of reach of people like Elena and Molotov.

Molotov can be considered a sequel to *Bourgeois Happiness*. Yegor Molotov is now a 32-year-old archivist in an unspecified government department. He is a close friend of the Dorogov family and, it turns out, in love with their daughter, Nadya. Her father, a government functionary and head of a clan of civil servants, wants Nadya to marry a middle-aged general in order to ensure the clan's continued prosperity. With the help of Molotov's friend, a painter named Cherevanin, Nadya manages to resist her father's threats and attempts at intimidation. After a very unpleasant interlude the general decides to withdraw his offer, and Nadya's father gives her permission to marry Molotov. This anti-climactic, apparently happy ending contains the central truth of Pomyalovsky's vision: life is dreary rather than tragic, and is filled with "absurd suffering and unnecessary trouble."

The plot is largely a pretext to present various attitudes toward life. Cherevanin, the Bohemian artist, is a particularly interesting figure. Honest thought, he explains to Molotov, has led him to the morose, "cemetery" realization that life is meaningless and absurd. Although sensitive to social injustice and aware of contemporary issues, he does not believe that human beings are capable of changing the world for the better. So he retires from society and spends his time drinking and painting. One might be tempted to see Cherevanin as the victim of romantic ennui and, indeed, Molotov calls his attitude a "homebred Byronism." But actually Cherevanin is a desperately honest individual, much like Pomyalovsky himself, whose passionate indifference to life results from a painful sense of frustration and helplessness.

The corrosive effects of age and experience have also left their mark on Molotov. His goal is "bourgeois happiness," that is, financial security, which will give him independence and personal comfort, his reward for years of hard work. He is totally indifferent to everything outside his own private world. His love for Nadya is stripped of romantic decoration: she is the companion who will share the fruits of his labor and put an end to his loneliness. Molotov insists that he and Nadya are not made for greatness, they are "simple people, part of the crowd." Pomyalovsky is careful to point out the redeeming features of Molotov's attitude. Given his ordinary talents and plebeian birth, he has no choice but make the best of what government service has to offer. In its sympathetic portrait of self-indulgence and careerism, Pomyalovsky's portrait of Molotov is unique in Russian literature.

Ever since his school days he had wanted to describe his experiences in the seminary. He revived this idea early in 1862 and wrote "A Winter Evening in the Seminary." It was published in Dostoevsky's journal, *Time*, and its success caused Pomyalovsky to continue his sketches. With this idea in mind, he withdrew to Malaya Okhta for the summer. It was childhood revisited, paradise regained. He stopped drinking. When he was not writing, he relaxed by boating and fishing. The interlude restored his strength and his confidence. He completed a second sketch, which Dostoevsky also published, and began a novel called *Brother and Sister*. Then a series of disappointments brought this peaceful, productive idyll to an end. The censor had mutilated his first sketch. Then the government closed down the Sunday schools. *The Contemporary*, which had been paying him a regular stipend, received a temporary suspension. Chernyshevsky, whom Pomyalovsky credited with teaching him how to think, was arrested and imprisoned. These events were too much to bear. He became listless, bitter, morose. "Damn you," he cried out against the powers of darkness around him, "how I hate you. You have poisoned my life, you have shattered my best hopes." In the fall he went back to Petersburg and began drinking. His depressions became more acute, and his personality changed. "Earlier I drank vodka," he wrote in a letter in 1862, "now I devour it. I used to reject religion, now I blaspheme. I could not stand despotism, and now I am a despot myself. I used to talk, now I roar. Finally, I thought of killing myself." He did make several attempts at suicide, and spent most of the winter of 1862–1863 in the hospital, where he somehow managed to complete his third seminary sketch. When spring came, he made one last effort to break the habit that was robbing him of his health and, he thought, of his mind.

Intense feelings of guilt and inferiority (intellectual as well as social) together with a low tolerance for frustration, made Pomyalovsky particularly vulnerable to alcoholism. Feelings of guilt, or sinfulness, were connected with his very first drinking experience. "I was drunk for the first time," he wrote to a friend in 1862, "when I was seven. From then on until I finished my education my passion for vodka developed crescendo and diminuendo. . . . Indeed, it began with a sin (in the catechismal sense) that I was forcibly made to commit. . . . My conscience tormented me, and I agonized over losing the Kingdom of God. Having had a taste of wine, I felt my mood change, and from then on I began tasting it more and more frequently." What Pomyalovsky called the seminary's "Orthodox-punitive spirit" intensified his feelings of guilt and his dependence on alcohol. After he left the seminary, his next period of heavy drinking coincided with his painful religious crisis of 1859–1860. Breaking with his class and his religion may have had a liberating effect, but it left emotional and spiritual wounds that never healed. His hallucinations were invariably visions of judgment and retribution: his grandfather reading a book containing all his sins; fellow drunks screaming out his failings; priests forcing him to do penance; devils dragging him off to hell. These are not the nightmares of a man at one with his conscience.

Drunkenness was also his way of rebelling against the seminary's repressive routine and later against the proprieties of gentry society. It was the only way he could express the rage he felt toward his school and toward upper-class society, which he once called "the seminary all over again." When Pomyalovsky describes the dual nature of the seminarian personality in his sketches—outwardly acquiescent and passive but inwardly hostile and aggressive—he is also describing the passive-aggressive duality found in many alcoholics. His teachers drilled into his head that he was a worthless dolt, and a sense of inferiority and inadequacy tormented him for the rest of his life. He had a strong need to be loved, and he did manage to stop drinking while courting a young girl in 1860. The romance ended, however, and he went off on a lengthy binge. As he put it, "only love could have saved me," and it didn't. Like most chronic alcoholics, whenever his dreams fell apart he turned to the bottle and his drinking pals. Psychologists generally agree that heavy drinking can mask suicidal tendencies by providing a lesser kind of self-destruction. Significantly, it was during his struggle to stop drinking that he first thought of killing himself. Unsure of his identity and role in life, tormented by feelings of guilt and inferiority, lonely and unhappy, Pomyalovsky had good reason to forget himself and his troubles in drink.

Even though he never completed the novel, *Brother and Sister* convincingly testifies to his artistic skill and intellectual independence. What remains is a series of sketches linked together by the explanatory comments of his friend and literary executor, Blagovshchensky. Potesin, the hero of the unfinished novel, passes through every sector of Petersburg society, beginning with the city's aristocratic salons and ending in its slums. During his descent down the social scale, he becomes increasingly bitter, and eventually dies of tuberculosis, regretting that he did not go through life as a scoundrel. Despite the novel's Dostoevskian scope and social thematics, Pomyalovsky's attitude toward his material was his own and was certainly at odds with the radical view of literature as social criticism. Believing that "no one was guilty" for the evils of contemporary society, he did not set out to flail injustice. Instead, he wanted to examine the interplay of environment (or fate) and personality, and to describe the psychological effects of debauchery, poverty, and ignorance. He did not believe that suffering ennobled human beings, but that it led to the creation of vicious, desperate persons who sacrificed whatever dignity they still possessed in order to survive.

The last months of Pomyalovsky's life could not have been more pathetic. He felt that he was done for. Most of his friends deserted him, and he pleaded with the few that remained to keep him from going mad with drink. In the summer of 1863 he moved with his brother and a couple of medical students to the country, where at first everything went well. Pomyalovsky stayed away from vodka, wrote the fourth seminary sketch, began the fifth, and completed "River Folk," a lusty if ambivalent celebration of Malaya Okhta. But trivial misunderstandings broke up the company, and he went off on a binge that almost killed him. Recovery seemed to transform him: "I'll begin a new life, and the past can go to hell." A few days later he noticed a sore on his leg. Home remedies proved useless, and the pain grew worse. Finally, against his will, he was taken to a hospital. Doctors opened the sore and found gangrene. On October 5, 1863, at the age of twenty-eight, Nikolay Pomyalovsky died. Four days later he was buried beside the cemetery church in his native village.

Shortly after Pomyalovsky's death Chernyshevsky declared, in an excess of admiration, that he had been "the best of contemporary prose writers . . . a man of Gogolian and Lermontovian power." Although it overshoots the mark, this estimate is typical of the respectful attention Pomyalovsky has received in the hundred years following his death. Since Russian criticism in the last century was notorious for its divisive polemics, it is a testimony to his talent that critics of all political and literary persuasions admired his writing. They stressed, for the most part, the originality of his language, the freshness of his themes, and the accuracy of his descriptions. Dissenting voices remarked on the coldness of his supposedly photographic realism. In the beginning of this century the critical consensus held that he was a talented writer whose full promise was never realized, a writer, as one critic said, of possibilities. He was frequently mentioned as a precursor of Gorky, who, in acknowledging his debt to Pomyalovsky's "stern realism," did much to stimulate a scholarly if not popular interest in his work. Soviet critics portray him as a casualty of Czarist despotism while praising his pictures of misery at the bottom of pre-revolutionary society. Today Pomyalovsky is regarded as the foremost plebeian novelist.

Of all of his works, *Seminary Sketches* is the most impressive. For one thing, he avoided the romantic idealizations of seminary life that are found in earlier writers such as Narezhny and Gogol. For another, as Pomyalovsky tells us in *Molotov*, he knew that the lower classes led lives that were totally different from the way of life that was depicted, say, in Turgenev's novels: "In those books people have different habits, different ideas; for the most part they live without working, without worrying about their daily bread. Everyone is a landowner, the hero is a landowner, the writer is a landowner. They have different desires, different manners, the milieu is entirely different. They do not suffer or enjoy themselves as we do, they do not believe or disbelieve as we do. In our lives there are no duels, girls do not go to balls or parties, men do not want to change the world, and they do not suffer from failing to do so." In *Seminary Sketches* Pomyalovsky set out to write something distinct, in style and subject, from the popular fiction of his day that was set in drawing rooms and manor houses of the gentry, and to portray in unsettling detail a barbaric world known to no one except other seminarians.

As its title indicates, *Seminary Sketches* belongs to a popular nineteenth-century genre. Balzac and Dickens wrote brilliant sketches of city life, and during the 1840s Russian writers such as Nekrasov and Grigorovich attempted to imitate their character essays and urban scenes. Whatever the documentary accuracy of these "physiological sketches," as they were called at the time, they had few literary merits. In the

1850s, however, Turgenev's *A Sportsman's Notes* and Salty-kov-Shchedrin's *Provincial Sketches* raised the sketch to the level of genuine art. By the 1860s the genre had all but disappeared, except with plebeian writers who were drawn to it because they wanted to underscore the actuality of the scenes described, and they also wanted to avoid subjects and genres favored by the literary establishment. There is nothing new, then, about Pomyalovsky's genre, but he did use it in original ways.

Pomyalovsky's basic innovation is the creative control he exercises over his material. In the usual sketch the author is subordinate to his subject. He walks through a village, for example, and then records what he sees and hears. The result is a wholly external description of events observed. The relationship between Pomyalovsky and his material is quite different. The fifteen to twenty years separating him from his early schooldays force him to be more selective and, although he would dislike the word, more imaginative in shaping his memories of things long past. His task it not simply to describe his seminarians from the outside; he must create (or re-create) them as a novelist might, hence his unusual interest in their interior lives, in how they think and feel. He constructs scenes that are psychologically revealing, and the dramatic delineation of character is more the stuff of fiction than of the sketch. And in tying these scenes together, he provides each of his sketches with a stronger narrative framework than is normally found in slice-of-life descriptions. The freedom with which Pomyalovsky organizes his sketches is particularly evident in his frequent journalistic digressions about education, atheism, and other current topics. His controlling presence is most strongly felt, of course, in the introspective, autobiographical fourth sketch. In brief, Pomyalovsky blended elements of fiction, journalism, and autobiography into an original version of a hackneyed genre.

Pomyalovsky's style is equally unconventional. Gone are the pallid imitations of Turgenev in *Bourgeois Happiness*. The syntax is gnarled, the vocabulary unexpected. Schoolboy slang, the argot of thieves, Church Slavonicisms, the peculiar jargon of seminarians, the language of journalism, and coarsely detailed descriptions clash in a verbal cacophony that will jar readers raised on Pushkin or Tolstoy. It would be a mistake, however, to consider his awkward, rough, unruly prose as a sign of incompetence, for his style was a deliberate slap in the face of accepted literary norms. The most derogatory term in Pomyalovsky's critical vocabulary was "novelistic," by which he meant anything that seemed decorative, contrived, artificial, in a word, anything that seemed "literary." He wanted to tell the truth about seminary life, and his bitter insistence on the authenticity of that experience led him to reject the polished style of the literary establishment. Indeed, at times he shows remarkable bad taste, but that is precisely his aim.

His quarrel with contemporary fiction extends beyond questions of style. He objected to the descriptions of childhood found in Tolstoy's *Childhood, Boyhood, and Youth* and Aksakov's *Childhood Years of Bagrov's Grandson*. Each is a sensitive, probing reconstruction of what Tolstoy called "the golden years of childhood happiness." Pomyalovsky knew firsthand that sons of Russian clerics did not grow up, as did Aksakov and Tolstoy, in the leisured luxury of the privileged class. "Everyone is certain," Pomyalovsky wrote, "that childhood is the most innocent, most joyful period of life, but that is a lie. . . . Childhood is the most dangerous period of life, a time when it is easy to be corrupted and to perish forever." He did not mean that Tolstoy, for example, had lied. Pomyalovsky only wished to set the record straight that seminarians grew up under different, much less fortunate circumstances.

The first sketch, "A Winter Evening in the Seminary," takes the reader into a huge, gloomy, crowded classroom and describes what becomes of human beings under a degrading, dehumanizing educational system. Tavlya, the worst of the lot, is a bully, extortionist, and loan shark who tears baby sparrows to pieces. To curry favor with his superiors, Semyonov spies on his classmates. He is not a mean lad, but weak and cowardly. By the end of the evening he is cheated, beaten up, whipped, and almost murdered. Goroblagodatsky, the class leader, is a "goner," that is, a wild, defiant enemy of the system. He is one of the few whose spirit does not break. Pomyalovsky implies that these boys represent three types of possible response to their environment: depravity, servility, or rebellion. Everyone lives in an atmosphere of fear and hatred, of boredom and violence. Seminarians pass the time in brutish or senseless ways. Their games invariably involve physical pain, and one of the high points of the evening is the vicious beating of a class of eight-year-olds by "knights" twice their age.

The second sketch, "Seminary Types," opens with the school's visit to the local bathhouse. This scene need not suffer from comparison with Dostoevsky's famous description of a communal bath in *Notes from the House of the Dead*. Here Pomyalovsky displays his remarkable gift for handling physical action and colorful dialogue. The rest of the sketch moves in two directions. Pomyalovsky celebrates seminarian cunning and audacity. They get the better of everyone, whether robbing a bakery, duping a creditor, stealing a barge, or ambushing a policeman. On the other hand, Pomyalovsky again draws attention to the darker sides of seminary life. We meet Aksyutka, an unusually gifted and intelligent lad who is well on his way to becoming a hardened criminal; Satan, a good-natured buffoon who takes nothing seriously, least of all himself; Mekhalka, a depressing composite of cruelty and self-contempt, who bludgeons dogs and eats wax candles. We are told the story of a young boy who, after slashing his wrist, sells his soul to the devil in a note written in his own blood. For this he is whipped, and he dies. The teachers are no better, and no worse, than their students. Lobov falls asleep in class, but not before he can put into practice his favorite punishment: whipping students "on the clouds," that is, while they are held horizontally off the ground. Dolbezhin and The Old Man both come to class drunk. Dolbezhin considers it his sacred duty to birch every boy in class whether he deserves it or not. The Old Man, in one of the most terrifying scenes in the book, slowly tears the hair from the head of a student who did not prepare his lesson.

"Suitors from the Seminary" is a somewhat static indictment of a practice whereby the Church pretended to help the families of deceased clergymen. A daughter or relative is assigned a vacancy in a parish with the understanding that she marry someone to fill the vacancy. And so, a sexton's widow brings her thirty-year-old daughter to the seminary and bribes the inspector to arrange introductions to three or four seminarians about to be expelled. The daughter eventually selects an empty-headed lummox nicknamed Azinus. Ten years her junior, he agrees to marry only as a means of escaping the seminary and finding a job. Pomyalovsky makes it clear that neither party has a choice. Either they join together, or they starve separately. Although this sketch contains several comic if slightly grotesque moments, such as the mock marriage of two boys, Pomyalovsky never loses sight of his central theme: the precarious and brutalizing existence led by all who enter the seminary.

The fourth sketch, "Runaways and Survivors," is the longest and in many ways the most moving. In the previous sketches Pomyalovsky presented examples of misshapen human beings. Here he looks at the process of psychological and moral disintegration. The center of attention is Carp, a bright, energetic lad who is really young Pomyalovsky. During his first days in school Carp receives the customary abuse from older students. He reacts by abusing others and by retreating into his private fantasies. Soon he comes to trust no one except his "fools," kindly simpletons who are mistreated by everyone. Hypocritically deferential to his superiors, he develops a sense of shame akin to self-hatred. Two circumstances save him from being totally corrupted. Muscles, one of the strongest boys in class, protects him from the worst humiliations reserved for new students, thus allowing Carp to retain some sense of human dignity. And Carp is not infected by the nonsense of his non-studies since he is smart enough not to take them seriously. He has one hope: to spend Easter with his family. When a teacher threatens to detain him if he does not learn to sing correctly, Carp deliberately makes himself ill. He is sent to the infirmary, misses his singing class, and is allowed to go home. There is nothing extraordinary here, nothing tragic in the classical sense, and yet Carp has turned into a sullen, revengeful adolescent who is at peace neither with his classmates nor with himself.

The unfinished fifth sketch concerns a school superintendent nicknamed "Stargazer." To seminarians he was a mysterious figure around whom legends grew concerning his supernatural powers and enormous knowledge. Actually, Stargazer was too squeamish to stand the horrors of seminary life, and too weak-willed to do anything about them, so he rarely appeared in school. Stargazer probably represents, at least for Pomyalovsky, the attitude of educated society toward seminarians: close your eyes and do not become involved. Although the sketch ends with an ambiguous tribute to certain improvements in the treatment and education of seminarians, the reader realizes that these reforms were too late and too few, for they can never undo the damage already done.

When *Seminary Sketches* first appeared, some critics complained that Pomyalovsky presented his seminarians in an unsympathetic light. At first glance, it is true; most of them seem little better than brutes or thugs. Teachers make every class a torture, but their persecution is nothing compared to the jungle warfare between the classmates themselves. Pomyalovsky traces his seminarians' grotesque behavior to three interrelated causes: the wretchedness of their lives, their sense of helplessness, and their instinct for self-preservation. It was one of the insights Pomyalovsky shared with Dostoevsky that human suffering and humiliation find their easiest outlet in the creation of more suffering and humiliation. A seminarian leads a miserable life, so he makes others miserable. He has no control over his fate, so with his fists and wits he tries to exercise control over weaker classmates. The instinct for survival finds expression in stealing, cheating, begging, eating garbage, or marrying a girl who brings a job as her dowry. Pomyalovsky undoubtedly sympathizes with his characters, but, refusing to idealize them, he presents them as being totally unaware of their own ugliness and degradation. And it is precisely this lack of awareness that so saddens and horrifies.

The weak are destroyed, the strong corrupted, but no one escapes with his moral sensibility intact. Pomyalovsky's vision is bleak, but it is also painfully honest. His sketches, rooted as they are in his own wounds, are cries from the heart: screams, as Pomyalovsky said once, from a lost soul in hell.

SEMINARY SKETCHES

N. G. Pomyalovsky

A Winter Evening in the Seminary

FIRST SKETCH

DEDICATED TO N. A. BLAGOVESHCHENSKY [1]

Class is over. Boys are playing.

As in all public institutions, the enormous room accommodating the fourth form of the school lacks any semblance of snugness or hominess. The dirty walls, moldy and mildewed, are covered with dark brown streaks and stains; the corners are caked with ice. Wooden columns prop up the ceiling. It began buckling long ago and without support threatened to cave in. During the winter, sand or sawdust was scattered across the floor: otherwise it would be permanently covered with mud and slush students brought in from the street on their boots. Rows of long, slanting desks and benches begin at the back wall; the teacher's desk is near the front wall between two windows; on the right, there is a blackboard; on the left, a pail of drinking water stands on a stool in the corner near the door; in the opposite corner there is a stove; between the stove and the door is a coat-rack with a whole row of rags hanging from its hooks: overcoats, fur coats, robes and cloaks of every description, all sewn from mama's dressing gown or papa's cassock. Some coats are made of raw fur, others are covered with cloth, wool, or ticking; everything is torn and tattered. And many are the vermin that feed on the seminarian's poorly nourished body in this place of coolness, verdure, and repose.[2] Not much light penetrates the bubbly, greenish panes of the five windows. Stench and soot fill the room. The air is dank, almost rancid, damp and cold.

We are describing the school at a time when *the period of compulsory education* was ending and *the law of overage* beginning to take effect.[3] There was a time, long since passed, when not only very young but even bearded children were forcibly driven from their villages by order of the authorities, more often than not from positions as sextons and sacristans, and sent to seminaries where they were taught writing, reading, arithmetic, and church rubrics. Some were engaged to be married and dreaming sweet dreams of their honeymoons when lightning struck and they were married instead to Pozharsky's grammar, Memorsky's arithmetic, the Psalter, and church singing. At the seminary they were frozen, starved within an inch of their lives, and introduced to *May bugs* (birch rods). In those days even the first form consisted mainly of adults; in the other forms, especially in the seminary proper, it went without saying. If you were well along in years, you were not detained for long: after studying reading and writing for *three* or *four* years, you were released to become a sexton. The younger, more diligent students of thirty or so, and frequently even older, passed on to the *theological course* (the upper form of the seminary). Parents sent their fledglings off to school amidst tears, wails, and laments. These fledglings returned home with a deep hatred for and disgust with their school. But all this happened very long ago.

Times changed. An awareness, if not of the utility of education, then of its inevitability, gradually penetrated society. You had to complete at least four years of schooling to qualify even for the post of village sacristan. Fathers themselves would bring their children to school, desks were quickly occupied,

4

the number of students increased, and finally the point was reached where the school had no more space. Then the famous *law of overage* was devised. Some fathers were still in the habit of sending grown-up sons to school, and frequently they would bring lads as old as sixteen. After two years of study in each of the school's four forms they became overage. This was the reason given in their certificates when they were dispatched *beyond the gates* (expelled). As many as five hundred students were enrolled in the school; each year a hundred or more received certificates; then, to take their place, a new crowd arrived from villages (the majority) and towns; a year later another hundred students were dispatched beyond the gates. Those receiving certificates normally became novices, sextons, church wardens or consistorial scribes, but many simply wandered about the diocese with no definite occupation; they did not know what to do with their certificates, and from time to time there was a terrifying rumor that all those without positions would be conscripted into the army. Now we can understand how the school's enrollment was maintained and why half of the students we meet in this dark, dirty classroom are quite grown up.

A cutting wind whips across the slushy courtyard. No one even thinks of going outside. You can see at a glance more than one hundred students in the enormous classroom. What a variety of personalities, what a mixture of clothes and faces! . . .[4] There are men of twenty-four and boys of twelve. Students have broken up into many small groups; they are playing games, original ones, just as everything is original in the seminary; some students are walking by themselves; others are sleeping, despite the noise, not only on the floor but also above their classmates' heads on desks. The sound of voices moans through the room.

Most of the students in our sketch will bear nicknames the

brotherhood bestowed upon them: Mitakha, Elpakha, Tavlya, Six-eared Chabrya, Polecat, Spitter, Omega, Erra-Koksta, Katka and so forth, but it is impossible to mention Semyonov's; the seminarians gave him a nickname that no censor would pass. It was quite obscene.[5]

Semyonov is a good-looking boy of about sixteen. The son of a town priest, he is well-behaved and neatly dressed; it is immediately apparent that the school had not yet succeeded in completely erasing the influence of his home. Semyonov senses he is a *townie;* the brotherhood [6] despises townies and calls them sissies; they love their mama as well as mama's cookies and rolls, do not know how to fight, and are afraid of being birched, a helpless bunch protected by the administration. The brotherhood considers very few townies exceptions to this rule. Semyonov's face has a strange, enigmatic expression, at once melancholy and cunning; fear of his classmates mingles with concealed hatred. He is bored now, so he wanders from corner to corner, not knowing how to amuse himself. He deliberately tries to remain alone, far from his classmates; but, since the others are all doing something together—playing games, singing songs, talking—he suddenly feels like sharing his leisure with someone. He walks over to some boys playing stones and says meekly:

"Fellows, let me in."

"The goose is no friend to the pig," was the answer.

"Want some of this?" someone muttered, placing a beefy fico with its big, dirty thumbnail right under Semyonov's nose.

"If you don't want it in the neck, get moving!" added a third boy.

Semyonov walked away dejectedly even though his classmates had not made any special impression upon him; it was as if he had grown accustomed to such rude treatment and had learned to live with it.

"Gentlemen, *boilers!*"

"Who for, Tavlya?" several voices responded.

"For Goroblagodatsky."

Semyonov and some other boys went to the table where two overagers were playing stones, Goroblagodatsky, the second strongest student, and Tavlya, the fourth strongest. The faces surrounding the players grinned pleasantly in expectation of an entertaining spectacle.

"Well!" Tavlya said.

Goroblagodatsky placed his hand on the table and spread his fingers. Tavlya placed a small stone in the most awkward way possible on each finger.

"Go ahead!" he said.

Goroblagodatsky flipped the stones in the air and caught only three of five.

"Missed two!" the spectators yelled.

"Pal, it's time to write some letters home," Tavlya added.

Without replying, Goroblagodatsky placed his left hand on the table. Tavlya tossed a stone into the air; during its flight he managed to pinch Goroblagodatsky's hand with terrible force and also to catch the stone.

The crowd roared with laughter.

The game of stones is probably familiar to everyone, but in the school it had original variations; here the loser received different kinds of pinches: cool pinches, warm pinches, hot ones, and boilers. Only the youngest, least experienced boys in the first form played without pinches; now, however, the reader is present at a game with boilers.

Meanwhile, the queen (the most important stone) was flying through the air, and Tavlya's powerful hands were twisting the skin on his opponent's hand and tugging at it with a vengeance. After twenty pinches the hand became very red; after fifty it turned black and blue.

7

"How do you like it?" Tavlya asks, looking him in the eye. His opponent is silent.

"How do you like it?"

Again, no answer.

"Let him have it, let him have it!" the spectators say.

"Start crying and I'll let you go," Tavlya says.

"Watch out, or you'll be the one that's crying!" Goroblagodatsky answers. The husky lad's hand really hurt, but only his grim expression revealed how he felt.

"Well, uncle, does it hurt?"

Tavlya pinched him so hard that Goroblagodatsky involuntarily grated his teeth. Everyone roared with laughter.

"Give up?"

Another strong pinch, and the spectators roared. There was no gloating or malicious mockery in their laughter; students saw only the comic side of everything. Semyonov alone smiled in a rather peculiar way; his pleasure did not resemble the pleasure of his classmates; in fact, he was silently repeating to himself: "Serves him right, serves him right."

The count reached one hundred.

"Oh, the hell with you!" Tavlya finally concluded.

Goroblagodatsky hated Tavlya intensely and had agreed to play with him in hopes of winning so that he could give him something worse than boilers. Both were *second-termers*. Every educational institution has its own traditions. The school's aborigines, book-learning forced upon them, had banded together in a *brotherhood* that was hostile to the administration, and they bequeathed their hatred to subsequent generations. The administration, in turn, was hostile to the brotherhood and, in order to keep them within the bounds of the school manual (a set of rules pertaining to conduct and study), it devised a complete bureaucratic system for the seminary. Knowing that a kingdom divided against itself will not stand, the administration gave certain students power over others with the aim of fomenting discord among them. The bureaucratic posts were: dormitory wardens (chosen from the fourth form), senior guards (chosen from the wardens, they took weekly turns patrolling the whole school), censors (they kept order in the classroom), auditors (they heard recitations in the morning and entered grades in the register, a special book for grades), and, finally, the last and probably most terrible post: the whip (he whipped his classmates for the teacher). All these posts were filled by second-termers. A student who after two years of study remained in the same form for another two years because of laziness and poor grades was called a second-termer. It was only natural that such students got something out of their lessons; consequently, they knew more than other students did; the administration took this into account and its calculations proved correct: second-termers studied diligently in order to stay in power and most of them were at the head of their form since it was not lack of ability but sheer laziness that made them repeat the course. Such was the basis of the school bureaucracy that was supposed to help the administration destroy the brotherhood.

All this produced disgusting results. Second-termers enjoyed the complete trust of the administration; to complain about them was to insult the superintendent and the inspector. They were absolute despots, and nothing so corrupts the spirit of an educational institution as the power of one student over another. Censors, auditors, wardens, guards, and whips were completely free to do anything they pleased. The censor resembled a little king in his kingdom, auditors comprised the court retinue, and second-termers made up the aristocracy. Moreover, second-termers, having studied an extra two years, were growing up and, therefore, physical strength was on their side. Finally, they also were familiar with the rituals and customs of their form, the character of teachers, and ways of getting around them. A newcomer could not take a step without a second-termer's help. By introducing this despotic system the administration thought it would encourage back-biting and informing within the brotherhood. Things turned out quite differently: the school's second-termers either turned into reptiles, repulsive reptiles like Tavlya, or into wild individuals like Goroblagodatsky. They hated each other because each used his power for different ends. The other strong students, Lashezin and Benelyavdov, also hated Tavlya; everyone hated and despised him.

His physical strength and position as a second-term auditor turned Tavlya into an abominable bribe-taker. He extorted money, rolls, portions of meat, paper, and books from his subordinates. In addition, Tavlya was a shylock. The rate of interest in the school, because of its absurd organization, was unconscionable, brazen, and vicious. Such rates have never existed anywhere else, and they never will. It was by no means uncommon—on the contrary, it was the norm—that if you borrowed ten kopecks for a period of one week, you had to pay back fifteen; that is, in the generally accepted lending period of one year the capital would increase twenty-five fold. In this connection it should be noted that if a debtor did not repay his loan on schedule within one week, at the end of the second week he had to pay twenty kopecks instead of fifteen. Such interest rates had been an accepted fact of seminary life from time immemorial. Tavlya was not the only one who skinned his classmates, he was only more conspicuous than most. Someone always needed a loan. Censors and auditors demanded bribes; you'd catch it if you refused, so if a first-termer had no money, he would go to a classmate, a shylock, prepared to pay any interest whatsoever in order to escape a very vicious beating. Since credit was guaranteed by one's fist or by the ever-present possibility of playing a dirty trick on the debtor, only second-termers would risk lending money. It should be noted that townies bore the brunt of providing ready cash. They went home every Sunday and returned with a little money; consequently they were badgered by everyone, even though a townie was considered rich if he received a weekly allowance of five kopecks. Many students had unpaid debts and frequently they would run away. Tavlya's coarse, vile, depraved nature flourished in this despotic environment. He lived like a lord, despising everyone; other students prepared class notes and vocabulary lists for him to study from; he would not even get up for a drink of water; instead, he would yell: "Hey, Katka, I'm thirsty." His charges scratched his heels; he would order someone to take a penknife and scrape his hair in order to clean his filthy head of dandruff which, for some reason, was called flesh; he would force students to tell him fairy tales, invariably scary ones, and if the stories were not scary, Tavlya slugged the narrator; and in what way did Tavlya's charges not cater to his consummate depravity? Despite all this he treated his servants cruelly. "Do you want to eat a grouse," he would say to Katka and then he would begin plucking his subordinate's hair. "That's how mama pats you on the head; wait a second and I'll show you how papa does it"; he then would dig his fingers into a student's *fleece* (hair) and rub as hard as he could from the top of the forehead to the nape of the neck. He would ask a student: "Have you seen Moscow?" and then, pressing his large, sweaty, filthy palms against his charge's ears, he would squeeze his head, lift him off the ground, and say: "Do you see Moscow now? There it is!" He liked to bend his classmates into *runners*, that is, he would make a student lie on his back over a bench, pick up his legs and push them toward his face. It was an inner spiritual compulsion to spit in a classmate's face, to hit him and humiliate him in every possible way. His classmates knew that on one occasion Tavlya had taken some baby sparrows from their nest and, holding them by their skinny legs, had torn the sparrows to pieces. A minority of students only hated him; the majority feared him and hated him, too.

Goroblagodatsky had a strong but wild nature. Repeating the course had an entirely different effect on him than it had on Tavlya. He was positive proof that the administration had miscalculated in allowing some students to lord it over others in hopes of encouraging backbiting and informing within the brotherhood. The despotic system actually worked to the brotherhood's advantage. Second-termers became the custodians of school traditions and, having inherited a hatred for the administration, they used their power to harass the administration. The censor, auditors, and whip all sided with the brotherhood, and the leader of all of them in the class we are describing was Goroblagodatsky. Drunkenness, snufftaking, unexcused absences, fighting, noisiness, and various absurd games were all prohibited by the administration and practiced by the brotherhood. The absurd rote-learning and Spartan punishments embittered students, but no one was more embittered than Goroblagodatsky.

He was a *goner.*

A goner can be recognized by inward and outward marks. He walks with a defiant swagger, the peak of his cap pushed back, his arms folded, his right shoulder forward; his whole figure seems to say: "Do you want a punch in the kisser? Do you think I won't give it to you?" He rarely steps aside for anyone, although he steers clear of school officials just to keep from bowing. Goroblagodatsky would support the most unseemly scheme if it could harm the powers that be, and he pulled off the wildest things. Passionately devoted to the past and its traditions, a goner is the defender of student freedom and liberty; if necessary, he will spare neither his reputation nor his certificate in fighting for this sacred cause. He is the main pillar of the brotherhood.

Seminarians with such heroic qualities were usually called goners. There were, however, different types of goners. Some were called *blessed ones:* these were rather stupid persons who nevertheless adhered to the same principles; others were called *stragglers:* in general, they were not stupid, only lazy and lackadaisical. The goner Goroblagodatsky, however, was a *brain:* he stood first in studies and last in conduct. A brain or straggler harassed the administration in an intelligent way, a blessed one in a stupid way: for example, he would suddenly laugh in a teacher's face and show him the fico; he gets whipped but in a little while he again plays some other stupid, insolent trick.

No goner could equal Goroblagodatsky in harrying the administration. If the steward found his door smeared with some unpalatable gruel (a watery buckwheat porridge), if an unpopular teacher found lice * in his coat, if the inspector's pig had its legs broken or its tail torn off, if the superin-

---

* There was a huge quantity of these insects in the seminary. It is incredible, but true, that one student was almost eaten alive by them: he was a kind of huge nest for parasites; whole swarms could be seen crawling in his uncut, uncombed hair; once when his shirt was removed and taken out into the snow, the snow turned black because of them. In general, the slovenliness of seminarians was shocking: scrofula, fungi, and filth wore away at their bodies.

tendent's cellar was looted, if a row of windows was smashed during the night, you could be sure that Goroblagodatsky had a hand in it, together with blessed ones and stragglers whom he boldly led against the administration. When it became necessary to stage a revolt against the administration, once again the commander was Goroblagodatsky: under his direction goners would stir up recently-whipped and other disaffected students; these in turn would incite the whole form, the meekest and most timid students would begin making a racket and uttering threats, the brotherhood became excited, and there ripened a seminary disturbance known in the local language as a *mutiny*. Protesters knew beforehand they would not win a single concession from the administration: if, for example, they were being fed tainted beef resembling carrion, they knew they would eat the very same beef after the disturbance, but at least they would have vented their anger even if it meant a whipping.

Because he was a goner, Goroblagodatsky often caught it from the administration; in seven years he had been whipped approximately three hundred times, not to mention countless other seminary punishments; be that as it may, we should point out that he was not whipped as often as he deserved: for his different escapades he should have received at least five times the number of punishments he actually received, but he was shifty and cunning. Goners in the seminary devised many ways of duping the administration. Particularly remarkable was a tactic called *going in circles*. A snuffbox, for example, is found on A; A says it belongs to B; B says it belongs to D; D mentions A; A then says it belongs to B, and so forth —this is *going in circles:* try to find out who owns the snuffbox. About thirty students would join a circle and then Solomon himself could not decide who should be whipped.

Students always took advantage of the circle during mutinies. "Why were you yelling during class?" "So-an-so put me up to it." "Why did you put him up to it?" He in turn would name another student, and a run-around began in which the devil himself would break a leg. To dupe the brotherhood was considered a crime, to dupe the administration was considered an achievement and a virtue. It sometimes happened that the wrong student was whipped, but he rarely gave the guilty party away. Students considered a voluntary confession crass and cowardly; on the other hand, a lad who told the biggest and most audacious lies to the authorities, who shamelessly denied his guilt, who skillfully muddled everything, who vowed and swore to God that he was innocent—this lad stood high in the eyes of the seminary community. Goroblagodatsky stood higher than anyone else; long practice in various escapades had made him the most resourceful and skilled of evaders. Others merely refused to admit their guilt, but he, looking the authorities straight in the eye, snarled in his insolent, self-assured way, and at the same time his face expressed such outraged innocence that even an experienced physiognomist and psychologist would have been bewildered. He played the part of innocent victim so well that he actually believed himself innocent and never confessed during a whipping. Despising everything connected with the administration, he did not give a damn about anything: birchings, slaps to the back of the head, going without dinner, kneeling, bowing to the ground, and so forth had absolutely no moral influence on him. Punishments, being only a matter of suffering and screaming, were so meaningless and incurred so little disgrace that Goroblagodatsky, having been publicly whipped before five hundred students in the dining hall, not only did not hesitate to rejoin his classmates immediately after the flogging, he even bragged about it. This utter shamelessness with regard to the administrator's birch rod produced a local saying: "they're not planting turnips, only cleaning the plow." And what more could one ask: the whip, a student who flogged his fellow students, was respected and liked by them because he, too, did his job to their liking: skilled in his craft, he would thrash his classmates soundly, and the birches would whistle through the air when a stout lad lay beneath them. Goroblagodatsky was whipped a lot; on occasion he had tasted as many as one hundred strokes and therefore he could withstand birchings better than his classmates could; hence he looked on all punishments with absolute contempt. They made him kneel on the edge of a slanting desk, they forced· him to bow to the ground two hundred times while wearing two wolfskin coats, they sentenced him to hold a heavy rock in an upraised hand for a half-hour and longer (needless to say, the administration was inventive), they rapped his palms with a ruler, slapped his cheeks, poured salt on his beaten body (believe me, these are facts), and still he bore everything like a Spartan; his expression was ferocious and wild after a punishment, and his soul still full of hatred for the administration. We witnessed Goroblagodatsky's ability to bear physical pain when Tavlya gave him boilers.

Stealing, gossiping, vandalism, and other vile acts were considered vices only when they were not directed at the administration: the brotherhood itself was honest, and this fact places Goroblagodatsky in a new light. He never took a bribe, justly and fairly recorded the grades of his charges, did not bully them, frequently defended weaklings, liked to intervene in arguments, and although he decided them arbitrarily, he was always just; he continually baited shylocks and bride-takers. He was loved and respected by the brotherhood.

We said that Goroblagodatsky intensely hated Tavlya because of the latter's disgusting character, but he played stones
with him anyway: he wanted to win so he could make Tavlya
suffer.

When he stopped pinching, Tavlya proposed craftily:
"Want to try again?"

Tavlya was a very good player and full of confidence.

"Let's go," Goroblagodatsky answered stubbornly.

Once again the stones rattled.

Semyonov watched the players from a distance. Semyonov
was a third type of student created by the seminary administration. Today the brotherhood was to brand him a *squealer*.

The administration realized that its educational system had
not produced the desired result, but instead of abandoning
such practices, they instituted more absurdities. A new bureaucrat appeared, the squealer who secretly informed the administration about everything going on in the brotherhood.
Student hatred for such informers is quite understandable;
indeed, an enormous amount of baseness was required to become a squealer. Capable and industrious students never informed on others, they occupied a prominent place on the
honor role without doing that; secret informants invariably
were ungifted students and sneaky cowards; in return for
their vile services the administration would pass them from
one form to the next as if they were capable students. We
said, however, that the brotherhood itself was honest and
therefore did not respect those students who occupied an un-
deserved place on the honor roll because of bribes to the authorities, family connections, and patronage, to say nothing
of squealing. Moreover, students were absolutely right that
the informer not only communicated what actually happened
within the brotherhood, he also slandered them because a

squealer had to demonstrate his zeal to the administration in every way possible. Even when he told the truth to the inspector or superintendent, he still aroused hatred and bitterness in his form: for example, some boys would decide to go on a spree, or to cut off the tail of the steward's pig, or to sneak off to a friendly washerwoman, or simply to have fun in some other way, and suddenly, instead of having fun, they would be thrashed within an inch of their lives by the inspector who had been alerted in advance. In the majority of cases, it's true, these denunciations did not lead to punishment because of the seminarians' insuperable stubborness: nevertheless, the administration knew how to make effective use of such denunciations. Why would the inspector punish two students differently for the same offense? More often than not the reason was that squealers had denounced the student receiving the more severe punishment. The administration particularly disliked those persons who hated and persecuted informers. All the backbiting received from informers was entered into *the black book*. This book had an enormous influence when the time came to pass a student from one form to the next; at this time many students unexpectedly received so-called *wolf passports:* [7] these were certificates, but they contained a notation about bad conduct; such certificates could be explained only on the basis of the black book.

Even though he was terrified by the idea, Semyonov sensed the brotherhood had guessed he was a squealer. He was fully aware that no one wanted to talk to him, and the chief way of dealing with an informer was silence; an entire form, and sometimes the whole school, conspired not to exchange one word with a squealer unless it was abusive. It was a terrible situation to live week after week among other human beings without hearing one friendly sound, to see repellent contempt and disgust on every face, to be completely convinced that no one would give you any kind of help, that on the contrary, everyone would gladly hurt you. . . . Indeed, within the brotherhood a squealer stood beyond the protection of any law: he was slandered, subjected to punishments, his belongings were stolen and broken, his clothes and books were torn apart, he was beaten and persecuted. To act in any other way towards a squealer was considered *dishonorable*.

Nevertheless, the administration, permanently corrupting dozens of students by turning them into informers, gained nothing: school life continued its absurd development, and the brotherhood did as it pleased.

Watching the players, Semyonov grinned maliciously.

"Boilers!" Goroblagodatsky shouted.

There was something ominous in his voice. Tavlya panicked and momentarily turned pale. A crowd again gathered around the table. Again a stone was flying through the air, but now Tavlya's hand was on the table. He had misjudged his skill: Goroblagodatsky had a run of eight, and Tavlya missed after five.

"It'll last forever," Goroblagodatsky said sullenly.

Tavlya appeared to be frightened. The spectators were not laughing: they saw that the game had taken a serious turn and that Goroblagodatsky was getting his revenge.

The count reached one hundred. Tavlya's hand was swollen from the powerful pinches. He was in terrible pain; finally, he could stand it no longer and pleaded:

"Come on, that's enough!"

"Ask for mercy after two hundred," Goroblagodatsky replied.

"It really hurts!"

"It'll get worse."

At one hundred and seventy Tavlya's hand turned dark blue: the throbbing reached his shoulder.

"That's enough, Vanya. . . . When will it stop?"

Instead of answering, Goroblagodatsky pinched Tavlya's hand with a vengeance.

Tavlya knew that Goroblagodatsky always kept his word; nevertheless, his whole arm hurt so badly that he had to ask:

"Stop it. . . . You've had your fun."

"Another word out of you and I'll give you two hundred more."

Goroblagodatsky gave him a pinch that was worse than a boiler. Tavlya could not take it: tears began running down his cheeks.

The count finally reached two hundred.

"Now say you're sorry!"

Despite his pain, Tavlya was ashamed to say he was sorry.

"Come on, stop it!"

"Why were you grinning a little while ago?"

"I was just joking!"

"So *you* dare to make fun of me, you animal!"

He gave Tavlya a vicious pinch.

"Well, I'm sorry, Vanya. . . ."

It was as though Goroblagodatsky regretted stopping the torture of his hated Tavlya. He mustered all his strength, and the last pinch turned Tavlya's hand black.

"That's all for you. Had enough?" Goroblagodatsky asked.

As soon as Tavlya got free, his fear gave way to rage and anger.

"You scoundrel!" he said. "Leave me alone, you hear? I'll knock your teeth out."

"You?"

"Me."

"Here's my mug, go ahead," Goroblagodatsky said, sticking his head forward.

Enraged, Tavlya lost control of himself and gave his enemy a resounding blow, but the one he received in return was even more powerful.

A fight started.

"Serves him right, serves him right," stirred in Semyonov's soul.

Tavlya was so crazed with anger that despite his mangled arm he was still a match for Goroblagodatsky even though the latter was stronger. Anger so intoxicated Tavlya and so increased his strength that it was difficult to decide who came out the winner. This was one more grudge that Goroblagodatsky would hold against him.

After the fight Goroblagodatsky went to get a drink of water from the pail; Semyonov crossed his path. He slapped Semyonov and continued on his way as if nothing had happened. Semyonov looked angrily at him but did not dare utter a word.

Semyonov paused in the middle of the room, and then he began wandering aimlessly from corner to corner and between rows of desks, stopping here and there.

He watched a game of leapfrog, a game probably familiar to everyone, and therefore we will not describe it. In another place two lads were *breaking cookies*, that is, standing back to back and locking elbows, they took turns lifting each other off the ground; this was done quickly and the two bodies formed one rocking figure. The whip, known as *Supina*, was practicing his craft by the stove; holding some excellent birches in his hand, he waved them about and cracked the ends that were destined to strike a classmate's body. A game of *raps* was going on in the third row. This delicate game consists of one player closing his eyes and bowing his head while others flick their fingers at his head; he must guess who hit him; if he does not guess, he is hit again; if he guesses right, the hitter takes his place. Semyonov watched as one of his classmates received a whole barrage of raps; the latter clutched his head when he got up.

"Serves him right!" Semyonov repeated silently, and he walked toward the fifth row.

One group was playing *three-card monte,* and another was playing *little nose,* a popular card game in which the loser is beaten on the nose with a deck of cards. Semyonov went to the seventh row where he admired six students who were *rambling.* Grabbing hold of a desk, the six rocked back and forth.

In the next row Mitakha was *snapping a dogmatic,* that is, he sang "Glory of all the World" as loud as he could, and kept time by snapping his fingers.[8] Nearby *Nonsense* (a nickname) was playing his *smackers* by running his fingers across his fat lips which, slapping together, were smacking, to use the local expression. A third artist was trying to say as quickly as possible: "pick a peck of pickled peppers," "fresh flesh of fresh dried fish," "six thick thistle sticks."

Semyonov finally made his way to the wall. Omega and Six-eared Chabrya were playing *spits.* Both were trying to see how high they could spit up the wall. The loser received a *massage.* Six-eared Chabrya spit higher.

"Stick it out," he said, waving his outstretched hand in the air.

Omega stuck out his kisser.

"Puff it up!" Chabrya said.

Omega puffed up his cheeks.

"More!"

Omega puffed up his cheeks until he became red.

"Top," Chabrya began, placing his hand on Omega's forehead—"bottom," placing it on his chin—"two sides," placing his hand on one and then on the other cheek—"Puff it up!"

Omega puffed up his cheeks.

"And the whole works!" Six-eared Chabrya shouted triumphantly.

He then grasped Omega's face between his palms so that fat, shiny folds of skin oozed through his fingers, and he shook the well-fed jowls up and down.

Semyonov was bored. He did not know what to do.

"Candy and cookies! Cookies and candy!"

This was Elpakha's voice. He usually hawked candy and cookies, from which he derived a considerable profit since he bought by the pound and sold in small amounts.

Semyonov sidled up to him.

"How much do you want?" Elpakha asked, looking all around; for although the brotherhood had forbidden anyone to talk to Semyonov, merchant greed got the better of Elpakha.

"Five kopecks worth."

"Got cash?"

"Here it is!"

"Hold out your hands."

"Why are you giving me nibbled ones?"

"They're the best kind."

"Give me different ones, Elpakha."

"Candy and cookies," Elpakha shouted, turning aside.

Semyonov examined the candy lying in his palm, not knowing whether to eat it or throw it away; he had just decided to eat it when someone sneaked up from behind, snatched the sweets out of his hand and immediately disappeared. Semyonov glanced angrily at his classmates, but his anger was powerless, and at the same time listlessness replaced his boredom.

"Let's play *buttons*," Polecat said to him.

Semyonov was amazed that a classmate had spoken to him. He looked at Polecat suspiciously.

"Why are your peepers bulging? Don't be afraid."

"You'll trick me!"

"You're stupid. How could you say that?"

"Swear to God?"

"Sure, as Christ is my witness."

"Really, you won't fool me?"

"I swore to God, didn't I? What more do you want?"

"Well, alright," Semyonov answered, overjoyed that a human being had spoken to him, even if this being was only Polecat.

The school had its own currency: buttons from pants, vests, and jackets. The basic unit was a one-hole button; two one-holers equaled a four-holer or a pair, five pairs equaled a pile or a penny, five piles equaled a great pile. The value of buttons was permanently established, and you could always exchange five pairs for a penny. An enormous amount of button currency circulated in the seminary. It was used when students *spun tops* and played *odds-evens*. Some students accumulated a hundred or more great piles; you could recognize them because they always had a hand in their pocket, fingering their button wealth. The use of button money created a special kind of entrepreneur who would cut buttons from his classmates' clothing during the night or separate seminary currency from jackets by crawling under benches during class.

Polecat was such an entrepreneur. Polecat had nothing of his own, everything was issued by the State; if it were not for the State, you might well have seen a totally naked man walking the Russian land. He almost never had any money. In seven years less than seven rubles had passed through his hands; consequently, genuine money seemed less real to him than buttons. He was the beggar of the fourth form, and he was a real master at cadging. When he learned that a classmate had a roll or some sweets, he would pester him to death, wheedling and cajoling until he got what he wanted. Without family or relatives, an out-and-out orphan, he lived at the school all the time, never went anywhere during vacation, and became so involved in all aspects of seminary life that no other life existed for him. Only during vacation time would he visit the local market place, river and forest: this was the extent of his world. Polecat could not stand studying, but he did study because he could not stand being beaten either: of two evils (and a seminary education is an evil) he had to choose the lesser. He was a passionate gambler in buttons; but, having somehow accumulated a great pile, he either exchanged it for money that he squandered on food like a starving beggar, or he lost it again since he was not a very successful gambler. When he lost, he would set to work with his penknife under desks or, at night, under pillows where students hid their clothes. On one occasion he stripped every button from a classmate's clothes; thus the lad could not button his clothes and, try though he did, everything kept falling to the ground. On another occasion Benelyavdov, the strongest boy in the form, caught him by the hair under a desk during a lesson when the teacher was present and gave Polecat a *tousle*. It was impossible to ask for mercy: the teacher would notice. For a long time afterwards everyone made fun of Polecat, saying his hair was swollen. At present Polecat has but half a pair, that is, a one-holer.

"Odd or even?" he asked.

"Odd," Semyonov answered.

"You win, now it's your turn."

Semyonov took his turn but just as he opened his hand to see if Polecat's call of "odd" was correct, the rapacious Polecat grabbed the buttons and hid them in his pocket.

"What are you doing, Polecat?" Semyonov asked.

"I'm Polecat to you? Do you want it in the ear?"

"We have tricked him," someone said.

"We have transgressed," a second added.

"We have lied before thee," a third concluded.[9]

"Give them back, Polecat, come on, give them back."

"Polecat again. I'll punch your face in, I'll knock your teeth out!"

Semyonov did not continue the conversation. The unhappy lad walked away. There was no shelter anywhere. He remembered he had some kasha and the heel of a loaf of bread in his desk. Semyonov wanted to have breakfast, but the heel of bread was gone. Irritated by constant clashes with his classmates, he addressed them with the words:

"This is really a dirty trick."

"What's wrong?"

"Who took my heel?"

"With kasha?" someone said mockingly.

"Get took?"

"Someone swipe it?"

"Get fleeced?"

"Someone lift it?"

"Lafa! Brother!"

These words, translated from seminarian to human language, all mean "to steal," and *lafa* means "well done."

"Comedo!" Tavlya roared.

"I'm coming," was the reply.

After dinner Semyonov had overheard that Comedo and Tavlya had a strange bet, so, forgetting his bread, he hurried in the direction of Tavlya's voice.

"Is it ready?" Comedo asked.

"Here it is!" Tavlya answered, untying a bundle containing six three-kopeck loaves.

"You going to eat them?"

"I said I would."

A curious crowd surrounded them. Comedo was a youth of about nineteen, tall, round-shouldered, skinny, with an aged face.

"What are the conditions?"

"If you don't get them down, you pay for the loaves; if you do, then I'll give you twenty kopecks."

"Let's start."

"And watch it, no drinking until you're finished."

Instead of answering, Comedo began to bolt down the white bread seminarians so seldom eat.

"One!" the crowd counted, "two, three, four . . ."

"Here goes number five . . ."

Comedo smiled and ate the fifth one.

"I hope you choke on the sixth!"

Comedo smiled and ate the sixth one.

"Pig!" Tavlya said, handing him twenty kopecks.

"Now I can have a drink," Comedo said.

When he finished drinking, he was asked:

"Could you eat anything else?"

"I'd eat some bread and butter."

They got a chunk of bread and they got some butter.

"Try this out."

He ate it.

"Anything else?"

"I could eat a heel and some kasha."

The heel appeared. He was being fed out of curiosity. He ate the heel, too.

"I don't believe it! Where do you put it all, you animal. Beast! How come you don't burst, you scoundrel!"

"How's the belly?" someone asked.

"Packed," Comedo answered, looking blankly at everyone.

"Really packed?"

"Feel it."

They began feeling his belly.

"You vulture, it's like a drum."

"Could you eat two pounds of molasses?"

"Sure."

"And four bowls of kasha."

"Sure."

"And five turnips?"

"Could you drink four jugs of water?"

"I don't know, never tried . . . I want to sleep. . . ."

Comedo went to Kamchatka.[10] The crowd cursed Comedo for a long time, calling him a vulture, a pig, and many other names as well.

After feeding Comedo at his own expense, Tavlya was in his usual nasty frame of mind. He slapped one first-termer, bent another into runners, and massaged a third. Goroblagodatsky watched him and inwardly called Tavlya a beast. A little later Tavlya looked in on a game called *breaking the fast:* it was Vasenda's turn: he put his hand on the desk and Grishkets hit it with all his might. Vasenda tried to pull his hand away and make Grishkets miss: then Grishkets would have to put his hand on the table. Tavlya was not amused.

"Anyone want to play *fasting?*" he muttered. He began glancing around to see if anyone was *fasting.*

"Hey, there's a game," he said, finding what he wanted.

Eight or nine students had gathered in the back rows near Kamchatka. Hiding his head in his arms so as not to see anyone, one of them was taking a turn; his back was bare and bent forward. Hands rose over his back and crashed down upon it. Tavlya added his blow to the others. The player recognized who hit him by the force of the blow:

"Tavlya," he said.

It was Tavlya's turn to be beaten.

Meanwhile Goroblagodatsky, with his right shoulder forward, was walking bear like towards the same group. Seeing it was Tavlya's turn, he joined the players.

Tavlya was struck.

"That was a good one," some spectators remarked.

"Try this one, dear. I'll love you for it!"

"Who hit you?"

"You did."

"Give it to him. . . . Give it to him again!"

Tavlya bent forward.

"Whack him!"

"Smack him!"

"Bust him open!"

A mighty blow fell on Tavlya's back.

"Goroblagodatsky," Tavlya said, barely catching his breath.

"Stretch him out again!"

Another powerful blow.

"Benelyavdov," Tavlya indicated.

"Give it to him again!"

"Come on, fellows, you could kill someone . . ."

"Didn't you eat enough kasha?"

"Burn his backbone."

Another powerful blow, and again Tavlya guessed wrong.

"Come on, fellows, do you want to kill me?"

"This is how we show our love and respect," Goroblagodatsky said.

"Fellows, I won't play! . . . This is ridiculous! . . . No one else is beaten like this."

"But you are!"

"Lay him out again?"

"Let him have it!"

"I'll beat your face in," Goroblagodatsky said.

"Fellows . . ."

"Shut up!" Benelyavdov shouted menacingly.

Tavlya finally guessed right. The players broke out laughing when he said:

"I don't want to play any more . . ."

"Why not, old friend?" Goroblagodatsky asked.

Tavlya's glance was full of hate, but he withdrew without saying a word and went to amuse himself with first-termers. . . . The group continued to play "fasting." One of the players suddenly lifted his nose and sniffed the air.

"Who was it?" he asked.

The other players also lifted their noses. Then they all looked suspiciously at Polecat.

"Honest, fellows, it wasn't me. . . . Honest to Christ, not me . . . at least examine me. . . ."

"Stinker!" Goroblagodatsky proposed.

Nine or ten students dug into Polecat's hair and one of them began reciting:

"Stinker, dinker, in his lair, if you weren't at the fair we yank your hair: with blood, meat, liver, and guts. Cabbage or pie?"

"Pie," Polecat squeaked.

"Don't ask for pie, the flour's too high. Stinker, dinker, in his lair, if you weren't at the fair we yank your hair: with blood, meat, liver, and guts. Cabbage or pie?"

"Cabbage."

They roughed him up again while singing "stinker."

"Some of your hide or a fork in the side?"

"Hide," the exhausted Polecat answered.

After giving him a few fillips to the head, they released him, saying:

"Don't misbehave!"

"Such devils!" Polecat said, "Next time I'll make it worse!"

Watching Polecat's punishment, Semyonov whispered: "Serves him right, serves him right."

Goroblagodatsky grabbed Semyonov from behind and threw him over the desk in place of the boy whose turn it was; on the other side someone held Semyonov's head. Vicious blows rained on his back. He was staggering when he got up. A back like his could not take such a heavy pounding of fists. He looked around senselessly. Who had been beating him? Why? Semyonov dropped to the desk and began sobbing. The classroom was growing darker; in a few minutes it would be pitch black.

"Fellows," Semyonov said, getting hold of himself, "why do you hate me? Everyone! Everyone!"

A chorus of song drowned out his voice. Dusk was falling rapidly; one could barely make out the faces; line and color faded away; only sounds remained.

Semyonov made his way to the window and with a heavy heart looked bitterly at the uninviting courtyard and out into the impenetrable darkness of a miserable winter evening. He thought of his family. His father had long since gotten up from his afternoon nap; his kind mother (he was her favorite) carries a samovar into the living room; his brother and two little sisters are already at the table, chattering away and laughing; teaspoons and saucers jangle, a steamy mist rises from the invigorating liquid. "I'd like to go home! . . ." He covered his face with his hands, leaned against the window-pane and again began to sob. Suddenly he stopped crying. He was horror-stricken, and his whole body began to tremble. What he had gone through during the day had been terrible. He no sooner forgot his body's physical pain when something lodged in his chest, making it difficult to breathe. Numb with fear, he realized with perfect clarity: "Outcast! . . . Every-one hates you! And who knows what they'll do to you! Any second now they could hit you in the back, or pull a handful of hair from your head, or spit in your face . . ." The class-room was pitch-dark. The administration, for reasons of economy, lit lamps only during class periods. In such darkness they could do as they pleased with him, and he would never know who was venting his anger and avenging the brother-hood. "I won't do it any more," he whispered, without a shade of anger in his soul. "I deserve it," crept into his mind. He wanted to make peace with the brotherhood and sincerely ask for mercy. At this moment he hated the administration for making him a squealer, and he himself was ready to tear a handful of hair from the head of the classmate who would take his place. Semyonov decided to ask the entire form to forgive him and to make a public renunciation of spying. Suddenly, however, he thought he heard someone sneaking up on him; frightened, he hurried from the window and vanished somewhere in the darkness.

It was so dark in the classroom that you could not distin-guish a human face at two paces. All games stopped during these hours, and a seminarian could amuse himself only by making diverse and bizarre sounds. The general impression was grotesque. . . .

Sounds merge and intertwine. You hear the scream of an unfortunate lad who had probably been rammed in the back; someone hums the tune of "Lord, I cried unto Thee" in the eighth mode; [11] a pathetic note of high D breaks forth from the concert; someone is slugged in the face; near the stove the students sing: "Seminary lads, standing in the tavern, sang: come serve and fill our cups; we'll sell our books, we'll give you money"; someone is weeping; another creature is *guffawing*, that is, he whinnies like a horse: "hee-hee, ho-ho-ho-ho!" Obscenities hang in the air together with screams and laughter. Students are braying, guffawing, chanting, and fighting. In Kamchatka, under the direction of the inveterate Mitakha, the custodian of school tradition, a verse is being sung which was composed by the seminary's aborigines:

> Blessed are the creatures
> Whose fortunate natures
> Know neither our tortures
> Nor our teachers!
> You go to the dining hall
> And gulp down rotten cabbage soup
> And go to class again:
> You go to class even though you howl.
> And then archangels rush in
> And drag you from your seat;
> Torture the servant,
> Give him a whipping.

Wretched lads! Your grotesque behavior is not surprising. You are dragged about the room, tortured, and whipped! His classmates' sympathetic voices join with Mitakha's. Unfortunately, the end of the song, which is sung in a certain deep, funereal tone, has been forgotten and lost.

In another place you hear:

A peasant rides his nag
Over the priest's land,
Bringing grain,
Bringing grain.
Peasants run to the cart,
They stick their fists into the cart:
What are you selling, brother?
What are you selling, brother?
Oats, they are told;
A peasant shakes a handful
In his fist,
In his fist.

You also hear:

They grabbed the goat
By its stomach,
They threw the goat
Against damp mother earth;
His little legs
Lie on the road,
His head and tongue
Lie under a plank.

After each couplet there is a refrain:

Ti-li-li-li-li-li-li.

and then the second line is repeated.
Here is yet another excerpt:

Favorites of Apollo
Sit carelessly *in caupona*,
Eating herring, drinking *merum*,
Singing Bacchus' praises.

Oh, how powerful you are, good Bacchus!
We honor *tuum regnum* in our minds,
You visit *dum caput nostrum*,
From which you drive our *curas*.
You pour bliss into our hearts
And *diqnus domini* of a father.
We love Phoebus and the Muses;
They make us equal to the gods,
They pave the road to happiness
And give us what is best;
Sed omnes haec fruits of learning
Conjunctae sunt always with exhaustion.
Our youthful color would have faded long ago
If you did not give us strength.

The eight-stanza *Seminariad* was composed long ago and is handed down by tradition from one generation to the next. These local songs and verses reflect the brotherhood's attitude toward their studies and superiors.

From the popular repertoire students sang either sentimental romances like "The grey dove is grieving," "The dark night," "I am a poor shepherd girl," "The scorching sun is now on high," et cetera or they sang genuine folk songs like "The Hall," "Down the Volga," "Beyond the swift stream," and "Lads, we've had enough, we've had enough beer."

At present, however, a goner is reciting a homemade verse:

After eight o'clock in the morning
As soon as lamps are lit on the walls,
The peasant Sukovatov is hurrying,
Hurrying in his own boots.[12]

Laughter, jokes, and obscene remarks about the administration hang in the air. Some scoundrel is guffawing again. . . .

35

A dozen other students start guffawing. . . . Twenty. . . . And there is no end to it. . . . Students start barking, meeowing, growling, whistling, and shrieking. The seminary's cacophonic choir, consisting of about forty voices, joins in the nonsense: members divide among themselves the musical modes used in church singing, and everybody sings at the same time. Meanwhile, youngsters in the first form are chilled to the bone by the dampness and cold; they start to scream at the top of their voices: "It's cold, cold!"—this is a call to start warming up, after which students begin waving their arms to keep warm, as cabbies do, and their moans rend your soul: "It's cold, cold!" "Is a goblin being buried, is a witch being married?" [13] A hundred maws produce a wild uproar, and it all takes place in total darkness. If you brought a newcomer into the classroom and he had never heard the moans of seminarians, he might think he was listening to the screams of lost sinners in hell. They guffaw, howl "it's cold, cold," and bellow cacophonic songs in every mode; the sound of wailing, plaintive voices grows louder and louder, windowpanes begin to shake. . . . Is there any weird sound left in the world that cannot be found in this shouting, singing and droning? But now something new comes to life in the stifling, dank air of the pitch-dark classroom; something ascends above every head: his classmates hear Velikosvyatsky's famous, powerful bass voice chanting "Blissful and peaceful life. . . ." The unbridled power of the final words stuns his classmates: "Length of days to the class resting happily on its laurels!" [14] The song ends on a stupendous note. . . . Instantly, as if on cue, everyone becomes silent. The brotherhood is delighted; it has a passionate love for a powerful sound. A moment later a hundred voices chant "Length of days" in response to the basso. . . . It should be noted that besides goners, the brotherhood also respects physical strength, drinkers who hold

their liquor, and powerful bass voices. The seminary loves
good voices, protects and coddles them, and rescues them from
any trouble. At home students learn to chant in church where
they sing Christmas carols, serve at requiems and Te Deums,
and intone the Hours and the "Apostle"; [15] in this way they
develop both their voices and their love of singing. Our
schools often have outstanding choirs. Velikosvyatsky was
congratulated.

"Let's have a concert!" someone proposed.

"By the waters of Babylon." [16]

"We don't have the music!"

"We know it by heart!"

"Call the young choristers."

A concert begins a few minutes later. There is not one
raucous sound in the classroom. The sopranos weep like
children; the basso, like a despondent leader, moans his restrained reproach; a Babylonian cries: "Sing us one of the
songs of Zion!"; a fierce despot seems to be stamping his feet
in anger and impatience . . . "How shall we sing the Lord's
song in a foreign land?" answer the children's timid, weeping
voices; the little sopranos weep like women. The lament
ascends in high, soft, and passionate notes, and finally grows
into a powerful, menacing cry: "O daughter of Babylon, you
devastator! Happy shall he be who takes your little ones and
dashes them against the rock!"

After the concert everyone grows still. The students, temporarily subdued by the melodious singing, tell each other
fairy tales, recall their vacations, discuss the administration
and the brotherhood. From time to time someone is hit in the
neck. Mitakha, the custodian of tradition, sings in a sad voice:

> They grabbed the goat
> By its stomach . . .

The students do not remain meek and quiet for very long.
"Let's raid the first form," someone shouts.
"Let's go," others answer.

About twenty students gather together, and on this November evening sneak across the courtyard and into the first form. The pupils are also sitting in the shadow of death and do not expect visitors. The raiders from the fourth form scatter through the room, hitting youngsters in the face, bending them into runners, massaging them, punching them, slapping them, slugging them. Who is doing it? Why? Nobody knows and nobody gives a damn! Weeping, wailing, the slaughter of the Innocents! Woebegone youngsters are being annihilated everywhere. They are in pain. This vicious beating under cover of darkness expresses, on the one hand, a certain ridiculous bravado: "Charge on, O shoulder, swing out, O fist!"; [17] on the other hand, it expresses: "Tremble, children, and submit." In such cases, however, most students are only satisfying a need to beat up someone, to give him a hiding, to thrash him, to pull his hair, to slug him, to knock him down, to punch him, to bloody his nose, and they do so because they want to feel within their grasp a human being who is suffering and squealing and begging for mercy; such things are done not out of anger or revenge but simply out of love for the art. Having amused themselves to their heart's content, the knights return to their own quarters amidst triumphant laughter. The battered youngsters in the first form groan, weep, and rub their sides.

When the knights returned to their classroom, a new amusement had begun.
"The pile's too small!" several students shouted.
Some sort of commotion was going on in the dark in the middle of the room, not quite a fight but not quite a game

either. . . . There was a lot of laughing and swearing.

The commotion increased. When students yell "the pile's too small," it usually means someone had been knocked to the floor, then another on top of him, then a third, and so on. Those on the floor are kept from getting up. As many as thirty persons jumble together in a pile, entangling their arms and legs and pulling at each other's stomachs. Those who manage to break out of the pile and stand up try to knock down those who have not been on the floor, and several voices are always shouting: "The pile's too small!"

The commotion had not yet ended when a new game began. In the corner near the stove someone was yelling: "Let's squeeze oil."

A crowd could be heard making its way to the corner, pressing and crushing against the wall everyone in its path while yelling:

"Mikhalka, knock him down!"

"Vasenda, push."

"Get to work, Six-eared Chabrya."

"Squeeze, Polecat, squeeze!"

Those up against the wall could hardly breathe, and tried to break into the clear; if they did, they in turn squeezed oil.

Both games ended unexpectedly. . . . A piercing, imploring scream rang out, but not from the area of "the pile's too small" and not from where they were "squeezing oil."

"Fellows, what are you doing? Fellows, stop! . . . Help!"

At first no one recognized the voice. A mouth was gagged . . . someone was tossed to the floor . . . someone was spluttering. What was happening? Two or three minutes passed in dead silence. Then the whistle of a birch rod was clearly heard in the air, as were its blows against a human body. Obviously, someone was being whipped. The death-like stillness in the room was broken by a barely audible whisper:

"Ten . . . twenty . . . thirty."

The strokes were being counted.

"Forty . . fifty . . ."

"Aaaay," someone screamed.

Everyone now recognized Semyonov's voice and realized what was happening.

"Oh, so you like to bite, you bastard!" This was Tavlya's voice.

"Fellows I'm sorry! . . . I won't do it again! . . . Honest to God, I wo . . ."

Once again they muffled his mouth.

"Serves him right," the students whispered.

"From now on don't squeal!"

The count reached seventy . . .

My God, it's finally over!

At first Semyonov sobbed without saying a word. . . . The classroom was quiet because a completely unheard-of event had taken place. . . . Although tears brought some relief, Semyonov did not stop sobbing; humiliation and disgrace made him fearless, and he shouted at the whole form:

"You scoundrels! You can all . . ."

He then added an unprintable obscenity.

"Yap all you want!"

"To get even I'll tell the inspector everything . . . about everyone . . ."

Someone cuffed him and once more his howling sobs resounded throughout the room. Several students broke out laughing, but many were terrified. . . . Why? Because the brotherhood got very worked up during such incidents, sought out its enemies in the dark, and beat them up.

Semyonov countinued to sob. An inexpressible rancor was choking him; he picked up a book and tore it to shreds, bit his fingers, pulled his hair, and could not find words vile enough to vent his wrath. Exhausted, beaten, whipped, insulted, and humiliated several times during the evening, he now was completely benumbed by his misfortunes. It was both pathetic and terrifying to hear him whisper:

"I'll run away, I'll run away. . . . I'll cut my throat. . . . I can't go on! . . ."

We must do the students justice: a majority, particularly first-termers, sympathized with Semyonov's troubles. Several even had tears in their eyes; luckily, it was dark and no one would notice. Second-termers put on a brave front, but they, too, were depressed and partly afraid. Everyone realized that the affair would not pass unnoticed and that the seminary could expect a great whipping. The classroom was quiet except for Semyonov's sobbing. . . . There was something evil in his sobs. Suddenly the sobbing stopped, and it was deathly still.

"What's wrong with him?" students asked.

"Has something bad happened?"

"Is he alive?"

"Hey, fellows," Goroblagodatsky yelled after examining Semyonov's desk, "he's gone to complain!"

"Squealing again!" several voices shouted.

The students' mood changed immediately; angry curses poured down on Semyonov.

"Fellows, we've got to keep our mouths shut!"

"We are not planting turnips! . . ." several voices answered.

"Tavlya, what are you going to do?"

"I'll say I wanted to protect him but, while I was pulling someone's hand from his mouth, he bit me, too!"

"Good idea, Tavlya!"

Nevertheless, Tavlya was shaking like a dry leaf.

"What will the censor say? He's got to make a report, otherwise he'll answer for it!"

"I'll say I wasn't in class, and that's that."

Just then the bell rang announcing study hour. The door opened and a three-pronged lamp was brought into the room. The pillars cast undulating shadows across the room, and a gloomy, unfriendly light fell on the sturdy, bulky desks, bare, mildewed walls, and dirty windows.

Second-termers assembled in the front rows and deliberated upon the recent events. Study hour began; curiously, despite the teachers' vicious rod, at least forty students did not even think to pick up a book. Some hoped to receive a good mark in the register by bribing their auditor; others thought carelessly: "I'll get by somehow," and about fifteen students in the back rows of Kamchatka had no fears whatsoever because they knew the teachers would not bother them: the teachers had given up on them long ago, having learned by experience that whippings would never make them study: these lucky ones were getting ready to be expelled and did not give a damn about anything. Since they were extremely lazy and did absolutely nothing during study hours, they were forced to cultivate that schoolboy activity known as "fooling around," an activity common to all educational institutions but which here, like everything else in the seminary, took on original forms.

Kamchatkites enjoyed certain privileges; the censor, entrusted with maintaining peace and quiet, would wink at their pranks as long as they did not make any noise. Enjoying such prerogatives, Kamchatkites amused themselves as best they could. Grishkets elbows Vasenda and whispers: "pass it on"; Vasenda elbows Carp, Carp elbows Six-eared Chabrya and so forth down the row; the elbowing moves to the next row, then to a third, and finally covers the entire classroom. Having gorged himself, Comedo is sleeping; Polecat makes a spitball and tosses it in the face of his sleeping friend. Comedo wakes up and writes Polecat a note: "When study hour ends, I'll break your back, so don't bother me as long as I don't bother you." He then goes back to sleep. Many notes travel around the room; one says: "Give me a knife or a pencil"; another: "Hey, Slave-girl, later let's choose up sides for leapfrog"; a third: "Buddy, let me have some tobacco, I'll pay you back later, honest"; Khitonov receives an anonymous insult: "You have red hair, Khitonov, and red brings dread; a red-headed lout burnt down the stone house." Replies and desired objects travel by the same post. The boys do what they can to amuse themselves. Many of them make faces, touch their noses with their tongues, cross their eyes, and make wry mouths, then they either show their contorted faces to classmates or they look at themselves in a cheap mirror. *Spitter* has given numbers to the faces he makes: he sticks out his tongue to the left, pushes his nose to the right, rolls his eyes and puffs up his cheeks: this is face number five. He has a repertoire of twelve different faces.

An auditor known as *The Goddess* has been chewing an eraser constantly for three days; it will turn soft before long and he will puff it up, squeeze it with his fingers, and make a bubble; then this overager will slam the bubble against his forehead to hear it pop; he works diligently to enjoy such bliss, and he does not spare his jaw; when he gets tired, he allows one of his charges to do the chewing. *Mumbles* has made a panorama out of pictures on candy wrappers; he has been admiring it for a whole hour, for the hundredth time; he has also made an oracle out of candy wrappers: beautiful maidens use such wrappers to divine their future husbands, but he uses them to see whether or not he will be birched tomorrow. His neighbor has made a *sawyer*, that is, a wooden doll with a saw; balancing it on the edge of a desk, he rocks it back and forth. *Garlic* has stuck a string up his nose and by inhaling deeply he draws it into his mouth; jerking the string back and forth, he shows the trick to his *prodder* (friend), Mumbles. One overaged Kamchatkite, having sharpened a penknife, is shaving his upper lip and cheeks. After shaving, he begins whittling a little slot in his desk. Another overager makes a chain from a piece of wire. A third has twisted some paper into a narrow funnel and tickles his nose with it; his face screws up, he sneezes loudly, and he is happy. Two Kamchatkites are studying foreign languages. One says: "Her-I, her-know, her-noth, her-ing, her-for, her-to, her-row"; you only have to put "her" before each syllable and it comes out not in Russian but in Herite. The answer is even trickier: "Shee-not, do-see, shee-ry, wor-see," that is, "Do not worry." This is not Russian either but *Sheesee*. Words are split in two, for example, "swat-ter"; "shee" is added to the last syllable which is pronounced first, and "see" is added to the first syllable which is pronounced last: the result is "shee-ter swat-see." In the last row Lummox is practicing the art of typography: he spits on a knuckle, rubs it against a letter in his textbook, and then tears it out; he takes the letter from his finger and transfers it to a piece of paper; in this way he prints a word. Lying down on the winter coats they have spread under the last row of desks, five or six students are telling each other fairy tales and stories. The boring, monotonous, vacuous study hour inevitably puts many students to sleep; students are sleeping on desks in the fifth row, they are sleeping in the seventh row, they are sleeping in the twelfth row, they are sleeping under desks as well. This is how Kamchatkites and second-termers, having prepared their lessons, spend the study hour. A gay life!

Only inveterate, hopeless loafers, ready to receive their certificates, enjoyed the right to amuse themselves during study hours. There were many other loafers who were candidates for Kamchatka but not yet Kamchatkites. These students passed the time in even drabber ways. They also amused themselves after a fashion, but since they had to pretend they were doing something, their amusements were of a different sort. *Heron* is zealously writing something; from a distance he seems a most diligent student, but this is what he is doing: he writes down a number, another beneath it, and multiplies them; then he places the first number under the product and multiplies again, repeating the procedure again and again to see what he comes up with. *Porker* pokes a finger into his eyeball so as to enjoy seeing double and even treble; next, listening to the buzzing and murmuring of his classmates, he blocks and unblocks his ears in order to hear the disconnected sounds reverberate in his head; or he will put his ear to the desk and wonder why noise intensifies when it passes through wood. One first-termer is pinching himself, trying to inure his hand at least to warm pinches. Another ties a string around his finger and admires his finger puffed with blood. A third sucks his hand until blood appears. . . . They invent the most vacuous and, it would seem, most uninteresting activities; for example, they listen to their pulse; they inhale deeply and try to hold their breath as long as possible; they try to count to one thousand without blinking; they collect spittle in their mouths and then spit it out on the floor; they read a page backwards and then from bottom to top; they offer to pull one hundred hairs from their own heads, and they do it;

one lad dangles his legs, another picks his nose, others exchange winks and make various signs to one another; others perform various acrobatic tricks. . . . Someone sits with his head propped in his hands, looking aimlessly into space: he is dreaming about his mother and sisters, about the neighboring landowner's garden and the pond where he used to catch carp . . . and he can not keep his mind on the lesson. By shutting their eyes and trying to touch their fingertips together, several students are divining if the teacher will whip them tomorrow; and when it turns out he will, they wonder where they can borrow money to bribe the auditor, but they never think of opening their books. Others sit blankly, languishing in everlasting sorrow, staring vacantly at the dimly burning lamp and waiting for the end of the three hours of prescribed study and for the beneficent sound of the supper bell. These seminarians do not have the will power to study the lesson. The reader might ask: what does this mean? Could it be more entertaining to read a page from bottom to top, as some students do for amusement, than from top to bottom? . . . Yes, possibly it is more entertaining. It is no accident that one seminary song says that "blessed are those creatures who do not know our teachers"; that one must have "a fortunate nature" to bear the "tortures" of school life; that a student "howls" when he goes to class; that he is a "servant" and is "tortured." This song, handed down from generation to generation, was not composed by accident.

The principal pedagogical method in the seminary was rote-learning, a terrifying, deadening rote-learning. It became part of a student's flesh and blood. To omit a letter or misplace a word was considered a crime. Sitting before their books, students would endlessly and senselessly repeat "shame and disgrace, shame and disgrace, shame and disgrace . . .

later, later . . . befell, fell, fell . . . shame and disgrace later befell . . ." Such slave labor continued until the phrase "shame and disgrace" was indelibly imprinted in the student's head forever. Students were so miserable during a lesson that studying produced physical suffering expressed by the song: "Blessed are those creatures who do not know our teachers." Together with the blind rote-learning, another remarkable feature of the educational system was its *disputations*. The teachers received a scholastic education, employed all sorts of synechdoche and hyperbole, were nourished on the niceties of church rhetoric and raised on a philosophy that teaches "All men are mortal, Caius is a man, therefore Caius is mortal"; or, "All men are immortal, Caius is a man, therefore Caius is immortal"; or, "The soul is joined to the body by a previously established law"; or, "Laws of similarity and contrariety invariably derive from our *I* or from our self-awareness"; or, "Light destroys darkness"; or, "Submissiveness is the source of every good, but freethinking is ruinous and disgraceful," and so forth. [They practiced dialectics, resolving such questions as "Can the devil commit sin?"; "Is the essence of man's spirit affected in the afterlife by the state of death?"; "Does original sin contain in embryo, as it were, all mortal sins, voluntary and involuntary?"; "Which comes first, faith before love or love before faith?"; and so forth.] Their brains eventually ossified in debates where they triumphantly orated *pro and contra* on the same proposition, depending on the orders of their superiors, and put to use all one hundred rhetorical devices as well as every known sophistry and paralogism. Even during childhood they displayed a propensity for solving such questions as "What is an essence?"; "What is a whole?"; "Will Socrates and other virtuous philosophers of paganism be saved?"; and they earnestly wished that the answer would be no. The teachers were especially fond of proving that man is an immortal being gifted with a free soul, the king of the universe, even though, strangely enough, in real life they could barely conceal their conviction that man was nothing but a featherless rooster. All this was implied in their disputations. A student racked his brain until his head hurt when he had to solve the great questions posed by these philosopher-teachers; fortunately for him, disputations were rare events and generally they were considered an academic luxury. The all-devouring rote-learning reigned supreme . . .

Is it surprising that such learning only repelled students and that they preferred spitting contests or drawing a string through their nose to studying the lesson? Entering school from under his parents' wing, a student quickly sensed that something new was happening to him, something he had never before experienced, as if one net after another was falling over his eyes in endless succession and preventing him from seeing things clearly; he sensed that his mind, having lost its curiosity and boldness, had turned into some sort of machine where one only has to push a button for a mouth to open and begin spewing forth words; and these words—strange to say—no longer made sense. The only students who never had trouble with their lessons were those who combined a gift for memorization with a talent for disputations. But for this you had to be a born *brain*. There were some amazing brains. Thus, a certain Svetozarov memorized the words and phrases under the first four letters in Rozanov's Latin lexicon: beginning with "A, ab, abc," he covered forty or fifty pages without omitting a single word; he undertook this project solely out of love for the art.

Only a few students, however, were capable of school work; the majority found it difficult, and only birches made them study. For example, take Danilo Peskov, a lad both industrious and intelligent, but definitely incapable of memorizing anything word for word: after spending two hours and a half over his book, he blinks his bleary eyes. . . . And what does he see? He sees this: many students are even more exhausted than he, many are still trying to finish their portion of the textbook, anxiously reciting the lesson with heads upraised like chickens drinking water. Others are on the verge of tears because a low grade will be entered by their names in the register. One student tries to work up some energy by tousling his hair. Hey, poor lad, at least take pity on yourself! Throw the book under a desk or spit in it. In any event your body will suffer under the birches tomorrow. Go, good friend, to Kamchatka; life is easier there; and Kamchatkites have as much practical knowledge as the most dedicated brain. Looking at the faces of classmates exhausted by the rote-learning, a student involuntarily would ask himself: "What is this work and suffering for? Why all this fussing from morning till night over a loathsome textbook? Aren't we human beings?" In the midst of such reflections a bit of the lesson would pop into his head unawares, by itself, and all the words would knock about in his head. Near the end of the study hour a diligent student would find his brain exhausted; it did not contain a single thought despite the fact that thoughts would appear, as it happens in dreams, through association. The class presents a gloomy picture. . . . Every face is bored and apathetic, the last half-hour drags slowly by, and it seems the study hour will never end. . . . A student is indeed fortunate if he can fall asleep at his desk: supper time will come before he knows it.

The evening came to a very entertaining conclusion. Thirty minutes or so before the bell Semyonov reappeared. Pale and trembling with nervousness, he entered the room with down-cast eyes and, looking at no one, went to his seat. The study hall came alive; everyone was looking at him. Semyonov felt hundreds of curious, malevolent eyes turned towards him, his blood ran cold, and he stood transfixed in some sort of petrified state. He was waiting for something. In four or five minutes the door opened again; four military figures, employees of the school, were standing in the cold vapor pouring into the classroom from outside. One was Zakharenko, another Kropchenko: it was their duty to whip students; [18] the other two, Fetter and Fir, usually held students by the head and feet during whippings. A death-like silence descended on the classroom. . . . Tavlya turned pale and was breathing heavily. Soon the inspector appeared, an enormous man with a sullen look. Everyone stood up. He walked about the classroom without a word, occasionally stopping by a desk, and the student there would tremble and shake all over. . . . Finally the inspector stopped beside Tavlya. . . . Tavlya was ready to fall through the ground.

"To the door!" the inspector told him after a short silence.

"I . . ." Tavlya started to defend himself.

"To the door!" the inspector shouted.

"I was protecting him . . . he didn't understand . . ."

The inspector was stronger than any seminarian. He grabbed Tavlya by the hair and thrashed him; with one hand he then pulled Tavlya's head to the desk by the hair, with the other he hit him so hard in the back that his powerful fist boomed against the stout back; then, after pulling Tavlya up, the inspector yelled:

"To the door!"

After this Tavlya did not dare open his mouth. He went to the door, slowly undressed, and lay down on the dirty floor on his naked belly. Fetter and Fir sat on his legs and shoulders. . . .

"A good going-over!" the inspector said.

Zakharenko and Kropchenko swung the birches from either side; they dug into Tavlya's body, and he began defending himself, screaming wildly that he wanted to help Semyonov, but the latter did not understand and bit his hand. The inspector paid no attention to his howling; Tavlya received a vicious, prolonged whipping. Intensely angry, the inspector walked around the classroom without saying a word, and this was a bad sign: when he shouted and cursed, cursing and shouting dissipated his wrath. . . . Students were whispering the number of strokes and already had counted to eighty. Tavlya kept shouting "not guilty," swearing by the Lord God, his father and his mother that he was innocent. Goroblagodatsky cast a malevolent glance first at the inspector, then at Semyonov; Semyonov did not even understand himself: there was not a trace of revengeful pleasure in his heart, nearly his whole body trembled with a foreboding of something terrible and uncanny. God knows what he would have agreed to if only Tavlya were not being whipped at this moment. Tavlya had already taken more than a hundred strokes, his voice began to grow hoarse from shouting, but he continued to shout: "Not guilty, honest to God, not guilty . . . it's a mistake!" Nevertheless, he had to take one hundred and fifty.

"Enough," the inspector said and walked around the room. Everyone was waiting to see what would be next.

"Censor!" the inspector said.

"Here," the censor answered.

"Who else whipped Semyonov?"

"I don't know . . . I wasn't . . ."

"What?" the inspector yelled menacingly.

"I wasn't in the room . . ."

"Ah, you weren't in the room, you pig! Tomorrow I'll whip every tenth boy and I'll begin with you. . . . And you'll get it too," he told Goroblagodatsky, "and you," he told Polecat. The inspector then pointed to several others.

Goroblagodatsky answered rather rudely:

"I'm not guilty of anything."

"You're always guilty, you scoundrel, and you ought to be thrashed every minute."

"I'm not guilty," Goroblagodatsky answered sharply.

"So you want to be rude, do you, you pig," the inspector screamed in a rage.

Goroblagodatsky stopped talking; nevertheless, gritting his teeth, he gazed hatefully at the inspector.

Having reviled the whole form, the inspector left for home. The brotherhood was panic-stricken. There were instances in school when not only every tenth student was whipped, but a whole form, one after the other. No one could say for sure whether he would be whipped tomorrow. Faces drooped; several were pale; two townies were crying softly to hide their tears from their classmates: what if I'm tenth on the inspector's list? . . . Only Goroblagodatsky grumbled: "They're not planting turnips." He was inwardly enraged, but he delighted in the sight of Tavlya who could neither stand up nor sit down after the flogging. Goroblagodatsky intended to go over to Semyonov and finish him off; he had already told himself: "Seven crimes, one answering," but suddenly his face lit up with a new idea, he grinned maliciously and said:

"*Pfimfa.*"

Semyonov stood stock-still. . . . He was like a man who

senses a raised fist may fall on his skull at any moment and every moment he awaits the heavy blow. He was literally squeezed and crushed from all sides . . . it was almost impossible to breathe . . . Damn it, damn it! What moments a seminarian had to live through . . .

"Pfimfa," Goroblagodatsky said, going up to the censor, and they began whispering . . .

The supper bell rang. Hearts grew somewhat more cheerful. "Two by two!" the censor shouted.

A few minutes later the form set off for the dining hall and, five hundred voices having sung "Our Father," began eating their meager meal. As the crowd poured out of the dining hall, the censor went up to Benelyavdov and repeated the enigmatic word: "Pfimfa."

"He deserves it!" Benelyavdov answered.

> The porter has securely locked
> The entrance to the holy domicile.
> And the hermit in his lonely cell
> Says his *preces* before retiring.
> Morpheus scatters poppy seeds around the city,
> Working people have gone to sleep,
> Only dogs are awake,
> Here and there a sentry yells. . . .
> The cocks have crowed a second time.
> It was the deep of night;
> Everyone was sleeping soundly.

Thus does *The Seminariad* describe night . . .

Bedrooms 6, 7, 8, 9, and 10 are located on the second floor along the right side of the huge school courtyard. These rooms are interconnected. The back section, consisting of three rooms, was called *The Boot*. These were the bedrooms of paying students; consequently, in the morning and evening, especially during the first weeks after important holidays, a veritable food market opened in The Boot and two adjoining rooms. The whole school flocked there; crowds of students went from one bed to another; trunks were dragged out from under the two hundred or so beds in these rooms; in addition to books, these trunks were filled with food supplies of various kinds. Huge loaves of white bread, butter, oatmeal, mushrooms in sour cream, and pickled apples had been brought from home, especially from the countryside. These supplies gave off special aromas that filled the air; these aromas mingled with foul miasmas; the walls, which would freeze inside and out during cold waves in wintertime, reeked of dampness; tallow candles in heavy girandoles made the air sour and pungent; add to all this a huge tub standing in the corner by the door and half-filled with a certain liquid, a substitute for an outhouse. A student had to get used to this poisonous atmosphere, and would anyone believe that the majority, living in this polluted air, eventually lost the capacity to be sickened by it! . . . The cold made matters worse, and students found it more unbearable than the stench. The administration sometimes did not heat the stoves for a week; students would steal firewood, but this was not always possible, and they had to sleep under cold blankets and cover themselves with fur coats and overcoats. The huge dormitory rooms, with pillars down the middle as in the classrooms, were poorly lighted, and dark shadows fell in strips across the beds. Students snored and talked in their sleep: some sleepers ground their teeth.

Now for the final incident of this winter evening in the seminary. A figure unexpectedly emerged from The Boot and went to a corner of Room Nine; there two more figures got up . . . A conference began.

"Do you have the pfimfa?" one of them asked.

"I do."

"Give it here."

All three figures went to a corner and stopped by Sem-yonov's bed. . . . One of the accomplices held a paper cone packed with cotton. This was the pfimfa, one of the barbarous inventions of the seminary.[19] The lad with the pfimfa crept up to Semyonov in his bare feet. He lit the cotton in the wide opening of the cone and carefully placed the pointed end into Semyonov's nose. Semyonov twitched a bit in his sleep, but the lad with the pfimfa blew hard into the burning cotton; a thick steam of sulphurous smoke enveloped Semyonov's brain; he moaned in his sleep. After a second, even stronger puff, Semyonov jumped up like a madman. He tried to shout, but his lungs had been completely scorched and blackened by the smoke. Gasping for breath, he fell on the bed. The accomplices in this inquisitorial act immediately vanished. Semyonov's loud snoring was punctuated by heavy moans. The next day he was carried unconscious to the infirmary. The doctor could not understand what had happened to Semyonov, and when Semyonov himself regained conscious-ness and got his voice back, it turned out that he, too, could not remember what happened. The administration suspected that Semyonov's enemies had done something to him, but they could not uncover any proof. The next day many students were whipped in school, and many for no reason at all. . . .

1862

Seminary Types

Three o'clock in the morning. In the bedroom known as *The Boot* everyone is asleep. Some students are snoring, others mumble incoherently in their sleep. Several are grinding their teeth (something seminarians found unbearable—often they would stuff ashes into the grinder's mouth to break him of his bad habit); others moan because their heads and lungs are congested, and tomorrow they will say a gremlin tried to smother them. Only after peering intently into the darkness pervading The Boot can you see many bodies sprawled on beds and covered with coats, robes, cloaks, and various other ragged hand-me-downs over their blankets.

Someone got up in the corner and began creeping cautiously from one bed to another in his bare feet. Occasionally he would stop somewhere before continuing on his way. This was the school thief, the once renowned Aksyutka. One youth was sleeping under a wolfskin coat. This coat teemed with vermin, and they finally got the better of the seminarian. He tossed and turned, the coat slipped to the floor, leaving him half-covered. Aksyutka bent down to the head of his classmate's bed, found the coat collar, yanked it away in an instant, and immediately vanished. The victim's bite-ridden body was on fire, the chilly air cooled it, and, thanks to Aksyutka, he fell into a sweet, peaceful sleep. In the meantime Aksyutka managed to hide the coat until he could dispose of it; he then returned to his corner and slept the sleep of the innocent and just.

Four o'clock. Zakharenko entered. (Besides whipping students it was also his duty to wake them up and to ring the bell announcing the beginning and end of classes.) As he walked between rows of cots, he rang the bell wildly left and right over the sleeping heads.

Students jumped up, scratched their sides and the *fleece* on their heads, spat, yawned, or made the sign of the cross over their open mouths; some were staring vacantly, uncertain why they had been roused at such an ungodly hour, and then fell heavily back on their beds.

"To the bathhouse! To the bathhouse!" Zakharenko announced.

"Hey, you! Hee-ho-ho-ho!" someone guffawed.

Students were admitted to the bathhouse very early in the morning. It would have been disgraceful to let this horde of seminarians into town during the day; like the rabble led by Peter of Amiens,[1] these dirty, shabby, insolent ragamuffins in their motley dress never behaved themselves; they were always whistling, guffawing, and doing their best to strew disorder throughout the neighborhood. In the whole history of the school there was but one instance when seminarians were allowed to go to the bathhouse during the day, and the administration regretted its decision long afterwards. But more about that later.

"Be quick!" the dormitory warden shouted.

"Arise!" someone roared with an ear-splitting, soul-rending fury.

"To cleanse our sinful bodies!" was the thundering response.

The Boot filled with noise. The seminarians dressed quickly and willingly because going to the bathhouse was something like a student holiday. They pulled out trunks; those with clean linen were tying up bundles; those with money were setting aside a few kopecks, everyone was cheerful because for the first time in two weeks they at least would breathe fresh air and see some faces unconnected with the seminary; but the main thing was that for a seminarian a day at the bathhouse was a day of various enterprises and adventures.

"Two by two!" the warden commanded.

They stood in pairs.

"Forward march!"

They set out from The Boot in a long file. They met paying students on the staircase, and then several more rooms fell in line; students maintained by the State were waiting at the gate. Only townies remained in school. They went to the bathhouse on Saturdays. Heading the contingent was *Fir*, a soldier stationed at the school. The administration entrusted him with maintaining peace and quiet. Of course, peace and quiet could not be maintained by a pedagogue like the soldier Fir. An enormous snake consisting of about two hundred pairs curled along the wooden pavement that led from the school gates to the courtyard of the monastery. The racket, laughter, and dirty jokes shook the air of the shrine. A hermit in his "lonely cell," hearing the din and worldly noise, began praying more ardently and zealously for the sins of mankind.

The students ran into a ruddy, grotesquely tall monastery guard. The guard rarely missed an opportunity to make fun of seminarians when they went to the bathhouse or into town on a holiday: the students had played some dirty trick on him.

"Ah, here's the lice brigade!" he said to the passing students.

"Choke on your pancakes!" they answered.

The students knew that once during Shrovetide the guard had eaten seventy-three pancakes in one sitting and had drunk a gallon of rotgut, that is, vodka.[2]

"Why is lumber so expensive?" the guard asked.

"They need it to cook your pancakes."

"Devils! They used it to whip you!"

"Red, are you riding a horse? Or are you really that long?"

"Golden Fleece!"

"Signpost!"

"Watchtower!"

A hail of taunts poured down on the guard. How could one man outtalk more than two hundred keen-witted seminarians? He barely managed to get a word in edgewise:

"Listen, lice brigade, no stealing at the marketplace."

Satan tossed a handful of mud at him. The guard began cursing to high heaven.

As the last seventy pairs passed by, they orchestrated their invective.

"Pankcake, pancake, pancake!" someone began singing.

The guard did not know what to do: no one could hear his voice. When everyone had passed by and the word "pancake" was echoing in the distance, he shouted after the receding seminary:

"Worthless trash! You should all be flogged!"

Somewhere in the distance one could barely hear: "Pa-an-cake!"

The guard spit; the church bell rang, he piously crossed himself and went to matins.

Seminarians, most of them with their right shoulders forward, moved through the marketplace. The town was still asleep. A whole series of disorders took place. Dogs, of which there is such an abundance in the towns of Holy Russia, were out early to look for something to fill their animal bellies; a seminarian would throw a rock at a dog whenever he had a chance. The procession was marked by a senseless, useless destruction of property; it was all done simply for the aesthetic pleasure obtained from vandalism and mischief. Mekhalka loosened a post, pulled it out of the ground, and threw it in the middle of the street. He roared with laughter, the animal. Some students passed a house with windows at street level and drummed on the windowpanes, disturbing the peaceful slumber of townspeople. An old woman was trudging somewhere; she met the seminary, made the sign of the cross, hurried to the other side of the street, and whispered:

"Good Lord! The seminary must be in town!"

It was a good thing she thought to cross the street, otherwise certain students would have been glad to give her a massage from head to foot.

A carter was passing by. Aksyutka addressed him very seriously:

"Uncle, hey uncle!"

"You want something?" he answered amiably.

"Tell me, fellow, why did you eat the harness?"

Haulers, corn-chandlers, and carters cannot stand to be called harness-eaters.

"He had a bite of his mitten, too!" someone added.

The peasant lost his temper and let loose a barrage of invective.

As they walked by the river bank where spring ships were already moored, Satan proposed:

"Let's all yell 'look out!' "

"You begin!"

Satan began, then the sound of forty maws reverberated across the river: "Look out!"

The peasants on barges jumped up with alarm, not knowing what to make of such a tremendous yell. When they realized what was going on, they began swearing; they even said:

"Hey fellows, let's club them!"

The students replied:

"Big mouths. You eat spars for breakfast!"

"Look out!" the seminarians yelled with all their might.

Obscenities hung over the river.

Under the leadership of Fir, the soldier-pedagogue, students at last reached the public bathhouses. The marchers stopped. Fir stood at the door and admitted two students at a time, distributing tiny pieces of soap to students maintained by the State. Paying students received nothing. The pairs then went to the anteroom, buying switches and pieces of bast on their way since the State issued neither. Pair after pair raced headlong through the entrance to the anteroom. There was a crush at the door: everyone rushed to grab a pail since there were at least three times as many students as there were pails; consequently, many students had to sit around for an hour or so and wait for someone to finish. Aksyutka and Satan, of course, had pails. Within fifteen minutes the bathhouse was filled with people and the air shook with a wild uproar. The bathhouse was packed tighter than a drum; every bench was taken; some students sat on the floor, others crawled into cubbyholes designed for the bathers' clothes. Senior guards, censors, and others with authority occupied a rather clean, separate room that the proprietor reserved for dignitaries. The boys playfully slapped each other's naked bodies. Most of them had gone to the steamroom. Seminarians are passionately fond of steaming themselves. The wooden ledge was taken by storm. Every now and then the whacks of switches ring out, of which a seminarian will taste his fair share no matter what he does. Tavlya dragged someone by the hair from his *personal*, as he put it, place.

"Katka," Tavlya shouted.

"What?" was the servile answer.

"Give us more steam!"

"We've got enough," voices answered.

"I'll give you 'we've got enough!' "

"Do you want a punch in the pudding?"

That was Benelyavdov's voice. Tavlya ignored him. He shouted again:

"Katka! Hear and obey! I call thee nigh to do or die!" [3]

Katka appeared.

"Douse me."

Katka doused him.

"Whip me!"

Katka whipped him. Tavlya uttered terrible squeals of delight.

The uproar continued on the ledge: groans, screams, shrieks, whistling, and the crack of hot birch twigs. Presently the unfortunate *Toadfish* made his appearance. He was the seminary pariah. Toadfish had a repulsive, positively putrescent face, blotched and pock-marked; seminarians said about his face that one could sharpen knives on it. Wherever he went, the air became repulsive and detrimental to the lungs because of the odor on his chest, on his back, in his pockets, and in his hair. Indeed, it seemed that this unfortunate creature had ceased being a human being; he was simply a human body that could breathe and walk. The damned seminary putrefied Toadfish, literally putrefied him. The students did not really hate him, but they found him repellent and rarely did anyone find pleasure even in insulting him. No one will believe that in the course of eight years not one student out of five hundred said a kind word to him, much less shook his hand. Even the administration and servants despised him as much as the students did. We said the seminary putrefied his body: this has to be understood in the exact sense of the word. The administration and brotherhood sentenced him to live and sleep in a bedroom set aside for a dozen or so students like himself, seminary castoffs. The fact is that some students suffered from a certain disease that in childhood is not yet a disease but the result of physical immaturity. Nobody cared about them, nobody treated them. The seminary did not even buy them oilcloths to protect their mattresses from dampness and rot; moreover, in school those who suffered from this disease were usually whipped with leggings. I give you my word that worms nested in the mattresses, and these unfortunates had to sleep directly on their own discharges. It will be asked, why did these students not take care of themselves and air out their mattresses in the morning? Placed in a cell where they had to breathe positively infectious, noxious air, feeling a swarm of worms beneath their bodies every day, despised by everyone, they became slovenly to the point of cynicism and totally careless of their appearance: they, too, despised themselves. This is a fact: Toadfish reached the point where he swallowed flies and other insects, on one occasion he ate a piece of paper smeared with lamp-oil, and sometimes he would eat the ends of tallow candles.

Toadfish wandered dejectedly through the bathhouse, looking for a pail. He walked up to Polecat and muttered in a depressed, flaccid tone:

"Let me have the pail when you're finished."

Polecat, the beggar of the fourth form, knew how to keep up his beggar's role even before Toadfish. He answered:

"Three kopecks and it's yours."

"All I have is two."

"Give them to me."

"What will I have left?"

"Alright, give me five pairs of buttons."

"I don't have any."

"Go to hell, then, *fraterculus!*"

He walked up to Satan, who also had a second nickname: Ipse (himself). He was never called by his real name, and we will not use it either. Devils, depending on the nation to which they belong, come in various kinds. There is a German devil, an English devil, a French devil, and so forth. He does not resemble any of them. Ipse was not even a Russian devil; our national demon is honest, gay, and somewhat stupid: thus is he represented in folk tales and legends. Ipse was a self-made devil, a spirit of that hell known as the seminary. In the capacity of a devil he served such a man as the thief Aksyutka. He was called Satan because of his character.

In school there existed an absurd custom of *pestering* classmates, especially newcomers. I'll explain presently what this means. Three or four students would agree to pester someone. They would stick to their victim like leeches. At first they abused and made fun of him, then the pinching began, and finally the episode would end with raps, massages, and punches. The aim of such innocent diversions was to enrage the victim and drive him to tears. When they reached their goal, the tormentors laughingly abandoned their victim, whom they often drove to a state of insensibility and frenzy; thus, after *Idol* had exasperated *Azinus*, he cracked Idol's head with a poker. Satan always took an active part in such amusements; hardly anyone could pester as well as Ipse. He even ventured to antagonize those who were stronger than he was. It is difficult to imagine a bigger or more annoying pest than

Ipse. Sometimes he systematically attached himself to someone from morning till night for three or four days at a stretch without giving his victim a moment's peace. He was frequently beaten up, and viciously too, but he did not give a damn. Beatings somehow had made him as impervious as wood. Aksyutka was the only one who could calm him down, but that was because Satan worshipped Aksyutka's seminary genius.

This was the sort of man Toadfish had asked for a pail.

"Let me wring your hair!" Satan answered him.

"I'm not ready."

"Your hair's wet, isn't it?"

"I haven't rinsed yet."

"Rinse it! Here, I'll give you a pail."

"No, I can't."

Toadfish stood deep in thought, not knowing whether to wring his hair or not. When someone suggested a *wringing*, one student bowed his head and his partner grabbed a handful of hair. The student had to pull his hair free. His partner had only one opportunity to dig his fingers into his classmate's hair and, as the hair gradually slipped through, he did not have the right to grab a second handful. Many students could wriggle free very easily if their hair was wet. There were artists, however, who ventured a wringing even when their hair was dry; Satan was one of the latter. Seeing that Toadfish could not make up his mind, Ipse said:

"Alright, wait till I finish washing."

"Thanks a lot!" Toadfish answered joyfully.

He brought Satan some water and rinsed him off, trying to play up to Satan and get a pail; Satan finally finished washing, and with a joyful expression on his face Toadfish reached for the pail.

"Hey, lads!" Satan shouted.

"What are you doing, Ipse?"

But Toadfish's voice was crying in a wilderness. About fifteen students responded to Satan's call.

"Up for grabs!"

Satan rolled the pail along the slippery floor. Like wild animals, everyone dove after it, bumping into one another, shouting, swearing, and fighting.

Finally, after most students had finished washing, there were enough pails to go around. Toadfish got hold of a pail and began vigorously soaping his head, but just when his face and hair were covered with a thick foam of soap, Satan returned for some reason to the bathhouse, grabbed the pail from him, and gave him a massage. Frightened, Toadfish opened his eyes wide, the soapy foam spilled over his eyelashes, and he felt a sharp stinging sensation; there was nothing he could do about it; rubbing his eyes and squinting, he somehow reached the tap and washed them out.

Meanwhile, many others had already finished washing; the bathhouse became much quieter although you could still hear some occasional guffawing, swearing, and so forth; the reader, somewhat familiar with the ways of the seminary, can imagine this for himself.

Let's go to the anteroom. The attendant was handing out linen to students maintained by the State. Seminarians did not return to school in pairs; when someone finished washing, he went his own way.

The seminary's holiday was now beginning.

"Now, old man, it is time to deliver us out of all our troubles," Benelyavdov said to Goroblagodatsky.[4]

"You mean, a jug of vodka mightier than any known god or shrine?"

"Let's make for *The Greenery* (a tavern)."

"Only one thing: Dolbezhin has the first class."

"So what?"

"If he notices, he'll whip our tails."

"Why should he notice?"

"After the bathhouse we'll really feel it on an empty stomach."

"We'll have a bite first and then we'll drink just one bottle."

"Alright, come what may, let's give it a try!"

"Get moving, let's be quick!"

At bathhouses there are always vendors who sell *sbiten*,[5] beet cider, milk, cabbage soup, kvass, rolls, pastry, pretzels, and cookies. A great feast is now going on. About twenty students are eating and drinking. Shamelessly, indeed with pride and a sense of their own worth, second-termers are eating and drinking at someone else's expense. The seminarians' flushed faces beam with pleasure. Polecat, the beggar of the fourth form, wanders among the guests, cadging as usual. Today he is in luck: one lad breaks off a bit of his roll for him; he asks another: "Let me have a sip, sweetheart," and, after complying with his request, the donor goes on drinking from the same glass. Only aristocrats assemble in taverns, inns, or pothouses, depending on their taste and disposition. The great majority, however, cannot afford a one-kopeck glass of beet cider or a roll costing a kopeck and a half. These students gaze enviously and greedily at the diners, especially at second-termers, and smack their lips. A rather large number of these students, however, did not stop to gape near the stand or try to cadge food; they ventured forth into the streets and marketplace, looking for a spot where they could filch something. Aksyutka, however, managed to sneak a pastry from the stand itself.

Students were walking alone or in small groups. Every merchant in town was trembling at this moment. I should mention a characteristic feature of seminary morality: stealing was considered reprehensible only when it was done within the brotherhood. A seminarian's moral sense distinguished three completely separate spheres of activity. The first sphere is the brotherhood; the second is society, that is, everything beyond the school walls; here the seminary commune approved of thievery and mischief-making, particularly when it was done with cunning, cleverness, and wit. Nevertheless, there was nothing malicious or vengeful in this attitude toward society; you were allowed to steal only food: consequently, no one cared if you robbed a shopkeeper, peddler, or hawker; on the other hand, the brotherhood considered it despicable to steal money, clothing, and so forth even on the outside. The third sphere is the administration: students played dirty tricks on it out of malice and a desire for revenge. Thus was fashioned the seminarian code of ethics. Now we can understand why none of his classmates stopped Aksyutka when they saw him filching a pastry: in the eyes of the seminary this would have been squealing. Now we can also understand why there are so many original phrases and expressions for the concept of stealing in the language of the seminary, all those swipings, coppings, filchings, snatchings, connings, and so forth.

Our heroes had gone forth to swipe, cop, filch, snatch, and con what they could.

The principal heroes were Aksyutka and Satan, the *one*, and, as it were, the *only* (an expression from an absurd, atrociously written textbook used in the seminary).

"Satan!"

"What do you want?"

"Ipse!" Aksyutka shouted.

"What do you want?"

"Rub your hands!"

"You mean we can pull a leg (to dupe someone, to steal)?"

"You'd better keep quiet."

"We'll spend small and eat big!"

"Here's ten kopecks." Aksyutka said.

"Why so generous all of a sudden?"

"Let's go to the shop: you see, it's already open. You do the buying, but be careful, just a little bit of everything: a kopeck's worth of flour, say it's for soup, a half-kopeck of chicory, a kopeck of pepper, a half-kopeck of onions, a kopeck of glue, a half-kopeck of shag, and two kopecks of candy and vegetable oil."

"What should I put the oil in?"

"Are you Satan? Are you my dear Ipse?"

Aksyutka gave him a message. Anticipating a profit, Satan did not get angry at him. As usual, he only made a tail out of the skirts of his nankeen coat and drew three circles with it in the air, saying each time:

"I am Ipse."

Aksyutka began explaining:

"You'll buy little bits and it'll take more time. When you ask for oil, say that you left your bottle at home and don't quit, keep asking for a jar."

"We'll fool him! Aksyon, you're smarter than Satan!"

"You should call me: Akyson Ivanych."

Saying this, Aksyutka gave him another massage. Satan stood at attention, made horns on his head with his fingers, gave his own broad face a wild massage, and in conclusion shook his tail three times. He was not called Satan for nothing: he had horns and a tail, a perfect devil.

Their plan was a complete success. Fifteen minutes later

Aksyutka had the stolen property: two rolls, a jar of raspberry jam, a hunk of whitish bread, and about two dozen potatoes. Aksyutka's nostrils flared like tiny sails, a sure sign he wanted to steal or had already stolen something.

"Now let's dance with leaping and hasten to the tavern with happy feet," commanded Aksyutka, that innocent lad.[6]

The other innocent child, the boy Ipse, made face number seven, which expressed joy and approval.

"Know what I pulled off?"

"What?"

"I spit into a barrel of sauerkraut."

"Ho, ho, ho!" bellowed the satanical throat.

Aksyutka, a thief in school and on the streets, was an unusual person, talented, strong-willed and highly intelligent, but the seminary (and, partly, his home life) destroyed him just as it destroyed hundreds and hundreds of unfortunate human beings. The very style and method of his stealing reflected a powerful nature, powerful but morally degenerate. Aksyutka was a creative thief. This lad, a convict's son, could not steal anything without playing some clever, malicious trick on his victim. After rifling a trunk, snatching a roll, filching some paper, or copping a book, or what not, anyone else would have run away, but not Aksyutka: he would go and find some rocks or mud and stuff them into the trunk in place of the stolen proprety. Some students, knowing he was a thief, would try to get on his good side by bringing him offerings (after all, even outside the seminary we sometimes try to get on the good side of thieves to keep them from hurting us), but he would refuse, playing the role of the honest man who is insulted by a bribe. Here is an example. A certain student received a bag of oatmeal from the country. He knew Aksyutka had seen the package and was absolutely convinced Aksyutka would steal the oatmeal; consequently, the student hurried to Aksyutka with his donation, offering him two or three handfuls of oatmeal. Aksyutka said: "I cannot eat oatmeal," but his nostrils quivered. Aksyutka wanted to play a clever, thievish trick. After the reassured student had stuffed the sack of oatmeal into his desk, Aksyutka crawled up to the *oatmealer's* desk as quietly as a flea across a floor and stole the sack. Immediately thereafter he walked up to the *oatmealer* and addressed him in a plaintive tone: "Fellow, you promised me a little oatmeal, now give it here." The student reached into his desk; the oatmeal was gone. Aksyutka cursed him, saying: "Swine, you promise but you don't deliver; I'll pay you back for this!" He turned away; his nostrils were puffed out like sails, and his face beamed with an awareness of his power as a thief. A half-hour later he walked up to the classmate he had robbed and said: "Want some oatmeal?" Aksyutka held the oatmeal in his palm. "It this mine?" "No, my mother sent it to me!" "Pig, you don't even have a mother!" "I meant my godmother." That's Aksyutka for you. He was especially skilled at *trading knives*. Here we will describe one more typical custom in the seminary. Usually someone would shout: "Who wants to trade knives?" When someone else agrees to trade, then the sport begins. They show each other nothing but the ends of their knives; then each must decide whether it is worthwhile to trade since no one wants to exchange a good knife for a bad one. Aksyutka was especially skilled at this.

We are convinced he will wind up in jail. When he was expelled from school, he first found lodgings in an inn where, for room, board, and three kopecks a day, he chopped cabbages, carried firewood, tended stoves, kneaded dough, and so forth. Honest work quickly bored him, however, and he robbed his employer and ran away. Later, he was seen on separate occasions wearing a cassock, a sheepskin coat, and a frock coat. In short, the school thief had turned into an all-around rogue. Having gained experience in *the fifth form* (thus did seminarians of long ago refer to the school of life that followed the four forms of the seminary), he took a position as sexton but, because of drunkeness and rowdiness (he smashed the mayor's windows), he soon was exiled to manual labor at some poor monastery. After passing this course in church penitence, Aksyutka joined a cathedral choir, but he was kicked out for something resembling highway robbery. This incident forced Aksyutka to leave the clergy and enter the ranks of the bourgeoisie. His most serious trouble came when he threatened to slit the throat of his former dean. For this he was placed under surveillance. He is a terrifying man, and one can foresee but a single path remaining for him: the Vladimir road, on which hundreds of our convicts travel to Siberia; Aksyutka will be one of the most incorrigible among them.

Now we shall return to the other students.

The rapacious seminary scattered in all directions.

An old ragged woman, formerly one of those third-rate courtesans known as night-rats, was selling peeled lemons, cookies as brittle as dried clay, piebald rolls, and other indigestible refuse in order to maintain her decrepit body. When she caught sight of the seminary returning home, like a mother protecting her child from a wolf, she covered her rotten, stale food with a dirty rag and a tattered apron.

She had been robbed once before, but today the seminarians could not filch even one stale roll from under the aging woman's tatters. This time the seminarians had to be content with insulting the unfortunate woman.

In a different spot student projects met with success.

Bakers had opened a long, wide window. The light steam of freshly baked bread was rising from the shelves. Although the seminarians' keen, thieving eyes had seen immediately that it would be difficult to turn a profit here, they continued nosing around the place; soon they made the happy discovery that fresh dough had been left on the shelves in another part of the bakery. The bakers did not expect an assault at this point, and they left it undefended. Under the leadership of the rapacious Polecat, seminarians sneaked into the bakery and began grabbing the dough, hastily hiding it in the pockets of their coats and pants. They vanished immediately as soon as they heard the bakers' footsteps, and a minute later they were not even in the marketplace. Why would students want fresh dough? They would not eat it uncooked, would they? No, but when stoves were fired in the morning, they would manage to bake it on dampers in the flues; although it would be covered with soot, who cares! Seminarians aren't choosy.

Now we shall describe another incident.

Three overagers dropped in on a chorister, a classmate who had been expelled. They found him lying on his bed, suffering from a hangover. A shoemaker was due to drop in on him in order to collect a debt of three rubles. A day earlier the chorister had vowed and sworn to pay him, but now he had only half of his savings left.

"Well, fellows, what can I do?" the anxious chorister shouted.

"Get over here!" one of the overagers answered.

"Why?"

"We'll con him. Lie down on the table."

"What for?"

"Lie down, don't argue."

They placed a table in the front corner beneath the icons. When the chorister stretched out on the table, they placed a burning wax candle at the head of the table and covered him with a white sheet; one overager picked up the Psalter, walked over to the singer, and said:

"Die!"

The lad pretended he was dead. A seminarian began reading psalms over him, as if over a corpse, with a look of deep mourning.

The shoemaker entered, heard the monotonous reading, and realized a corpse was in the house. He crossed himself piously.

"Who is it?" he asked.

"A classmate," they answered glumly.

"What's his name?"

"Barsuk."

At first the shoemaker scratched his head and thought to himself: "There goes my money!" Then his heart softened and he said to the seminarians:

"Gentlemen, the deceased left a small debt, but I'll forget it: it's a sin to dun a dead man."

"A good man, to be sure!" someone answered. "To tell the truth, there's no money to bury him. Friend, you began a good deed, so why not finish it? Give us something for the poor lad's wake."

The shoemaker took out a fifty-kopeck coin and gave it to them. They thanked him

The shoemaker, naturally, wanted to take a look at the deceased. Making the sign of the cross, he said:

"At least let me look at him."

Barsuk played the role of a corpse so well that you would have taken him straight to the cemetery. They uncovered his face: it was pale and deathlike from the hangover.

When the shoemaker kissed the chorister's forehead in keeping with the Orthodox custom, the latter made a fico under the sheet and thought to himself:

"Here's a fig instead of a candle!" [7]

After the shoemaker left, the dead lad was resurrected and, laughing wildly, he jumped up on the table.

"Now, lads, let's have a wake!"

"A bottle of vodka!"

"Pickles and herring!"

Food and drink were on the table in no time; laughing and joking as they sang various religious chants, they conducted a memorial service for the repose of God's servant, Barsuk.

Seminarians proudly and triumphantly told each other the story of this incident.

But the affair did not end here. One evening a month later the shoemaker ran into Barsuk.

Barsuk kept his wits even here.

Arms crossed and eyes flashing, he walked menacingly towards the shoemaker and shrieked in a wild voice:

"Let the ungodly perish!" [8]

The shoemaker was unnerved. He thought he saw a corpse who had returned from the nether world to punish him for presuming to visit the deceased and demand his money. He made the sign of the cross and, terrified, took to his heels. Long afterwards he still told the story of how a corpse appeared before him and tried to drag him off to hell.

This incident gave the seminary even more satisfaction.

Here is the last of the seminarians' outrageous adventures on the day they went to the bathhouse.

Prowling around the marketplace like a thief, Mekhalka noticed the door to the pastry shop was open, and he looked inside. The shopkeeper was standing in the far corner with his back to the door. Mekhalka was not a tactitian but a strategist and, without giving it a second thought, he pounced on a gingerbread as large as a good-sized board, and raced out of the shop. The shopkeeper rushed after him, shouting "thief!" Mekhalka, weighed down my his burden, ran slowly and was dangerously close to being punched in the neck. He used the following strategy: he waited until the shopkeeper came close to him and then, turning suddenly, he raised the gingerbread above his head and smashed it in the shopkeeper's face. He then raced away with what remained of the cake.

Mekhalka was a remarkable individual. He was not a thief, but a real bandit. Everyone knew that on one occasion, coming out of church, he grabbed the first cur he came across, bashed its head against a post, and afterward celebrated his feat by eating a wax candle. For this they wanted to flog him within an inch of his life. But because it was Easter Week, the punishment was delayed until the feast of Saint Thomas. When the day of retribution arrived and four soldiers, led by the superintendent, came into the classroom with an enormous number of birches, Mekhalka's eyes flashed like a wild animal's and, resolutely clenching his fists and gritting his teeth, he ran to the open window and jumped on the window sill as quickly as a cat. (The room was on the second floor.)

"If you come any closer, I'll bash my brains out on the cobblestones!" he cried out. When the superintendent tried to persuade him to surrender, he replied he would punish the administration by jumping from the second floor. The superintendent spit and walked out. For such outbursts Mekhalka received a wolf passport.

We know that subsequently Mekhalka, Aksyutka, and one more artist hired out as laborers in a blacksmith's shop. Working at the anvil with his lusty hammer, Mekhalka tried to earn some extra money in his own way with the help of his friends. He climbed into a neighboring yard, dismantled a cabby's droshky, and carried all the metal back to the blacksmith's. He ended up as a sexton, and he became the bane of his priest's existence.

This, gentlemen, is the merry picture of seminarians at a bathhouse, a tale containing only the bare facts. There is nothing to add, the facts speak for themselves.

Having eaten everything they stole, the seminarians were in good spirits after the bathhouse; there was less hitting and punching, fewer massages, and in general the classroom was relatively quiet and peaceful.

In Kamchatka several fellows got together to discuss bygone times and the seminary's ancient heroes. Mitakha led the discussion.

"Yes, gentlemen, those were the good old days."

"In olden times they had more fun than we do."

"On the other hand, floggings were worse," Mitakha said.

"You don't say."

"I can tell you about one case."

"Tell us, Mitakha, tell us."

"One thing, don't interrupt."

Mitakha began:

"Three brothers were here: *Kalya*, *Milya*, and *Zhulya*. They were the strongest students of the time and they used to make boots. Twice they went to town with some classmates to do some real carousing on the outside. And they did it up fine. On the way home they were singing so loudly that you could hear them five streets away, and they met some cossacks who invited them to shut up. Our lads told them to go to hell. A fight started. They drubbed the cossacks and returned to school, certain that their secret was safe. It wasn't:

an investigation began the next day. Everything came out. And was there a flogging! They whipped you then under the bell in the middle of the courtyard,[9] on the right side of your body and then on the left, and they gave you up to three hundred whacks."

"Fellows, I also heard about . . ." someone started to speak.

"I said, no interruptions."

"Bastard."

"Animal."

"*Mazepa!*"

It is worth remarking that *Mazepa* was a swear word in the seminary and the reason is probably historical; during the period we are describing no more than five of five hundred students knew of Mazepa's existence.[10] His name was merely a derogatory word, not a proper noun. Fat-faced boys were usually called *mazepas*. Everything in the seminary is unique and original.

The seminarian who interrupted the story fell quiet.

"And so what happened, Mitakha?"

"Listen. All the students assembled in the courtyard, the inspector arrived, guards appeared, and a huge pile of hot birches was brought in. Kalya, Milya, and Zhulya stood in the crowd. Their classmates, you see, had managed to fill them full of vodka before the whipping. Kalya was stretched out, then Milya, then Zhulya. But even though they were drunk during the whipping, even though they bit right through the skin of their arms, nevertheless they were doused with water after the flogging and carried unconscious to the infirmary on a piece of matting. That's how tails were whipped!"

"Why did they bite their arms?"

"Numskull!"

"Lout!"

"If you bite your arm, it distracts you: when you bite your arm, the arm hurts, but you don't feel anything in your behind."

"And afterwards, fellows, a fantastic thing happened."

"Go on."

"A boy in the first form was present at this terrible flogging; he was fresh from home, where his mother used to pat him on the head, but he saw that here they pat you on a different spot. He was skinny, short, pale, in a word, scum, not a seminarian at all. When he witnessed this fine flogging, he just about died from fright. He became an excellent student and watched his every step so as to escape birchings. He would tremble and grow pale whenever someone was whipped. A teacher noticed this and came to hate him since he could not stand a student who yelled a lot under the rod. The teacher wanted to see how the greenhorn would react to a birching. He found fault with something and gave the greenhorn such a flogging that long afterwards he was still pulling splinters out of his body. After the flogging the student fainted. This set the teacher completely against him; he began persecuting the boy, and he always flogged him viciously. The student's life was so miserable that he decided to run away from school. They caught him. At first he wanted to hang himself, but later he decided on something else. He waited until night, got hold of a penknife, slashed his wrist, and wrote a note in his own blood: "Devil, I'll sell you my soul if you'll save me from being whipped."

The listeners were all ears.

"At midnight," Mitakha continued, "he took this note and crawled under the stove. What happened there, nobody knows. They dragged him out unconscious. He said he had seen the devil. When the administration learned of his escapade, they whipped him under the bell; afterwards, so they say, he was carried to the infirmary where he gave up the ghost."

The story made a strong impression even on the seminarians' lively imagination. Conversation ceased, and everyone became pensive. At this moment students understood and realized with particular clarity that, given their sort of life, there were times when you would sell your soul to the devil.

After the impact of the story had faded slightly, a student asked: "Have any of you fellows seen a devil?"

No one responded.

"Anyone seen a goblin?"

It turned out that many had seen goblins, and if someone had not, he knew someone who had. Superstition and misconceptions were just as strong in the seminary as they are in the peasantry: students believed in wood demons, goblins, water sprites, nymphs, witches, sorcerers, spells, and omens. In short, this side of the seminarian personality revealed a deep-rooted ignorance that the administration never even thought of eradicating because it, too, was not always free of superstition.

A home-bred occultism even existed in the seminary. Thus, almost the whole seminary believed that if you took the dried membrane of a feather and placed it in a book, you would forget the lesson in that book; if you placed the same membrane under someone's mattress, the boy would have an accident in his sleep, for which he would be forced to kiss Toadfish. It was considered bad luck to leave your book open after a lesson because then you would forget the lesson. When someone played a hoax by saying that the teacher was coming, other students would shout: "Why are you lying, you bastard? Do you want to put him in a bad mood?" Some students believed the teacher would not ask them any questions if they held on to certain parts of the body. . . . At one time the school even had its own sorcerer. This was a student named *Beguti* who came to the seminary from Kiev. He got his nickname because he used to say *beguti* (they ran) rather than *bezhali* when he told a fairy tale. He would guess how many cows someone had in his village, how many sisters in his family, how much money he had in his pocket, and so on. Many took him seriously.

In this connection we will describe how Aksyutka tricked Grishkets. For a whole week Aksyutka induced his classmates to pretend they seriously believed that Grishkets was a sorcerer. When this goal was reached, many students began asking him to tell their fortunes. At first Grishkets thought it all a joke, but his classmates played their role so well that Grishkets finally took their game seriously. Then he became frightened and pleaded with his classmates to stop thinking he was a sorcerer. When they saw he was worried, they pestered him even more. Grishkets almost lost his mind. When Aksyutka, sitting next to him in the dining hall, begged Grishkets to teach him how to be a sorcerer, Grishkets went to the inspector and said: "Honest to God, sir, I'm not a sorcerer. Would I take such a sin on my soul?" And, crossing himself, he insisted that Aksyutka had made it all up.

Seminarians found devilry an inexhaustible topic of conversation.

We have, however, imperceptibly reverted once again to memories of bygone days. We shall tell two stories.

The administration forbade students from swimming; complying with this order, the police would harass students along the river. Seeing that the students did not stop swimming, a policeman decided to catch them at any cost and take them to the administration. Kalya, Milya, and Zhulya were furious, and together with several classmates they intentionally went swimming the next day. The policeman swooped down and caught them at the scene of the crime; but they grabbed him, gagged his mouth to keep him from shouting, and then tossed him into the river. After this operation they tied his pants to his boots, thus making two sacks, and stuffed them full of sand up to his waist; after this they laughingly abandoned him and went on their way. Unable to stand up, the poor man floundered on the ground for a long time. When he was set free, he swore never to bother seminarians again.

A certain student wanted to celebrate his name day, but he had only five rubles. It was summertime. Our poor lad was walking with friends along the river bank, and he was sad. In one spot they came across a bunch of workers who had left their barge and were cooking kasha on the bank. "Have a good meal!" they said. "Please join us." "What's food without vodka?" "Where can we get some?" "Here's the money," the seminarian said, giving them enough for six liters. The peasants were overjoyed, and they got the vodka immediately. The seminarians made them dead drunk; when they went back to the barge to sleep, the seminarians pirated it and sold it, peasants and all.

Students always listened with enthusiasm and complete approval to these stories and reminiscences of the exploits of seminarians.

But the bell rang and classes began.

We said that classes began, and they began in the following way.

"I caught a louse," a Kamchatkite said.

"Rain on the house."

"I've two by the tail."

"It's going to hail."

"Four's the number."

"Comes the thunder."

For no reason at all, some overager began rattling off the words: "One-two: ahead of you, three-four: one cart more, Five-six: pile up sticks, seven-eight: hay can't wait, nine-ten: hay again, eleven-twelve: curse like hell."

Then another overager pulled a birch snuffbox out of his boot, began to chant a psalm at the top of his lungs, and, wheezing, loaded his nose with snuff.

Snuff-taking was extremely popular in school. It could not have been otherwise: during study hours with one three-pronged lamp providing light for over one hundred students, eyes naturally grew bleary; but after a student took a pinch of snuff, he was clear-eyed for a few minutes. During classes, each one lasting two hours, the monotonous recitations inevitably would put you to sleep, but when you took snuff, you would open your eyes in spite of yourself. Snuff was prohibited by the administration, but the brotherhood paid no attention to that prohibition. They bought snuff from Zakharenko who sold it rather cheaply since he ground it from shag. Snuff-taking in the seminary also had its peculiarities. They would flick it up the nose or take it in pinches; particularly remarkable, however, was the method of spreading snuff from the tip of the index finger to the wrist and drawing it into the nose with a deep breath. Students would bet on who could inhale the most snuff in one try, and sometimes an enthusiastic contestant would overreach himself and, taking too much, faint dead away.

The students managed to play a game of *paints* before the

teacher arrived. They chose an *angel* and a *devil*, as well as a shopkeeper; other players were designated by certain colors which were not revealed to the devil or the angel. The angel stepped forward and knocked on the door.

"Who's there?" the shopkeeper asked.

"An angel."

"What do you want?"

"Paint."

"What kind?"

"Green."

"Whoever is green, go to the angel."

The devil in turn went to the shopkeeper, chose a color, and led it away.

The game continued until every color was chosen. Then the angel's forces stood on the right hand of the shopkeeper, the devil's forces on the left. Each team formed a chain by grabbing one another around the stomach. The angel and the devil locked arms, angels and devils let out a roar, and a tug of war began. The struggle lasted a long time, but the devil finally prevailed.

Suddenly the door opened. A huge gentleman in a brown greatcoat entered the room. There was absolute silence. This was the teacher, Ivan Mikhaylych Lobov. The censor read the prayer "Heavenly King." [11] The students stood and waited for the order to sit down. They sat down. The great teacher went to the desk and sat down on a dirty chair. He picked up the register. Many students shuddered. After a moment's silence Lobov shouted.

"Aksyutka!"

"Here," Aksyutka answered boldly.

"Up to your old tricks?"

"I can't study."

"Then why did you study up to now?"

"Now I can't."

"To the stove! Give him a ride *on the clouds!*" [12]

Aksyutka made the teacher furious. He played tricks on him that no one else would have dared. This thief, whom we already have partially described, was extremely able, had a fantastic memory, and was probably the smartest student in the form; it was nothing for him to read a lesson a couple of times and repeat it word for word. Studying came easy to him. Suddenly, however, he would stop studying and make fun of the teacher just to spite him. They would whip him, but it did absolutely no good. He would then be sent to Kamchatka. But as soon as he got what he wanted, he again started doing excellent work and was transferred to the front row; and as soon as he was transferred, he would break out singing:

"Ta-ra-ra-boom-dee-ay!"

"And zeroes every day!"

After this song Aksyutka again would stop studying. The whippings were resumed. Lobov had transferred Aksyutka several times back and forth between Kamchatka and the front row.

Lobov finally flew into a rage and shouted the ominous *on the clouds.*

Four lads immediately jumped up, grabbed Aksyutka, took off his clothes, picked him up by his arms and legs, and held him in a horizontal position; birches whistled from either side.

Aksyutka screamed, yet he managed to shout:

"I can't study, honest-to-God, I can't!"

"Put a book under his nose."

They put it there.

"Study!"

"I can't! You can take the icon off the wall, I still can't." [13]

"Study right now!"

This time Aksyutka shouted the truth that he could not study because he was being birched; the teacher realized this, but he still kept Aksyutka hanging over the book for a fairly long time.

"Drop that creature."

Aksyutka made his way to Kamchatka.

"Redouble the beating!" [14]

Several classmates hopped up from their seats, fell on Aksyutka and loaded his head with *case shot*, that is, they rapped him about the head.

Aksyutka shrieked:

"Go ahead and kill me, but I can't study."

Lobov was in the habit of walking through the classroom with a long birch switch. He got up from the desk and struck Aksyutka along the back. Aksyutka shrieked:

"Honest-to-God, I can't study!"

Lobov gradually calmed down, and the class went on as usual. A little while later he shouted:

"Censor, some kvass."

The censor went for the kvass and brought it back.

Sipping kvass from a tin cup, Lobov looked over the register and indicated by name who should go to the stove for a whipping, who should kneel in front of the blackboard, who should kneel on the edge of a desk, who should go without dinner, and who was not allowed into town. Lobov's class became decorated with figures placed in a variety of positions. He then began questioning students who knew their lesson, correcting them when they did not answer word for word, and washing down seminarian erudition with a strongly fermented kvass. Usually he wore galoshes and did not remove his reddish greatcoat. When the student finished his recitation, Lobov reached into his coat pocket, took out a rather large pie, and began devouring it with gusto. The seminarians greedily watched the disappearing pie. Lobov was in the habit of breakfasting in class, combining food for the spirit with food for the body.

After examining five students, he began dozing off and finally fell asleep, snoring softly. The student he was questioning had to wait for the great teacher to awake and begin again. Lobov would never explain his assignments; that would be, as he put it, extravagant, and so he would indicate with his fingernail *from those to these* in a book, leaving it up to the student to learn the lesson by the next class.

Was this great pedagogue whipped too often in his youth, or not enough?

Morpheus whistled softly through the pedagogue's nose, and the students who were kneeling or standing at attention took advantage of the opportunity. A low murmuring broke out, and the seminarians' innocent games got under way: checkers, *feast days* (a card game), buttons, pinches, raps, and so forth.

The bell rang, the teacher woke up, the usual prayer was said, the teacher left, and the classroom filled with the usual noise.

The second class, Latin, was taught by Dolbezhin. Dolbezhin, too, was a huge man, tubercular, irritable, and extraordinarily strict. Nobody liked to joke with him, and he used such obscene curses in class that you would not believe your ears. He considered it a most sacred duty to whip everyone in his class by the end of the term, well-behaved and diligent students included, so that no one escaped a birching. The demon of seminary envy tormented him at the end of one term when there were still two students in his class who had not been whipped because they had behaved extremely cautiously. Although he could find fault with nothing, he nevertheless hunted up an excuse. On one occasion it seemed he would miss class and his students were gaily awaiting the bell when, with five minutes to go, Dolbezhin suddenly appeared at the far corner of the courtyard; his face was particularly menacing (he was very drunk), and his eyes were fixed on the windows of his classroom. Many students were scared to death. One of the students who had not been whipped looked out the window and then quickly hid himself in the room.

"Yeleonsky!" Dolbezhin shouted, walking into the room.

Yeleonsky (the one who had not been whipped), shaking from head to toe, went up to him.

Dolbezhin hit him in the face with his fist and bloodied it; blood started flowing from his nose and mouth.

Yeleonsky did not say a word. Pale and trembling, he looked blankly at the teacher.

"Flog him!"

They flogged Yeleonsky.

There remained but one boy who had not been whipped. Dolbezhin flogged him, unlike the first, in a most cheerful frame of mind.

"My dear," he said with a smile, "go to the door."

"What for?"

"Because you haven't been whipped yet."

The lad did not even consider replying that this was not a reason, and he went to the door.

There was not a single boy in his class who had not been whipped.

Nevertheless, despite all this, difficult as it is to believe, the brotherhood not only respected Dolbezhin, they also liked him. Dolbezhin was in reality a goner himself. Like the brotherhood, he could not stand *townies*, and he gave one of them a most obscene nickname; when a squealer came to him with gossip, he thrashed him within an inch of his life; students like Goroblagodatsky were his favorites. Once *Flea* decided to amaze his comrades by remaining silent while Dolbezhin birched him, as if someone else were being whipped; Dolbezhin congratulated him before the whole form, whereas Lobov, for the same prank, "gave him a ride on the clouds" and then sprinkled salt over his lacerated body. Dolbezhin did not take bribes from parents, and he was so honest that at the end of the term he would read his final grades to his class and allow students to dispute them if they thought they deserved higher marks. For these reasons students liked him.

In class today there were only two incidents. He called on *Hoofs*. The latter picked up his Latin book, intending to do his translation at his seat.

"To the middle of the room!" Dolbezhin said.

It was worse to recite *in the middle* than at your seat because in the latter case classmates would prompt you. A student was able to hear the slightest sound, but if he did not hear it, he could glance sideways and guess the word by reading lips.

Hoofs walked to the middle of the room. He *flunked* (in the gymnasium it is called *failing*), and could not translate one sentence.

"Wrong!" Dolbezhin said.

He translated it differently.

"Wrong!"

Hoofs tried a new variation.

"To the stove!"

Hoofs was given *only* ten strokes. He was overjoyed he had gotten off so lightly, and had already started for his desk when he heard Dolbezhin's voice:

"Translate it again."

He translated the passage in a new way.

"Once more to the stove!"

Hoofs was given ten more strokes and again made to translate. This time Hoofs said he was unable to think up any more new variations, for which he was told:

"To the stove!"

He got ten more, and had to translate again. Hoofs racked his memory and brains. Nothing happened.

"Well!" Dolbezhin said, and his index finger pointed toward the stove.

Hoofs' faculties were strained to the limit, his brain was working at a hundred horsepower; suddenly, like an illumination from above, a new variation formed in his head. He recited it.

"At last!" Dolbezhin gave his approval. "That's enough from you. Take your seat. Wood should sit on wood!" Dolbezhin next turned to Trezorka:

"Did you prepare the vocabulary?"

"No."

"What? How many times has this happened?"

"If you wish, I'll prepare it," Trezorka answered smartly.

Trezorka was a townie and accustomed to treating people rather freely. His casual familiarity infuriated Dolbezhin. He grew pale, and veins bulged on his forehead.

"Oh, you scoundrel," he shouted, and his powerful hand picked up Kroneberg's bulky lexicon. The lexicon flew aloft and soared across the room; a little further and it would have actually cracked the lively lad's skull. Dolbezhin then began cursing and spitting; phlegm rattled in his tubercular chest; he was dumbfounded by Trezorka's audacity, but for some reason he did not dare to whip him, probably because Trezorka's father was a rather influential figure in town. And, in fact, some trouble almost erupted, but nothing came of it.

After this scene the classroom became deathly still. Everyone was trembling. Carefree Carp was the one person who had managed to fall asleep before the eyes of the enraged teacher; moreover, he was sitting in the front row. The teacher suddenly asked him a question, but he did not hear it and went on snoring softly. A friend nudged him but it was too late: the teacher's eyes were blazing.

"To the stove!"

"There're no more birches," the whip said.

"What were you using a few minutes ago?"

"They broke."

"Go get some new ones."

Meanwhile Carp swore and vowed that he got up at three o'clock to prepare his lesson and that he had a headache; the fact of the matter was that the Latin had put him in a stupor and he had shut his carp-like eyes.

"I'll show you!"

The whip appeared, but without the birches.

"The birches are all gone," he said.

Once again the teacher exploded, got up from his chair and went to where the whip was sitting. He found some fresh birches. Carp squeaked:

"Forgive me! . . ."

In the meantime the teacher had forgotten Carp and went after the whip. Grabbing the narrow ends of a bunch of birches, he started beating the stubs against his back, stomach, shoulders, and legs.

The bell rang. They sang the prayer "Meet is it . . ." [15] Carp had been saved. This very teacher, who flew into a rage over the slight trace of audacity in Rover's reply, would forgive and even welcome audacities of a much stronger sort. Thus, a certain *Blacking* once took a public examination. Dolbezhin raised his fist from under the table and said quietly: "If you flunk, I'll get you!" Blacking waved his own fist at him and whispered an unprintable obscenity. This only amused the teacher.

Finally, Dolbezhin was a cynic. He used to discuss the dirtiest things with the very same Blacking. The latter responded unabashedly and frankly, and they both improvised on various themes in the dirtiest way imaginable.

The seminary went to the dining hall, "gulped down some rotten cabbage soup and went to class again." The food was terrible: chaff was mixed with flour; helpings of beef frequently flew out the window and rotted in the courtyard; Comedo used to collect five or six helpings of meat and eat them, but he was the only who did so; there were small, whitish worms in the soup and mouse droppings in the kasha; only one steward provided irreproachable food, but such stewards were rare in the seminary. (Incidentally, we will discuss this steward later.)

Lobov's character resembled Tavlya's, and Dolbezhin's resembled Goroblagodatsky's. We now will describe a third person who, strictly speaking, was not a separate type but rather a combination of the two we have mentioned. This gentleman was called The Old Man.

He was a handsome man with a deep, expansive, open bass voice and a complexion of peaches and cream. Incidentally, he taught the so-called *Rubrics*, that is, the science of performing church services. He presented this subject in the strangest possible way. Instead of giving church books to students and showing when, what, and where something was read or sung, thus acquainting them with these books firsthand, he would pass out notes containing the first words of each prayer or hymn in their order of succession. Whole sheets of writing paper were filled with such headings. It was so difficult and tedious to study and memorize them that perhaps only four out of more than one hundred students would know the lesson. This was clearly not the students' fault. It is true that students sometimes would go on strike to spite a teacher and refuse to study their lesson, but such strikes were termed mutinies and ended with the whole class getting whipped; in this case it was not a question of going on strike, but simply of the physical and mental impossibility of memorizing all these things. Even the Old Man himself understood this. Nevertheless, he would whip every boy in the form: row upon row would trudge to the stove. Even though whips were extremely lenient in such cases, they were lenient only toward those they liked. Whips were very inventive, being specialists in their profession. When the Old Man suspected a whip of connivance and personally supervised a flogging, he would find the lad's body covered with blue stripes: the secret was that the whip would smear the birches with ink and then wipe them off a little: a light touch was sufficient to make a counterfeit scar. A student would waste his mind on the damnedest things! When these three teachers held classes on the same day, the same student could be whipped several times. Thus, Carp once received four floggings in one day (and at least four hundred while in school).

Today, however, there were no "Rubrics." They studied

a different subject. When the Old Man came in drunk, look out! His face was pale, and his huge black eyes were especially deep and bright. This misfortune happened today. Everyone shuddered as soon as he entered. The look on his face told everyone that his class was in for much misery. He picked up the register. The students passed a painful and terrible minute. The Old Man called on Elpakha. His body shaking and his soul shuddering, Elpakha went to the middle of the room.

"I . . ." his voice gave out.

"What's wrong?" The Old Man asked in a calm but intensely malevolent tone.

"Today's . . . my . . . name day. . . ."

"Congratulations!" His voice dropped two notes lower, but he was inwardly furious, and bloodthirsty animal instincts welled up inside him. . . . At that moment he was terrifying.

"I . . ." the sufferer said, "was in church . . ."

"Good for you!"

"And so I didn't manage to learn the lesson," Elpakha continued in a sinking voice, aware of the fixed, flashing eyes staring at him with intense hatred from a deathly pale face. . .

"Do you think your angel is rejoicing in heaven?"

Elpakha was silent; he felt a faint hope that he would not be punished since The Old Man's wrath sometimes dissipated itself in moralizing that could last for a half-hour or more. Elpakha was waiting to see what would happen.

"He's crying over your laziness."

Elpakha was more dead than alive.

"And you must cry. Come here."

Elpakha did not stir.

"Get over here!" The Old Man repeated in the same calm, even voice.

Elpakha walked up to him.

"Kneel here beside me."

The trembling Elpakha knelt down.

"Your angel is crying, and you're going to cry. Put your head on my knees."

Elpakha slowly obeyed, but he did not understand what The Old Man wanted to do to him. Suddenly he screamed, raised his head, and clutched it with his hands.

"Lie still, lie still," The Old Man told him.

Why did Elpakha scream? Because The Old Man grabbed a handful of hair, yanked it upward with his powerful hand, and tore it from its roots: then, slowly spreading his beautiful fingers, he began blowing the hair away and continued blowing as the hair flew through the air.

"Lie still, lie still!" The Old Man repeated.

Elpakha howled and lowered his head to The Old Man's knees as if they were an executioner's block.

The Old Man grabbed a second handful of Elpakha's hair and again yanked it from its roots and again blew it into the air.

"Forgive me, for God's sake," the sufferer implored.

"Lie still, lie still," The Old Man answered. There was something satanic in the measured tone of his voice. . . .

He repeated the same operation a third time even more slowly and coldbloodedly.

Elpakha sobbed in agony.

"Now go kneel in the middle of the room!" The Old Man said as the last strand of Elpakha's hair flew away and disappeared.

The Old Man sat for a long time afterward with head bowed. Did he feel pangs of remorse?

"Kneel for a *whole year!*"

His conscience was clear. The Old Man was in the habit of making students kneel for a whole year, for a term, for a month: when it was his class, you had to kneel. A merciless man!

The Old Man was on a rampage during the whole class. What didn't he think of: he made students *bow to the stove* and *kiss the birches*, he *salted* the wounds of those he whipped, in a word, he was an artist in his work even when he was drunk.

Nevertheless, it must be said that most of the brotherhood respected him for the same reasons they respected Dolbezhin, and only a minority hated and feared him. During the period we are describing, the moral level of the brotherhood and administration was almost identical. But later we shall see that both the brotherhood and the best part of the administration developed different principles. What we are describing now is vile, but as time passed the brotherhood became better and the administration became kinder. I am both distressed and irritated by several writers who stated that I had exhausted the whole of seminary life in "A Winter Evening in the Seminary." In the very next sketch, you will see good omens for the future, although even there you will find much that is really foul. The seminary, as it did in real life, will gradually improve in my sketches; only allow me to describe it as it was without adding or subtracting anything. Nothing is built quickly, and everything must pass through many phases of development. After about eight more sketches the seminary, God willing, will be described in full. If we were to limit ourselves only to these two sketches, "A Winter in the Seminary" and "Seminary Types," it would be most unfortunate: the reader would not have a complete picture of what a seminary is like and therefore he would form a relatively wrong impression of it.

1862

Suitors from the Seminary

THIRD SKETCH

Aksyutka's game finally drove Lobov to play a vile trick. The seminary went to the dining hall, gulped down some rotten cabbage soup, and went back to the classroom. Aksyutka alone grits his teeth.

Be that as it may, everyone more or less fortified himself: Aksyutka alone hungrily grits his teeth, or as the local expression has it, "his belly is growling, his belly is beating a tattoo." Aksyutka's situation had never been more helpless, in a moral as well as a physical sense than it was now. After making fun of Lobov, as was his habit, he no sooner landed in Kamchatka than he began getting fives in the register, that is, the very best marks.

This only enraged the teacher. "You animal," Lobov told him, "are you making fun of me? When they flog you, you get zeroes; when you're sent to Kamchatka, you get fives! You don't fool me: you're trying to move back to the first row so you can again make me furious with your zeroes. Forget it! You won't sit in the first row anymore, and until you start getting zeroes again, stay out of the dining hall." Aksyutka vowed and swore that he had repented, and promised to study regularly from now on. Lobov paid no attention. "To hell with your studying," he said, "stay in Kamchatka." Aksyutka's pride was severely hurt and, nostrils flaring, he thought: "We'll see who comes out on top." He began getting excellent marks, but after every class Lobov told him: "Don't eat today!"

Aksyutka somehow managed to get by for three days, here and there stealing a bun, a roll, a hunk of bread, oatmeal, peas, and so on. Yesterday he sneaked into the confectionery where *Vanka the Red* sold *shiten*, buns, rolls, brown bread, rusks, pretzels, apples, turnips, molasses, honey, red caviar, and, to the elite, *vodka* (of course, at twice the regular price); Aksyutka stole several rolls there by hammering a nail into a stick and using it to reach across the counter for food when Vanka the Red was on the other side of the room. But today was Wednesday; the confectionery was crowded only on Mondays and Tuesdays when seminarians still had the pocket money they brought from home; stealing was a risky business when the confectionery was empty. What could he do? Knowing that Aksyutka's belly was growling, seminarians carefully hid their hunks of bread and kept a close eye on him. Most of them had no desire to share their extra bread with him; moreover, they had nothing to spare: the seminary did not serve morning or evening snacks; dinner consisted of two hunks of bread, of which one was eaten in the dining hall, and the other pocketed for later on.[1]

Meanwhile, the whole school had spilled out into the courtyard. Students were building a toboggan slide. Since boards were unavailable, the slide was made entirely of snow. Snowballs the size of a man were rolling across the school's immense courtyard. While one boy directed them, ten others worked on each ball. They rolled the balls to the slide, and students swarmed around it like ants around an anthill. In a couple of days the entire seminary would fly headfirst down the long, smooth slope, a little smaller than the wooden slopes in Petersburg, on sleds, toboggans, iced boards, mats, skates, or simply on their natural scooters, that is, flat on their stomachs. The seminarians presented a gay and cheerful sight: the supervisor elected by them shouted his order to begin work, resonant bass and tenor voices responded; laughter and jokes filled the air. A good time.

Aksyutka grits his teeth.

About eighty persons were playing *kickball* on the left side of the courtyard, using a leather ball that was the size of a human head and stuffed with hair. Two teams lined up opposite each other; one student kicked the ball, slowly advancing it with his foot; this was the most difficult part of the game since a powerful kick might send the ball to the other side, into the enemy camp where it might be captured. You were not allowed *to toe the ball* since you might strike an opponent's foot. You were not allowed *to kick from behind the line*, that is, to run into the enemy camp, wait for the ball, and then drive it *to town*, that is, across the goal line. Anyone who broke the rules of the game was hit in the neck.

"Kickball," one team shouted. This meant they had *captured the town* (scored).

The victors, proud and delighted, returned to their positions. They were having a good time.

But Aksyutka is gritting his teeth.

In a corner of the courtyard near the confectionery and bakery several persons had made tunnels in a huge pile of snow and were crawling through these tunnels on their stomachs. In another corner of the courtyard students were playing war, trying to dislodge each other from the positions they had taken on a pile of snow, and using snowballs for ammunition. Grishkets and Vasenda knocked Sashkets down in the snow and piled snow over his arms and legs so that only his head stuck out—Sashkets was defenseless, and they gave him a massage. Grishkets and Vasenda roared with laughter, and so did Sashkets; this was a friendly joke. Everyone was having a good time.

Aksyutka grits his teeth.

Two women entered the courtyard; one was an old woman, the other somewhere past thirty. After asking to see the *enspictor*, that is, the inspector, they headed for a two-story building that had on its roof a spire topped by a star. Presently they were standing in the inspector's reception room. The old woman was decrepit, her wrinkled face so scorched by the summer sun that even during winter it kept its tan; her small eyes darted back and forth like two frightened mice, and their melancholy expression evoked compassion. This hunched-over old lady, balding at the temples, had a wool shawl over her grey hair, a shabby coat on her shoulders, and men's boots on her feet. The other woman was about thirty-two, tall and pock-marked, with long, calloused hands. She had the sullen, indifferent look of those who are facing something inevitable in their lives and have become reconciled to it. She wore a new coat made of rabbit fur, a new shawl, and goatskin shoes instead of boots.

They waited half an hour or so for the inspector. He finally appeared, but he was obviously in a bad mood.

"What do you want?" he asked brusquely.

Both women fell at his feet. The old one began to cry

and, as if she were wailing a lament for the dead, began speaking:

"Father, dear father. . . . Oh, benefactor, our sorrow is great . . . we've lost our last crust of bread . . . father, don't be angry! . . ."

The old woman struck her head against the floor.

Such servility somewhat mollified the inspector, but his bad mood had not entirely disappeared.

"Say why you came."

The inspector's threatening voice made the old woman tremble, she became confused and began talking gibberish:

"Our dear one passed away . . . our loved one was struck down . . . he sipped some kvass, at first everything was just fine . . ."

The inspector lost his temper.

"You can go to hell, you wretched hags," he shouted, stamping his foot, . .

Both women froze. . . .

"On your feet at once and talk sense, otherwise I'll have you chased out of here with a broom! . . . Sluts! . . . You've interrupted my nap!"

"Father! . . ." the old woman started to say something.

"Ivan!" yelled the inspector. "Throw them out! . . ."

Both women jumped to their feet. The old woman rushed from the reception room into the vestibule. An onlooker might find all this very strange, especially the old woman's last maneuver; we could now expect, apparently, the inspector to really lose his temper; but something quite different happened, his face brightened, and he began pacing calmly up and down the room, patiently awaiting the old woman.

She returned shortly, a bag in one hand, a bundle in the other. She placed both of them at the inspector's feet. . . .

"What's this?" he asked.

"Don't spurn, father, gifts from the countryside, and . . ."

"Show me what you have there."

Hastily untying the bag, the old woman removed sugar, tea, a bottle of rum, dried mushrooms, and apples; the bundle contained about thirty-five yards of cloth. . . .

The inspector said, not without pleasure but not without dignity either: "All right, thank you. . . . What do you want?"

"This is my daughter," the old woman said, "She's an orphan . . . we've been to the bishop . . . he's assigned her a church, her father's . . ."

"So?"

"He sent us to you."

"For suitors?"

"For suitors, father," and the old woman again plopped down at his feet.

"Very well, very well."

"But no rascals, father!" Then the old woman stuck out her hand and unclenched her fist: a silver ruble was in her palm.

The inspector took the old woman's ruble and put it in his pocket with complete composure, exactly as an auditor would when he takes bribes from his charges.

"I have two fellows in mind and perhaps we'll find some others who are interested."

The inspector then inquired about the location of the church, the duties involved, its revenues, and the number of other clerics; he asked for the old woman's address, and promised to let the students go to the bride-showing on the following day.[2]

The old woman and the bride thanked the inspector and went on their way. They stopped in the courtyard and glanced at the colorful, swarming crowd of students.

"Which one will God send as our provider?" thought the old woman.

"Which one will I marry?" thought the bride.

This bride was an *assigned bride* who was marrying solely to avoid starving to death. In Russia marriages are often arranged so that the bridegroom will receive a promotion and a dowry, and the bride a roof over her head as well as her husband's name and rank. But this all takes place more or less within the bounds of propriety, it is disguised in one way or another, and therefore its ugliness and its perversion of the honorable goals of marriage are not very shocking. Such cases are frequent everywhere. But nowhere is the sanctity of marriage so violated as it is among seminarians. In the seminary the desecration of marriage and its perversion are legalized and hallowed by tradition. In the course of fourteen years [3] a seminarian is flogged perhaps four hundred times, he is humiliated and corrupted morally, intellectually, and physically any number of times; after this educational training he at last earns a diploma that should give him, it would seem, the right to a position in a parish, but the only way he can get one is to agree to marry a *certain State* girl, an *assigned bride* designated by the *administration*. It's more or less the same as when *landowners* used to *marry off* their peasants instead of letting the peasants *marry of their own accord*. When a clergyman dies and leaves a family behind, what can it do? It might as well starve to death! . . . The house (if it belongs to the Church), land, gardens, meadows, family hearth—all these pass to his successor. Russian priests, deacons, and sacristans are members of the Orthodox proletariat. . . . They have no property. Every priest is hungry and cold until he finds a position; then his parish feeds him; he always dies with the oppressive thought that his sons and daughters will be destitute. The poverty, landlessness, and insecurity of the clergy have perverted its entire way of life. In order to prevent orphaned families of clergymen from starving to death, it was decided to sacrifice one of the highest human institutions, marriage. Churches are *assigned*, note the technical, almost official quality of this expression. When the head of a family dies, his position is given to someone who agrees to marry his daughter or relative. Announcements of a new vacancy stipulate that candidates must marry a *certain girl*. Suitors begin visiting the bride's home. For the most part, this is done in a rush, and a time limit is set for the bride's decision; consequently, *claimants* do not have time to get acquainted. There have been instances when the bride, living two hundred versts away, failed to arrive in the cathedral city on time; and the applicant for the priest's position had neither the money nor the time to visit the bride; in such cases both parties exchanged letters; agreement was reached through the mail and, after receiving the order to assume his position, the bridegroom went to see his bride. Such arrangements frequently produced outrageous confrontations: the bride turned out to be an old, pock-marked shrew; and the bridegroom attempted to beat her even before the wedding. But when the bride did come to town, even then everything went smoothly and the stale, defective merchandise was disposed of with remarkable dexterity; the bride's cheeks were plastered with cosmetics and the bride-showing was scheduled for the evening in poor light: the old, pock-marked face seemed young and smooth. . . . It even happened that a young, pretty relative, sometimes married herself, would play the bride's role until the very day of the wedding, and only in church did the bridegroom see on his left a monster straight out of those ancient drawings which long ago were first dried in smoke and darkened with soot, and then exchanged for onions and eggs.

What could he do? Having starved long enough after finishing school, the seminarian clenched his teeth and looked grudgingly at his future mate, but . . . he said to hell with it and followed Olga's admonition to Prince Igor; he stood before the altar and contemplated how he would break the ribs of his life's companion, damn her, on the very first night.[4] It goes without saying that under such conditions of deceit and hypocrisy marriage is an evil, the defilement of the most cherished and sacred of human rights. But even when the merchandise was displayed openly during the bride-showing and matchmaking, even then it was very rare that the marriage turned out happily. If marriages often fail after long acquaintance, what can be expected of one that is arranged purely by chance! In arranged, society marriages the insulted and humiliated party is, for the most part, the woman; but in seminarian marriages both the man and the woman are victims. . . . In society marriages the man says: "I am not starving, I have a good name, marry me and you will not starve and you will have a good name." Things are different in seminarian marriages. The bridegroom cries out: "I have nothing to eat." The bride cries out: "I'm starving to death." There is but one solution: both parties must unite. The origin of all this is the damned poverty of our clergy. Who is to blame?

And so a sexton's widow brought her impassive daughter and managed to have a position assigned to her. The bishop sent her to the school to select a bridegroom from students about to be expelled.

During the period that Lobov, The Old Man, Dolbezhin, and similar pedagogues were on a rampage in the seminary, a new type of teacher was emerging who seemed more humanitarian.

Among them was Pavel Fedorovich Krasnov.

Pavel Fedorovich was a young graduate of the theological academy. He was a handsome man with a likeable face, by nature kind and tactful. We would like to be wholly sympathetic towards him, but how is this possible?

It never entered his mind to abolish birchings; on the contrary, he defended them as an indispensable supplement to education.

On the other hand, when he punished a student, he never gave him more than ten lashes. He taught arithmetic, geography, and Greek but he did not make students memorize everything word for word, and in the seminary this was considered almost a sign that the arrival of the Antichrist was near and that the world was coming to its end. He allowed students to ask questions, make objections, and demand explanations of various topics; he condescended to answer them, and in the seminary this was the utmost liberalism. Carried away by a positively good heart, he sometimes interested himself in the needs of his students. Thus, in the first sketch we mentioned an unfortunate student who would have been almost eaten alive by ticks if it had not been for Pavel Fedorovich: he took him to the bathhouse, washed him, steamed him, cut his hair, burned all his clothes, gave him new ones, and treated him kindly. Once Lobov had to take over Krasnov's classes when the latter became ill. Lobov lifted Carp up and thrashed him *on the clouds.* He wanted to do the same thing to the class censor, a lad about twenty years old, but the censor ran off, whereupon Lobov recorded his name in the day-book, and a whipping still seemed in the offing.[5] When Krasnov learned how Lobov had gone wild in class, he lost his temper, tore the day-book to shreds, and quarreled with Lobov. His grades were fair, and he did not conceal them from students; on the contrary, he summoned dissatisfied students to argue their case. Only once did Krasnov beat a student mercilessly with his own hands, but that was because the seminarian had made an obscene joke during his recitation, and Pavel Fedorovich had delicate nerves. In short, as a private individual Krasnov was indisputably honest and kind.

But look what he was like as a seminary teacher.

"Ivanov!" he calls.

Ivanov gets up from a rear desk in Kamchatka, an area Krasnov watched continuously and carefully and, as a result, he was an insufferable teacher for those who wanted *to rest on their laurels*, that is, for sluggards. Krasnov harassed them not so much by floggings as by a systematic persecution; and this persecution, based on psychological tactics, had a strong Jesuitical flavor. Krasnov sees in the register that Ivanov has a zero for the day, but nevertheless he says:

"Recite the lesson, Ivanov."

Ivanov makes no response. He thinks to himself: "Krasnov knows I have a zero in the register. . . . Why's he calling on me? Just to torment me!"

"Well, why don't you answer?"

Ivanov is silent. It would have been better if Krasnov scolded him; then he would not have been ashamed before his classmates because scoldings from the authorities are never taken to heart. Now, however, Ivanov finds himself in a ludicrous position: his own friends are laughing at his embarrassment and thus for the time being he is without his chief ally against the administration, the brotherhood.

"Are you well?" Pavel Fedorovich asks tenderly.

"Yes," Ivanov answers, sullen and mistrustful.

"Nothing's happened to you?"

"Nothing."

"Nothing?"

"Nothing," Ivanov answers in a solemn, funereal tone.

"But you seem upset about something?"

Not a sound from Ivanov, not a whisper.

"Isn't that right?"

But it seems that Ivanov's mouth is sewn shut.

"Why are you silent? . . . Well, recite the lesson for me."

Ivanov finally gets hold of himself. Blushing and gasping, he shrieks wildly: "I . . . I . . . don't . . . know."

"What don't you know?"

"I . . . the lesson."

Pavel Fedorovich pretends not to hear the answer.

"What did you say?"

"The lesson . . . I don't know it!" Ivanov repeats with difficulty.

"I can't hear you, talk louder."

"I don't know!" Ivanov has to repeat again.

His classmates roar with laughter.

Ivanov thinks to himself: "I wish he'd go straight to hell! He's really got his hooks into me, the fiend."

Meanwhile, the teacher feigns surprise that *even* Ivanov has not prepared the lesson.

"You don't know? But that's impossible!"

More laughter.

Ivanov would have gladly fallen through the ground.

"Why don't you know the lesson?"

The baiting begins again and continues until Ivanov begins to lie.

"I had a headache."

"It was probably stuffed up?"

"It was stuffed up."

"And maybe you caught cold?"

"I caught cold."

"A stuffy head and a cold? What a pity, my boy!"

His classmates, seeing Ivanov's confusion, are breaking up with laughter. But the sufferer is thinking: "My God, when's he going to whip me?" And he decides to get it over with at once.

"I can't study."

"Why not, my friend?"

"I'm not smart enough."

"Did you try to study yesterday?"

"I tried."

"What were you studying?"

The most painful moment had arrived: even if his life depended on it, Ivanov could not have opened his mouth; it was as if his lips had been sealed with a padlock. Ivanov had not even bothered to find out the assignment, much less learn it. Afraid that classmates would prompt Ivanov, Pavel Fedorovich rose from his chair, walked toward Ivanov, and asked:

"Well, why don't you say something?"

Ivanov became mute; this unfortunate lad could not open his mouth.

Pavel Fedorovich placed a hand on him. While Ivanov was undergoing this painful moral torture, other Kamchatkites began to share his anxiety.

"Why are you looking at the desk? Look straight at me."

Ivanov is trembling nervously. He cannot lift up his head; it is as heavy as the beer barrel that only knocked against the *bogatyr's* shoulders.[6]

In the meantime Pavel Fedorovich had taken hold of Ivanov's chin.

"There's no need to be shy, my friend."

The measure of spiritual suffering overflowed. Ivanov just sighs heavily. After the long interrogation, with that feeling of deep despair that causes people to jump headfirst from third-story windows, Ivanov is finally forced to confess that he does not know what was assigned. But he now hopes that after this the scolding and flogging will begin, and so it is nearly over; it is a vain hope.

"Why have you settled in Kamchatka? Take a look at your fellow apostles. Krasnopevtsev, you tell me, what is a skerry?"

Someone prompts Krasnopevtsev.

"A skerry," he answers smartly, "is the same thing as a sea dog."

Everyone roars with laughter.

"Well, Vozdvizhensky . . . you go to the map and show me how many continents there are."

Vozdvizhensky walks up to a map hanging on the blackboard, picks up a pointer, and begins traveling across Europe.

"Well, get started, my friend."

"Europe," the friend begins.

"One," the teacher counts.

"Asia."

"Two." the teacher counts.

"Hispania," the Kamchatkite continues, moving his pointer into the White Sea straight at the walruses and polar bears.

Everybody roars with laughter. The teacher counts:

"Three."

But the scholar stopped at the White Sea, looking for his dear Hispania, and remained for the winter.

"Well, travel on. Or have you enumerated all the countries of the world?"

"All of them," our learned geographer answered.

"You're absolutely right. Go to your seat, wood should sit on wood," Pavel Fedorovich concluded.

He intentionally calls on the most notorious sluggards, remarkable for their extreme, mindless ignorance.

"Berezin, tell me where to place tenths."

"In the tenth place."

"Excellent. And how old are you?"

"Twenty-one."

"And how long have you been studying?"

"This is my ninth year."

"And it's plain that you have not been unsuccessful for eight years. And in the future keep up the good work. And now listen to how our Teterin translates. The translation should have gone: 'Diogenes, after seeing a small city with huge gates, said: Men of Myndus, bar your gates, lest the city should run away.' The Greek word for men is *andres*. Here is Teterin's translation: 'Andrey, shut the wicket, a wolf is coming,' He also signed for boots in the following way: Peters Teterins were given boots. "Well, listen, Peters Teterins, what is the sea?"

"Water."

"What does it taste like?"

"It's wet."

It was said of Peters Teterins that he translated *maximus* as *Maksim;* when they began to prompt him that *maximus* means very large, he came out with 'very large Maksim.'

"Well, Pototsky, conjugate *Virgin Mary!*"

"I am the Virgin, thou art the Virgin, he is the Virgin, we are Virgins, you are Virgins, they are Virgins."

"Well done. Conjugate 'blockhead.' "

"I am a blockhead . . ."

"Precisely. That's enough. Fedorov, go to the board and spell 'hunting.' "

He writes "huntun."

"Spell 'muddy.' "

He writes "dummy."

Pavel Fedorovich made fun of Kamchatkites by forcing them to talk nonsense. Ivanov inwardly rejoiced that the teacher's attention had been diverted. His joy was short-lived: the teacher was only starting a new maneuver.

"Well, Ivanov, what do you think of these fine fellows?"

Ivanov becomes alarmed once again.

"What would you call these gentlemen? Wouldn't you call them savages? Platonov, what is a savage?"

"A savage person."

"Do you know how to speak Greek?"

"No."

"And I heard that you did. You were walking along with another goose like yourself. You said: 'Alpha, Beta, Gamma, Delta'; the other goose said: 'Epsilon, Zeta, Eta, Theta.' Isn't that right? It was then that a baker called you all heathens. Once a fellow like you visited his father during vacation. His father asked him: 'How do you say in Latin: the horse fell from the bridge?' Our hero answered: 'horsendus fellendus from brigendus.' "

Ivanov once again began hoping he had been forgotten.

"Aren't you ashamed, Ivanov, of sitting with such dolts? I'm sure you wouldn't try conjugating blockhead, you wouldn't say that tenths stand in the tenth place, you wouldn't look for some kind of Hispania in the Arctic Ocean; why did you get mixed up with such savages?"

"Forgive me," Ivanov whispered.

"What is there to forgive you for?" And Pavel Fedorovich again forced Ivanov to condemn himself:

"I've been lazy."

"Will you work if I forgive you?"

A new maneuver began. It is well known that waiting to be punished causes a schoolboy more suffering than the punishment itself. Pavel Fedorovich understood this and put to full use his practical psychology.

"Forgive you? Then you'll scold me yourself for permitting you to be lazy; you'll say: 'I wasn't stupid but the teachers paid no attention to me.'"

"I'm sorry!" Ivanov said.

"Do you know what could happen to you if, God forbid, you were expelled? Do you know what lies ahead for all these Kamchatkites?"

Kamchatka pricked up its ears.

"There are a lot of people who are now wandering over the Russian land: unemployed sextons, sacristans, lay brothers from churches and consistories, dismissed novices, expelled students; do you know what the authorities want to do with them? They want to draft them into the army."

"I'm sorry!" Ivanov said, thinking dejectedly: "My God, when is the whipping going to start? . . . Damned Krasnov! . . . He's worn me out."

"I heard for a fact that there will be a conscription soon, a recruitment. Expect the worst . . ."

In the first sketch we had an opportunity to mention the recurrent, ominous rumor that all unemployed, expelled students would be drafted. Now we will add that the authorities frequently wanted to put this plan into operation, but the clergy always started grumbling, and understandably so: many of the powers that be were either sons of clerics or had sons and other relatives who were clerics. Be that as it may, the ominous rumor about military service frequently made seminarians tremble.

Pavel Fedorovich took full advantage of this fact.

"How can I forgive you?" he tells Ivanov. "Do you really want to put on a uniform?"

"I'll study."

"But you just said you couldn't study?"

Ivanov feels miserable because the teacher has forced him to confess:

"I told a lie."

The badgering continues. After a long interrogation he had to agree, in a sepulchral tone, that he deserved to be punished; he then had to set the number of blows. Only when a student was driven to the verge of spiritual collapse and close to losing his mind, only then did this teacher send him to the stove where he was given ten blows with the birches and advised that each time he did not know his lesson he would receive the same ten lashes on his backside. Determined to put sluggards on the path of truth, Pavel Fedorovich tirelessly and energetically pursued his goal, and he always brought his work to a favorable conclusion.

"Ivanov! Come to my apartment after class."

Having invited Ivanov to his apartment, Krasnov made him study the lesson during recreation period; if ever again he were to decide to take things easy, he would be made to study all the time, he would not be given a spare minute even on holidays, and the damned textbook would always be under his nose; and so our sluggard grit his teeth and plunged into the hated lines. Little by little the memorization sucked him in and swallowed him up.

Is this the end?

No, it is still not the end. Pavel Fedorovich had kept in touch with other teachers concerning a certain neophyte. Dolbezhin and the Old Man had told the neophyte: "You study for other teachers, my dear, but not for me? I'll flog you, you animal, I'll kill you." These teachers in turn began *birching* the sluggard *into shape* in their respective subjects. What could you do? You would involuntarily gulp down every bit of your seminary schooling even though deep hatred and irreconcilable aversion for this schooling would ripen in your soul and take root forever. It was true that a student would be grateful if his birchings earned him a diploma, but he would be grateful not for his seminary schooling, but for certain privileges the diploma granted.

My dear sirs, do you like the pedagogical barbarism to which even Pavel Fedorovich resorted, a man with a positively good heart? What can this mean? Since seminary courses are difficult and absurd, I assure you that few seminarians would have studied at all if Lobov, Dolbezhin, the Old Man, and Krasnov had not employed unnatural and dreadful methods in their teaching. Lobov, Dolbezhin, the Old Man, and Krasnov had no choice but to resort to spiritual and physical coercion. The main cause of all this lies not in the teachers or students but rather in the nature of a seminary education, may it vanish from the face of the earth! A seminarian with the least bit of sense always remembers his education with a feeling of horror.

Until today Kamchatka had been resting serenely and lightheartedly on its laurels; but today it was filled with noisy, frantic talk. Pavel Fedorovich's threats about military service provoked this talk and noise. The ominous rumor, however, did not make the same impression upon every Kamchatkite. Kamchatkites can be divided into two groups according to the curriculum in the seminary. This curriculum was either *sacred*, today called theological, or *profane*, today called secular. Certain Kamchatkites spurned only *profane* courses, and they diligently studied Divine Law.[7] Biblical history, church rubrics and church singing. These students were preparing specifically to become sextons and sacristans. Two good representatives of this type were *Vasenda* and *Azinus.* Vasenda was an overager who would have to finish school not as a youth but as a thirty-year-old adult. He said to hell with everything and took up sacred studies. He was a kind, honest man of enormous physical strength, and who, like all strong men, was calm and intense; above all, however, he was a remarkable skinflint and businessman. He even looked like a flinty sexton whose household would be every bit as good as a deacon's, and maybe better.

Let's peek into Vasenda's student trunk when he pulls it out from under the bed. In one corner is a small wooden icon of Saint Vasily, a blessing from his mother, a sexton's widow; two straps are nailed inside the top of the trunk and they hold several quires of writing paper; around the inside edge near the paper there is an art exhibit consisting of wrappers from candies and sweets: a general with a nose almost as wide as his face; a naked woman is breast-feeding a dove, standing behind her is a cupid who apparently suffers from dropsy; a cheap print cut out of "Bova" depicts this legendary hero routing an enormous army with a broom; [8] further on there is a picture from the Bible in which you can see the expulsion of our first parents from paradise, and other pictures of a similar sort; these pictures are interspersed with candy wrappers; here too, among other things, a calendar is glued to the lid and it shows the days and months for an entire year. In one corner of the trunk is a small tub containing mushrooms in sour cream, in another a bag of oatmeal. On the bottom are books, all of the sacred variety since Vasenda had sold all his profane ones, having no need of them. Clean linen and new clothes are carefully folded on the other side of the trunk. In addition, there is a small box under the icon where Vasenda keeps his money, letters, the most recent song book, snuff, an empty phial, a penknife, a comb, soap, and so forth. Such is Vasenda's trunk, girded with strong metal straps and fastened with a very strong lock. Vasenda owns an excellent, tanned sheepskin coat and a pair of indestructible boots complete with leggings. He was thrifty to the extreme: for example, he would write with the same pen for a whole year, barely touching it to the paper and carefully wrapping it up each time he used it. Even now he looks like a sedate, practical sexton; and, in fact, he does know how to buy and sell anything; his gait is imposing, his boots shine. . . . He represented the best type of Kamchatkite. And he actually did become an excellent and prosperous provincial sexton. The rumors about military service caused him little concern: he believed in his star.

Azinus was a tall, long-legged, round-shouldered student whose shoulder blades protruded from his back; his wide cheekbones, darting gray eyes, and constantly uplifted nose, which was always sniffing something, gave his face the scheming look we find on petty crooks with low foreheads. All year round he wore a robe made of ticking, boots that were full of holes, and a quilted cap. Azinus was the son of an unemployed sexton, an alcoholic living on charity. Azinus' mother, a poor old woman whose husband beat her all her life, had sent her son to school with a distant relative, but because of inexperience or senile absentmindedness she did not bother to give him the documents needed to enroll in the seminary. The relative brought Azinus, then an eight-year-old boy, to the school's enormous courtyard and set him free to obtain his education on his own. Azinus walked around the courtyard for a long time, not knowing where to go. By evening he was very hungry; at eight o'clock he saw a huge group of students, joined them, and found himself in the dining hall where, without giving it a second thought, he dug into the cabbage soup and kasha. After supper the students first went to prayers and then to their bedrooms. Azinus followed them; he found an empty cot in a bedroom and fell fast asleep. In the morning he went to prayers with the others; afterwards he happened to walk into the first form where he settled down in the back row. About three months passed before a teacher finally noticed him. Inquiries were made: Azinus' name was not on the roll. He was fed for the last time and ordered to leave the premises and go wherever he liked. And this is childhood, the best time of our lives! He lived on alms for several days, sleeping God knows where, until he bumped into another beggar, his own father, who took his little son to a sexton he knew; finally the sexton enrolled little Azinus in the seminary which was to cripple him forever.

At first he made progress, but soon he said to hell with everything and, having survived the usual number of whippings, settled permanently in Kamchatka. Here his personality was formed, and it was utterly erratic. He spent most of his time at odds-evens, tops, three-card monte, trading knives, and similar seminary games of chance. He became the school gypsy, trading and exchanging, buying and selling everything under the sun. The little money and various articles that he acquired slipped through his fingers without rhyme or reason. Every student who remained at school over Christmas or Easter managed to save something for the holidays; Azinus, however, would often spend all his money on food on the eve of the holiday, then he would wander through bedrooms where he would fawn, beg, grovel, curse, and lie in order to cadge a piece of a roll, an egg, or a chunk of butter from his classmates. With such a character he became an inveterate liar. His stories are repeated even today. For example, once he told how wolves attacked him as he went somewhere in a terrible blizzard during wintertime. What could he do? He said he was so scared that he hid in a field of rye. When he was asked how he landed in a field of rye in the wintertime, Azinus cursed, distributed a few massages, rolled a tail from the skirts of his robe, and twirled it in the air. He frequently told his audience that he had seen ghosts, goblins, dead men, and devils. Not only did he tell lies, he was also ready to steal anything. Once he traveled home, a distance of approximately one hundred and fifty versts, with four kopecks in his pocket; he slept in the forest and ate unripe berries; now and then he would drop into taverns where he would have dinner and then slip away without paying for it. When this fine fellow arrived home, he still had one kopeck left. Azinus was the exact opposite of Vasenda. He, too, paid no attention to the rumors about conscription, but this was solely because of his erratic personality.

In general, Kamchatkites who rejected profane subjects and studied only sacred ones were not greatly excited by Pavel Fedorovich's words. There were reasons for this. The administration looked on sacred Kamchatka with fairly benevolent eyes: at least it did do something. There were plans (and Kamchatkites knew about them) to turn the sacred back rows into a special class, a so-called *sexton class*. Consequently, students like Vasenda and Azinus were calm.

But something quite different took place in the other half of Kamchatka. Here absolute nihilists were resting on their laurels: they rejected both sacred and profane subjects.

Several wretched individuals were sitting there who had persuaded themselves and the administration that they had no ability and could not study, even though it is strange to think that such a limited elementary education could possibly be beyond the reach of anyone. One student, the son of a Finnish priest, spent six years in the first two forms and barely learned to read before being expelled. His nickname was *Primar Zabalder Gospells Church Calendar* since he called the primer "primar" and the psalter "zabalder." Such cases are not unusual in the seminary. Chabrya spent an equal amount of time in the same forms. Some students struggled fourteen years to reach the fourth form, which is enough time to receive a doctorate in any field and only a year less than the length of present-day military service. Poor wretches, you drudge like soldiers, and now they threaten you with military service! . . . The very thing to frighten you! . . . Nevertheless, you denounce the administration and tremble for your fate: you naturally have no desire to endure the same service a second time.

We have seen that really incompetent students were very worried today. But there were also some able students in profane Kamchatka, and they, too, shuddered at Krasnov's words, not so much because someone wanted to put them in uniform—these sluggards were a carefree bunch and thought little about the future—but rather because of the misfortune that their classmate Ivanov had experienced today. On the one hand, they had grown so lazy that they could not open a book; on the other, the more intelligent sluggards were instinctively and, indeed, rightly disgusted by their seminary education. Nevertheless, a nervous shudder still ran down their spines when they remembered Pavel Fedorovich. They felt that they were next in line after Ivanov, and that Krasnov's eagle eye would find them in Kamchatka and put them through the moral torture of his psycho-pedagogical system. Kamchatka today was sad and weary; however, if you, the reader, will wait a bit, you'll see what brought gay excitement not only to sacred Kamchatka, not only to profane Kamchatka, but to every seminarian in the form.

Only first allow me to describe a prank that Aksyutka and Ipse played today; otherwise, you will not understand our story.

Aksyutka is still gritting his teeth.

It grew dark. As we already have had occasion to mention, lamps were not lit in the classrooms until study hour began. Aksyutka sneaked into the third form where in the darkness he searched through the pockets and desks of students.

"Where can I filch something?" he whispered.

He went to the first form. He was no more successful there and angrily bent some poor lad into triple runners.

"They've guzzled up everything, the scoundrels."

As Aksyutka's hunger grew, so naturally did his insurmountable desire to steal something to eat; his cunning, resourcefulness, and inventiveness increased at the same time. He found his friend and faithful companion, Ipse, and together they set out for that corner of the courtyard, near the gates, where the bakery was located. They reached the bakery; Ipse hid in a dark corner while Aksyutka began pushing against the door with all his might.

"Fetter, dear, give us some bread!"

Fetter was a kind soldier. He frequently distributed bread to hungry seminarians, and, if he liked you, rye flapjacks. But this baker could not stand Aksyutka: he was convinced that Aksyutka had stolen his new leggings.

We will note here another curious fact of seminary life.

Students looked upon the servants at school more or less as their superiors; the inspector considered them much more important than any fourth-form warden. The administration always respected the testimony or complaints of a *guard* (the student term for servants). A student could take no action whatsoever against a guard. The reason is that the custodian, quartermaster, cook, baker, gatekeeper, and guard who administered whippings did what the administration wanted them to do. Come what might, all of them had to draw upon the limited supplies intended for students in order to provide the administration with bread, meat, grain, linen, cloth, and the like. It naturally followed that a complaint against any one of them was, as it were, a complaint against the administration itself; for example, if you accused the cook of serving skimpy portions of kasha, you were actually saying that the steward was stealing State grain and sharing it with the superintendent, that the school superintendent was sharing it with his counterpart in the seminary, that the latter was sharing it with the superintendent of the theological academy, and so on: it turned out that a complaint about the kasha was a complaint against the highest authorities and verged on conspiracy and mutiny.[9] In fact, in the seminary such complaints were actually called mutinies and dealt with as if that was what they were.

Servants recognized their position and took advantage of it. They lived much better than those they served: they wore clothing issued by the State, had plenty of good food, could air their grievances and threaten to quit; they always had rich cabbage soup with fresh meat, thickly buttered kasha, and, unlike seminarians whose bread was rationed, as much bread as they wanted. Besides getting room, board, and clothing, they received a salary of from eight to twelve rubles, and the custodian received seventeen in paper currency; [10] they were richer than the richest seminarians. Many of them had opportunities to steal from the State. The cook received a weekly stipend from certain students for feeding them kasha in the morning and in the evening. Zakharenko, the whip, openly took bribes; every holiday he went from form to form and announced: "What do you say, fellows, some tobacco money for Aleksey Grigorich (Zakharenko's name)?" Two- and five-kopeck coins dropped into his outstretched palms. Students noticed that he whipped them more conscientiously and zestfully if the collection had been small the week before. Zakharenko also sold students snuff, which he prepared himself. In short, the servants composed a secondary administration. If we add that several of them carried gossip to the inspector, then you can understand the influence they had over students. Consequently, there is nothing surprising about drunken Zakharenko rubbing his knuckles across a student's head, as if across a tambourine, and saying: "You rotten priestling, you make a mess, but we have to clean it up." Or what is surprising about Fir beating a student over the head with a broom, Loggerhead thrashing someone, and the like? In most cases students patiently bore such abuse.

But Aksyutka, because he was a goner, paid no attention to servant superiors. He kept trying to break into Fetter's bakery.

"Who's there?" Fetter asked.

"It's me, Fetter."

"You wouldn't eat the kind of bread I'd give you. . . . Go away!"

"Fetter, honest-to-God, I'm hungry."

"Go away! . . . Stop hanging around!"

Aksyutka changed his tone. He began calling Fetter names:

"Fetter, you devil, give me some bread! Does a little piece

mean that much to you? You dog, I hope you choke on those boots you are making!"

"You son of a bitch!" Fetter muttered.

Fetter stuck an awl into the wooden block he used as a table and, gritting his teeth, he grabbed a broom and dashed headlong to the door. He chased after Aksyutka. Aksyutka was a very good runner; he was an expert at playing tag and in a small area he knew how *to dodge*, making sudden turns first in one, than in another direction. The courtyard was large, and therefore Fetter would have had difficulty in catching Aksyutka if the latter had not run toward the gate. Fetter shouted at the gatekeeper: "Grab him."

The gatekeeper also grabbed a broom and went after Aksyutka. Aksyutka changed direction. Unfortunately for him it was six o'clock in the evening, the hour when servants swept out the bedrooms. They now began to appear in various corners of the courtyard.

"Grab him!"

Everyone knew Aksyutka. The servants took up brooms against him. Aksyutka was in a bad way. Hounded on four sides, he looked around like a rapacious wolf. "They'll break my neck, damn them!" he thought. But suddenly his nostrils quivered. He made a quick dash toward Fetter. Suspecting nothing in this new maneuver, Fetter ran toward him with outstretched arms. The other servants, seeing that Aksyutka was almost in Fetter's grasp, put down their brooms and shouted: "Get him!"

Flying straight at Fetter, Aksyutka suddenly dove under his feet. Fetter flew into the air and tumbled head over heels. Aksyutka raced away toward the classroom; it was already lit up, since study period had started. A dangerous man when angry, Fetter swore and vowed he would kill Aksyutka. He got up from the ground, grabbed the broom, and made for the classroom into which Aksyutka had disappeared.

"Now he'll get him . . . he's trapped!" the servants said, going their separate ways.

Fetter burst into the room, cursing wildly and brandishing his broom. When Aksyutka saw him, he jumped up on the first row of desks, then to the second, and raced over his classmates' heads. Fetter followed his example, and the huge soldier rushed around the temple of seminary learning, broom in hand. . . . It was a magnificent spectacle . . . The students enjoyed it: not every day could they witness such a performance. Books, slates, inkwells, and rulers rained down on the floor from beneath the feet of these furious antagonists.

"Ho-ho-ho!" some seminarians started laughing.

"Sick 'em!" others chimed in.

Others began whistling.

Someone threw a book at Fetter. Fetter paid no attention to the shouting, taunting, howling seminarians. He was in a terrible rage. His feet thundered across the twenty-two rows as if across a keyboard. Aksyutka suddenly leaped to the floor and hid under a desk; Fetter wanted to follow his example, but a seminarian grabbed his leg and he fell flat on his face in the middle of the room. It is impossible to reproduce here the savage abuse he heaped on the whole form.

Aksyutka, peeking from under the desk, told him: "Fetter, get up and take another tumble."

Fetter dashed toward him; but Aksyutka was already under another desk: "Really, Fetter, if you give me something, I'll give you a present, a pair of leggings."

Fetter realized it was pointless to chase under desks after

his enemy. Calling the students rotten priestlings and jack-anapes, he made for the door. He was accompanied by shouts, whistles, taunts, and jeers.

It might seem strange that the administration could not hear such a racket and uproar. The layout of the school was responsible. The building was divided into two wings, the old and the new. About three years prior to the period we are describing the seminary was still located in the old wing, and the grade school in the new one.[11] The seminary was then moved into a new building while the school remained where it was. The only members of the administration who lived in the school were the superintendent and inspector; the other teachers resided in the old wing.* Consequently, and of necessity, the school was governed by personnel chosen from among the students. Moreover, the apartments of the superintendent and inspector were at the opposite end of the courtyard, far away from the classrooms, so that no racket or uproar could reach them. Earlier we had occasion to say that servants comprised a secondary administration and, therefore, they were hated by the brotherhood; as a result, scenes like the one just described were never reported to the inspector or superintendent.

---

* Incidentally, in our description of the seminary we omitted a very important fact that has led to many misunderstandings. We forgot to say that the seminary we are describing was a boarding school. Its students did not live, as they do in other seminaries, in private lodgings. Everyone, approximately five hundred students, resided in huge brick buildings dating from the reign of Peter the Great. You should keep this fact in mind since in other seminaries private housing creates types of students and a way of life not found in a boarding school. This may be the reason that seminary life in our school developed such original and immutable characteristics. Because it was a boarding school, tradition played a powerful and vital role.

Everyone in the classroom gradually calmed down. Aksyutka made his way to Kamchatka. Soon Satan (he's also Ipse) made his appearance. . . .

"How'd it go, Satan?"

"We have tricked him!"

"Good work! . . . Come on, give it here!"

Ipse took out a whole loaf of bread. . . .

"Nice going! . . . For this I'll honor you with a massage. . . .

Satan accepted his massage and said: "I am Ipse!"

Aksyutka hungrily wolfed down the bread. But after his snack he was still uneasy. "Damn it," Aksyutka thought, "this way I may starve to death. Why not pull a zero in the register tomorrow? No, I'll wait a bit and have some more fun with Lobov. Still, things are in a bad way. So what—*God provided, no one spied it; but if someone did, he kept it hid*," Aksyutka concluded with a seminary proverb. "Let's see what tomorrow brings."

"Hey, Aksyon Ivanych," Ipse said to him, as if replying to his thoughts, "look at the birds of the air, they neither sow nor reap nor gather into barns, and yet our Heavenly Father feeds them." [12]

"Amen!" Aksyutka said and decided to continue playing pranks on Lobov.

The seminary's Homeric laughter had not yet died out when the inspector's lackey entered the class and asked:

"Where's the warden on duty?"

"Here," the warden answered.

"The inspector wants to see *you*."

The lackey left.

The same thought at once passed through everyone's mind:

Fetter had lodged a complaint with the inspector against Aksyutka, who, expecting the worst, was already shaking in his boots, but many others besides him were scared since they too had taken part in the scene.

The warden fastened all his buttons and set out for the inspector with some trepidation, since the high-spirited seminarians' little joke had taken place while he was on duty. Gloom descended on the classroom. The minutes dragged by as the form waited for the warden. He finally appeared. He was met with dead silence.

The warden glanced around the room. Everyone was waiting.

"Suitors!" he shouted.

Everyone breathed a sigh of relief.

"Suitors?" they answered.

A joyous murmur filled the classroom. The dreary expressions disappeared, and faces beamed. Everyone raised their heads a little higher. Everyone had the same thought: "There are suitors among us; this means we are boys no longer but independent human beings."

But what happened in Kamchatka? It is buzzing with talk because for Kamchatka its hour of triumph, its hour of greatness has arrived.

Everyone's gaze was turned to that happy land.

We've studied reading all our life
And over primers racked our brains!
Is it not time to take a wife
And throw our books into the flames?

The noise grew louder.

"Quiet," the censor shouted.

The room became a little quieter.

"Who are the suitors?"

Vasenda, Azinus, Erra-Koksta, and Grouse stepped forward.

"I'm a suitor, too," Aksyutka said, joining the others.

The form broke out laughing.

Ipse gleefully wagged the tail of his robe.

"Anyone else?"

There was no one else.

"Suitors, to the inspector! . . . Be quick about it!"

All five went to see the inspector. Watching Aksyutka make ludicrous faces, jump up and down, and slap his thighs, the form gaily laughed.

After the suitors had disappeared through the door, the room filled with loud talk, as if a marketplace were in full swing. The noise, however, was not the desperate racket of seminarians drawling "it's cold" or performing cacophonic songs; it was more like the noise filling the classroom when vacation passes were handed out. Kamchatka was positively ecstatic: it had sent forth its suitors, the heroes of the day. The event raised hopes in every mind: "Someday we, too, will get free of the seminary." From a twelve-year-old lad to a twenty-two-year-old man, from the worst sluggard to the best student, everyone had the same joyful thought. The whole school was throbbing with excitement. God only knows how the magic word "suitors" managed to fly through every form more swiftly than a swallow, bringing a sweet thrill to the hearts of seminarians. Lessons were forgotten, books stayed in the desks, students gathered in groups, and on this occasion the censor was indulgent: he did not break them up. For some reason everyone immediately thought of home, their house, father and mother, sisters and brothers. Even the youngest seminarians were discussing brides, weddings, positions as priests and sextons, salaries, caroling, and so forth. Many students were talking about the day they would be expelled: some intended to be sextons, others wanted to become novices or government clerks, and still others would be going into the army.

The suitors returned from the inspector.

"Well, what happened?" students asked, full of curiosity.

"Any luck, Aksyon Ivanych?" Ipse said.

"Here you are, read it."

Ipse took a piece of paper from Aksyutka's hand and began reading loudly:

PASS

The student Aksyon Ivanov is allowed into town for an appointment with his bride, Irina Voznesensky, from four in the afternoon until nine in the evening, on the 23d of October, 18——.

The inspector's signature followed.

"Bravo, Aksyutka!" his classmates shouted.

Vasenda and Azinus had identical passes.

But the remaining two candidates made their way to the sacred rows of Kamchatka with a depressed, crestfallen look.

"What about you?"

"First they'll put some rouge on them, and then they'll take them to the bride-showing."

Students laughed.

Humiliated and insulted, they sat down and despondently placed their defeated heads on their arms.

"To this one," Aksyutka explained as he pointed to an overager, "the inspector said: 'I have seen you intoxicated. What kind of husband would you make? No, instead of a wedding I'll give you a whipping!'"

Aksyutka added: "Congratulate the young couple on their lawful marriage."

Laughter.

"And this one," Aksyutka said, pointing to the other rejected suitor, "turned out to be only fourteen."

"A real bridegroom!"

"Let's give him a massage."

"Let's bend him into runners."

The unfortunate lad was even more insulted and humiliated by a most vigorous massage and a merciless bending. At a different time he would have protested, but now he was ashamed that he, a fourteen-year-old boy, had thought of *wedding* a thirty-two-year-old antique. Moreover, he was frightened by the impending rouging. Unhappy, ashamed, and afraid, he burst into tears.

Tavlya walked up to him, lifted up his head, squeezed the bridegroom's nose with two fingers, and pulled him across the desk.

"Ooh," he howled.

The form roared with laughter.

"Greenhorn!"

Tavlya then yanked his ears.

The poor fellow sobbed, but he was too ashamed to ask for mercy. Henceforth he was known as "the damp bridegroom." He ran away the same evening. When we discuss the runaways of the seminary, we will tell of his adventures.

A noisy, jostling crowd surrounded the suitors. They asked about the parish, the bride, the revenues; they gave advice and equipped them for tomorrow's meeting with the bride. The seminarians' attentive and considerate attitude was evidence of their excited frame of mind. Classmates expressed their excitement by gladly offering the suitors a new frock coat, a pair of pants, a vest, even boots and linen. Azinus discarded his tick robe and worn-out boots with pieces of wood for soles, and the next day he was a perfect dandy. All this reminds us of those fugitives Mr. Dostoevsky depicted in *Notes from the House of the Dead*.[13] Just as their comrades rejoiced at their escape from prison, so did students here rejoice when their comrades escaped the seminary.

The evening ended with a splendid scene. Tavlya married Katka. Students found some candles, bought some candy and cookies, got up a wedding procession, and traveled to Kamchatka for Katka. There sat the bride, a good-looking lad of about fourteen who was dressed in something resembling an improvised capote; a kerchief was tied around his head in peasant fashion, the rouge on his cheeks came from fading, red candy wrappers. Members of the wedding procession dressed up as men and women and accompanied Tavlya to his bride; then they went to the stove which Tavlya had designated as the altar. Priests, deacons, and sextons appeared, candles were lit, and the wedding ceremony began with the singing of "Rejoice, O Isaiah!" [14] Goroblagodatsky *knocked off the Apostle*, that is, at the conclusion he shouted at the top of his voice: "And the wife see that she reverence her husband." At the stove Tavlya kissed the mate sent to him by God. The procession then returned to Kamchatka for a great feast and celebration. The guests were served candy, cookies, oatmeal, and pickled peas; the wedding party and newlyweds were even treated to some of Aksyutka's stolen bread. There was dancing and singing. At the end of the study period they even drank some holy spirits (vodka). The inspector learned everything from his squealers the next day, which resulted in the rouging of a number of backsides.

The next day Vasenda, Azinus and Aksyutka went to the real bride-showing.

As befits a sensible, practical man, Vasenda found the

dowry, the assigned parish, and duties unsatisfactory, and the bride much too full of days, pock-marked, gangly, and spiritless. He decided to remain in Kamchatka until a better match came along.

Because of his erratic personality and partly because he was sick and tired of the seminary, Azinus said to hell with everything and decided to enter into lawful wedlock with a lady at least ten years his senior. He turned out to be the worst sort of husband, but his bride did not turn out any better.

Aksyutka had no thought of marrying. He went to the bride-showing solely to have some fun, to have a bite to eat, to steal something, and to carouse a bit on his own outside the school. He stole a silk scarf and thirty kopecks from his "betrothed."

One of the suitors, as we have already seen, ran away from school and was now a fugitive.

The next day the inspector gave the fifth suitor a rouging, that is, a splendid flogging.

1862

Runaways and Survivors

In this sketch the protagonist is Carp. What sort of fish is he?

Carp was a rather vain fish. His two brothers were already seminarians and they treated him like a *baby*, excluding him even from ordinary games, not to mention what they considered their serious enterprises, because *he had not yet tasted seminary kasha*, but in the meantime they sometimes told him stories about the various games seminarians played, about the seminary's legendary heroes, their adventures and clashes with the administration, and he found their stories very attractive: all this begot a passionate desire to plunge headlong, as completely and quickly as possible, into the swamp of seminary life.

The long-awaited day finally arrived. Carp's boy's shirt was taken off and replaced by a small frock coat, and from that moment on he felt a year older; he now had his *own* bed, his *own* trunk, his *own* books—this, too, made him feel bigger; when he was given twenty kopecks for rolls, an amount rarely in his possession, then Carp's pride knew no bounds. The hour came to leave home: prayers were said, Carp was blessed, his mother was in tears, his father solemn, his sisters pensive—

Carp was the only one who was happy, and he romped madly about the room, ecstatic because in a few more minutes he would be a seminarian, a seminarian from the top of his head to the tip of his toes, inside and out.

Carp was taken to the seminary. Here he bid his father a rather careless good-bye. He couldn't wait to join the students in the large courtyard, who were playing *stickball, catch, hopscotch, spike in the ring, heaven and hell, cossacks and brigands, stolen stick,* and so forth. After his father left, he hurried into the courtyard and joined a group of young seminarians playing *heaven and hell,* that is, they were hopping on one leg inside squares traced on the ground and trying to kick stones out of different squares with the toe of their boot.

"That's a lot of fun," Carp thought.

At the same time he heard a sneering voice:

"*Greenhorn!*"

"*Tommie!*" someone added.

"*Mama's boy!*"

"Who are they talking about?" Carp thought.

Somebody pinched him.

"Me," he decided. His heart stopped in expectation of something unpleasant. . . .

"A massage for the greenhorn!"

"What's that?" Carp thought.

A rather grown-up seminarian pounced on him and grabbed his face in his dirty palm. This kind of greeting caught Carp completely by surprise. It made him mad, but this ten-year-old who had just entered school was no match for husky seminarians. Carp, however, paid no attention to his lack of strength. He swung his leg and kicked the bully in the stomach. The seminarian let out a groan and wanted to give Carp a smack, but Carp ran off.

"Well done, greenhorn!" someone shouted in approval.

"And now they're praising me," Carp thought as he ran away.

At five o'clock in the evening his brothers took him to the second form where he settled down in the back row and quickly became acquainted with his neighbor, who was called *Fatstuff*.

"Are you going to study?" Fatstuff asked.

"Yes."

"Why?"

"The teacher will call on me."

"Maybe he won't."

"You mean people don't study?"

"It's not worth it."

"I won't study either."

Thus began Carp's religious training. But how would he pass the time? There were three hours left in the study period.

"What are we going to do?" Carp asked.

"Let's play *chimney sweep*."

"Alright."

But just as Fatstuff, hiding his slate, began asking riddles, a sharper came up to Carp, showed him a small phial, and asked:

"Want me to *put you in this little bottle?*"

"In that one? How?"

"You'll have to sit down. How about it?"

"You're joking! Go ahead and try!"

"Here, take this cap and rub yourself with it."

"And I'll sit in the little bottle?"

"Right."

Carp takes the cap offered to him and begins rubbing the cap very vigorously against his face.

"You're going into the little bottle, squeezing through," his classmates said, laughing all the while.

"What's so funny?" stupid Carp asked.

"That's enough," he was told, "you're in the little bottle."

"How's that?" Carp asked, removing the cap from his face.

The laughter was gay and friendly.

"I'm not in the little bottle."

"Give him a mirror."

They gave him a mirror. When he looked into it, Carp did not recognize himself: his whole face was as black as a chimney sweep's. Only then did he realize that the cap he had used had been smeared with soot and that the soot was difficult to notice on the black cloth. Carp was annoyed and embarrassed.

"You got yourself dirty," he was told.

"There's no one to blame."

"What if he squeals? We'll let him have it."

"I won't squeal," Carp answered, "but you fellows are scoundrels."

Carp was forced to bear his classmates' taunts. Having washed his face in the pail standing in the corner of the classroom, Carp turned to Fatstuff, hoping for his sympathy.

"Damn those fellows!" he said.

When Fatstuff heard this remark, he answered with a laugh that Carp found insulting.

"You fat pig," Carp muttered.

This was the beginning of his quarrel with Fatstuff. This quarrel grew stronger and stronger every time Carp was subjected to the various jokes and pranks his classmates played on greenhorns.

The censor walked up to Carp and asked him:

"Have you seen Moscow?"

"Never."

"Then I'll show it to you."

The censor then grabbed Carp's head, squeezed it between his palms, and lifted the greenhorn into the air . . .

"Hey, let me go," Carp squeaked.

The censor, having toyed with his fish, dropped him on a desk. Fatstuff laughed again. Carp was beginning to find his face repulsive.

"Fat face!" he said aloud.

This did not bother Fatstuff in the least. He only laughed louder. Carp found it made more sense to keep quiet for the time being; otherwise his irritation would only bring more taunts from his neighbors.

A little while later some lummox walked up to Carp. He gave him an order in a severe, officious tone of voice:

"Go to the first row. See the big student sitting there. Ask him for a *tousle*."

Carp obeyed the order.

"Give me a tousle," he said, walking up to the student.

"With pleasure. Say when," he replied and, having grabbed poor Carp's hair, he began yanking it about in a very painful way. . . . Carp screeched and tears came to his eyes.

When he returned to his place, he heard Fatstuff laughing again. Carp hated the sight of his neighbor's face.

"Take this!" the angry fish said and he punched his neighbor in the side.

It had no effect on Fatstuff either.

"Poke again," he said, offering his other side, and roared with offensive laughter.

"Pig," Carp replied, turning away with the firm intention of never saying another word to his neighbor.

Carp was sitting at his desk, frowning. The *massage, bottle,*

Moscow, and *tousle* all seemed like filthy tricks to him. . . .
He was afraid lest they put something else over on him. A
second-termer approached him. Carp watched him suspiciously.

"Poor lad, are they pestering you?" the second-termer said
tenderly.

Carp answered the question with an angry glance.

"They always pester greenhorns," the second-termer continued; "you tell me when someone bothers you."

Carp was hooked by the tender words.

"Why are they after me," he said pitifully; "I don't bother
them."

"Don't be afraid of anything now. I'll defend you."

"Defend me, friend . . ."

The second-termer sat down next to him and began asking
where he was from, where his father was, if he had a mother,
brothers or sisters. Carp trustingly bared his soul to his new
friend; such friendliness came to the distraught Carp at just
the right moment.

"Want a roll?" he asked, untying a small bundle.

The second-termer did not refuse and became even more
affectionate.

"Let me show you something," he said. "Write: 'Madam,
I'm Adam.' "

Carp wrote it down.

"Now read it backwards, from right to left."

From right to left it read: "Madam, I'm Adam."

Carp liked that a lot.

"Wait a second, I'll show you something else," the second-
termer said.

He left for a short time, returned, and again sat down next
to Carp.

"Write: *pour the water, pour; I swear I won't tell anybody.*"

Hoping that he would see something like "Madam, I'm Adam," Carp took a pencil and wrote what he was told.

But just as Carp finished the last word, the second-termer doused him with a dipper of water he had been holding behind his back. The wet Carp could not understand what this meant.

"What's this all about?" he asked.

"You signed a note yourself saying you wouldn't tell anybody," the second-termer replied.

"You're a scoundrel, a scoundrel . . ."

But the scoundrel only laughed. Repulsive Fatstuff also chimed in. Carp was insulted and humiliated. He could not stand Fatstuff's laughter and, overcome with anger, he gave him a rather hard punch in the neck. Fatstuff, however, was apparently invulnerable. After the punch he grabbed his stomach and broke into even louder peals of laughter. Carp grit his teeth and, covering his face with his hands, was about to cry.

At this moment *Muscles*, a lad of about eighteen who was a classmate of Carp, a ten-year-old boy, walked past him. Muscles stopped next to Carp, put one hand on his shoulder and with the other, for no reason at all, punched him sharply in the back. The blow landed over the heart and knocked the wind out of him. Groaning, he raised his head.

"Why did you do that?" he muttered.

"No reason," Muscles answered.

And in fact Muscles, a kind person as we shall see, did not know why he did such a vile thing. He hit Carp not from anger, not for amusement, not because his arm had fallen asleep and needed exercise, but precisely *for no reason*, unconsciously, the punch just happened by itself, accidentally. . . . He went calmly on his way, but Carp broke down and began to sob.

When Fatstuff saw this, he burst out laughing.

"Well, dearie, I'll bet you've never tasted anything like this before!"

All the anger that had been building up in Carp during study hour finally exploded.

"Just wait, you fat brute," Carp muttered and, saying this, he grabbed a ruler in one hand and a rather thick book in the other, and began working Fatstuff over, hitting him on his sides with the ruler and on his head with the book.

Fatstuff was older and stronger than Carp, but he was a coward. He did not even consider mounting an offensive.

"Well done, greenhorn!" classmates expressed their approval.

"A fine fellow!"

"Use the back of the book on him!"

Carp took this sound advice, turned the back of the book around, and slammed it against hated Fatstuff's temple.

"Bravo!"

"A strong one!"

"Hit him again!"

Carp took this advice, too.

Fatstuff finally broke loose from his grasp and shouted: "I'll tell the superintendent!" and disappeared through the door.

When Fatstuff left, the students' attitude towards Carp underwent a change.

"You're in for it, dearie," he was told.

"What do you mean?"

"They'll feed you a *dish of birches!*"

Carp was scared, but, not wanting to show it, he said bravely:

"Let them!" Still, he thought to himself: "Would they flog me on the very first day? That's all I need!"

A few minutes later Carp was summoned to the superintendent and, in fact, on the *very first day* of his baptism into the seminary faith he was annointed with five strokes of the rod and told: "We'll be easy on you only this first time; we'll hit harder from now on!"[1] Pondering the extent to which floggings would intensify in the future, Carp returned to class with a heavy heart. . . .

"What happened?" his classmates asked.

Once again not wanting to look like a coward, Carp answered:

"They flogged me, that's all."

"And you don't care?"

"They can flog me as much as they want, it's all the same to me!"

"That's the spirit!" his classmates praised him.

Carp's vanity was pleasantly flattered, and he continued to brag:

"They can't scare me even if they tear me in two."

"You don't say!"

"Honest to God, I don't care."

"You suckling," a second-termer lit into him, "have you been flogged *on the clouds?*"

"On the clouds?" Carp asked in bewilderment.

"That's right, have a taste of that dish, then say *they aren't sowing turnips, only cleaning the plow.*"

Having been the center of attention for several minutes,

Carp thought: "I guess I'm not so bad, am I?", but this thought led to another: "What does *on the clouds* mean? It must be something really cruel if they scare me with such a beating?" But the last question lost some of its significance when, a few minutes before supper, he overheard several second-termers talking about him. They said: "The greenhorn will probably turn out alright. He doesn't like to squeal, floggings don't scare him too much, and he really battered Fatstuff. He'll be a decent seminarian, only we'll have to really shape him up. We'll shape him up!" These remarks put Carp in a good mood. He reasoned: "All these massages, tousles, caps, and bottles are only meant to shape me up. They're testing me. So I've got to watch my step!" He resolved he would show his mettle, and he perked up, intending to prove to his new classmates that he had all the makings of a worthy seminarian. "What's this *on the clouds?* What else will they do to shape me up?" When such thoughts came to him, he would try to drive them away by remembering that "he would probably turn out alright." "Let's see what happens!" he said to himself.

He went to the dining hall, "gulped down some rotten cabbage soup," ate some kasha and, after prayers, went to a bedroom. . . .

"How's it going?" his brother, known as *Big Nose,* asked.

"They flogged me," Carp bragged.

"Already?"

"They sure did."

When his brother learned the details of the incident, he approved of Carp's behavior. But in telling his brother why he was whipped, Carp failed to mention the tears he shed when he was placed in the bottle, massaged, doused with water, and slapped around. He was beginning to develop the false seminarian shame that forbids one to be embarrassed by a whipping.

Carp, the protagonist of this sketch, will be described in particular detail since he was involved in many typical events of the school and seminary; moreover he spent fourteen years there, and this is the period we wish to examine in our articles on spiritual education. We might add that we are *personally* and *very* intimately acquainted with the person nicknamed Carp, and we are writing this true story from his own words.[2]

We said that Carp perked up, thinking that everything would be fine after he proved to his new classmates that he had all the makings of a worthy seminarian. "We'll get along," he thought. He did not even guess, however, that his greatest sorrow was yet to come. He was not called Carp when he entered the seminary. He received that nickname a few days later, and it was the cause of those misfortunes we are about to relate.

Here is what happened.

Not even four days had passed when Carp began to dream about home, to feel homesick, and to cry when he was by himself. He no longer wanted to be a seminarian. He found everything in the school rotten and revolting. Constantly exposed to all the filth described in our sketches, he quickly sensed the complete contrast between life at home and life in school. Home life now seemed like pure bliss, the best place in the world, whereas seminary life seemed like the kingdom of the damned. He gazed intently into that black abyss separating the two ways of life. . . . He wanted to go home, to go home! . . . His happiest moments were now those he spent with his brothers; but he had also misjudged his brothers if he thought he would be their equal once he entered the seminary; Carp was in the second form, which was looked down upon and held in contempt by the upper forms. He had not yet had the time to make friends with his classmates. Depression gnawed at his heart, and more than once he thought: "Why not make a run for it? But where can I run?" During this time Carp devised a plan that he thought to be quite good.

Even at home Carp knew that at school the so-called *choristers* led a soft life. In the cathedral town of his seminary there were several choirs: the school, seminary, theological academy, and cathedral each had its own choir, and in addition the town's churches had two. Sopranos and altos (and sometimes bassos and tenors) were recruited from students. Parents always objected to their children being impressed as choristers. Choirs definitely ruined children.* Boys missed classes for rehearsals, for masses performed *on request,* for weddings, and so forth. In the last sketch we presented examples of seminarian ignorance, but the most thickheaded ignorance reigned in choirs. Bright seminarians have said that they remember only *one* intelligent chorister during their *fourteen* years in the seminary, and he, too, came to grief: after finishing the seminary he became a psalmodist in a university town abroad where he intended to complete his education, but he ended up shooting himself. Choirs turn boys into dolts and corrupt them at the same time. Appearing quite frequently at wakes where, as we all know, our Orthodox brethren eat like pigs and drink like fishes, these children are not only exposed to drunkards, they also develop a taste for vodka themselves. Similarly, they are often present at sprees

* You must remember that our description does not apply equally to all choirs: a partial exception must be made for choirs in educational institutions although even these choirs are not completely innocuous. We will discuss them sometime in the future.

of older choristers where they listen to cynical tales of drunken sexual adventures, card playing, fights, and various other abominations. . . . Moreover, choirboys, especially the so-called *ispolatchiki*, earn a little extra money, and the money does them no good.[3] [In order to describe the corrupting influence of choir life in one stroke, we present the following fact. Once there was an old maid who, having begun to indulge her lust in the decline of life, enticed six young choristers, *ages eight to fifteen*, to her home and entered into a common-law marriage with all of them. She sometimes used the choristers for the same purpose that Nero used Sporus.[4] It is obviously very easy for a boy to perish in a choir.]

Carp knew nothing of this. He decided to join a choir. He joined the student choir, however, in which even though boys also wasted their time, they were not corrupted. Having joined the seminary choir, Carp could leave school twice a week for rehearsals and at least breathe a little fresh air; in addition, choristers in the seminary sometimes received tea and money; finally, choristers enjoyed the special protection of the seminary administration. Realizing all this, Carp joined the choir when the seminary became unbearable; he did not realize, however, that despite his powerful alto voice he had no talent for singing. He learned this the hard way. He actually would have been better off if he had remained a mute fish instead of becoming a chorister. For continually singing off-key they pulled his ears, kicked him, pinched him, and hit him over the head with a pitch pipe. Carp then resorted to ruses. While his colleagues sang, he only moved his lips. "No one will notice," he thought, "they'll say I'm singing, too." But it was difficult to fool the choirmaster with such tricks.

"Hey, jaybird, why do you just move your lips?" he asked Carp.

"I'm singing."

"You're lying, you rascal."

"Honest to God, I'm singing."

Carp made the sign of the cross.

Carp made the sign of the cross, but the choirmaster yanked his ear.

"Sing, you rogue, louder! . . . faster! . . ."

Carp roared at the top of his voice. He sang so well that everyone burst out laughing, and even the choirmaster could not restrain himself. One of the young choristers, a wiseacre called *Lyokha*, pointed his finger at the sufferer and, shaking with laughter, said:

"Ca . . . ca . . . ca . . . rp."

"A real carp, a mouth as big as a carp's," others chimed in.

"We should toss him in the pond."

The fun began.

Carp did not have enough sense to take all this as a joke. Lyokha teased him all the way home and, when they arrived at the school, the young seminarians surrounded Carp and began shouting:

"Carp!"

"Fish!"

"He fought with the ruff."[5]

Carp started cursing; his classmates began tugging at his clothes and pinching him; Carp then took up sticks and stones. The students started having fun; the crowd grew larger. Finally, someone knocked Carp off his feet.

"The pile's too small!"

Several students were knocked down on Carp, then some more on top of them, and the game began.

"Carp, where are you?" they shouted from above.

Carp's stomach was squashed, Carp gasped for air, Carp got a mouthful of dirt, Carp cried. . .

After a long struggle he broke loose somehow and made a run for the classroom. The seminarians chased after him. In the classroom they surrounded him once again.

"Let's *christen* Carp."

They grabbed his arms, and all sorts of yelling, screeching, yelping, groaning voices began shouting right into his ears:

"Carp, Carp, Carp!"

The racket was so terrible that the students did not hear the bell announcing the start of classes. Some time elapsed and a teacher, the famous Lobov, was already in the adjoining classroom, but the noise did not let up. Poor Carp was pinched, fillips rained down on his head, spitballs were tossed in his face. Carp felt as if he was being boiled alive; he gradually lost the ability to hear or feel anything. The joke went so far that it seemed to him that he had departed the real world and entered a semi-delirious, hideous dream. The roar was so unbearable that Carp imagined that someone was roaring inside his very head and chest. He was beginning to lose his senses, his vision became blurred, lines crossed, colors ran together. One minute more and he would have fainted. But someone pinched Carp so painfully that all his blood rushed to his face, veins stood out on his temples and neck, and, beside himself with rage, he attacked the first student he came across; his fingers dug into his victim's hair and would not let go.

The end of this incident was extremely disgusting. . . .

Lobov, infuriated by the seminarians' noise, came into the room. Everyone ran to his place. All by himself, Carp was tugging away at his victim who, unfortunately, was not strong enough to break loose.

"Grab him!" Lobov ordered.

No one moved.

"Grab him!"

Some big students jumped on Carp and instantly uncovered

those parts of the body that serve as conduits of human morality and ultimate justice in the seminary.

"Into the clouds with him!"

Carp hung in the air.

"Give it to him!"

Birch rods whistled from the right, they whistled from the left; blood spurted from the poor boy's body, and his terrible scream filled the seminary. His body took twenty-five lashes on its right side, the same number on its left; [fifty bloody, blue stripes were the repulsive ornament on the body of this child, and only his body was alive during these minutes when he experienced the absolute horror of a torture beyond the endurance of his ten-year-old organism.] His nerves had already been strained when he was pinched, slapped, and christened with the name Carp, but during the punishment his nerves were completely unable to register impressions; he lost his memory; his thoughts . . . there were no thoughts since reason does not operate at such moments; his moral humiliation . . . it, too, came later, but at the time he did not say one word in his defense, not once did he ask for mercy,—the only sound was the screaming of his living flesh as the sharp, burning, frenzied birches lacerated it with red and black welts. . . . His body suffered, his body screamed, his body sobbed. . . . This is why, when he was asked afterwards what he was thinking about during the punishment, Carp answered: "I don't remember." And there was nothing to remember because Carp's soul was dead during that time.

"Let him go!"

[With these words Lobov brought to an end his vile, Lobovian execution.]

In the life of every human being there is a period of time that determines his moral destiny, a turning point in his spiritual development. It is said that this period does not begin until adolescence; this is not true: for many it occurs during the full bloom of childhood. Such was the case with Carp. We once heard him express the following opinion: "Everyone is certain that childhood is the happiest, most innocent, and most joyful time of life, but that is a lie: given our horrifying educational system, which is headed by celibate, childless monks,[6] childhood is the most dangerous period of life, a time when it is easy to be corrupted and to perish forever." Carp spoke from experience . . .

Carp was dazed after the *christening* and flogging, and for a long time he was unable to think clearly. The following day his father visited him. As soon as he saw his father, tears poured from his eyes. A vivid picture arose in his imagination: his native village, the cemetery, his house and garden, his family, local friends, games. Now he fully realized how delightful was the home life that had seemed so ordinary, and how vile was the seminary life that had once been his goal.

"I want to go home," he said, swallowing a salty tear.

His father was the kindest of men. He felt sorry for his son. . .

"Papa, take me home."

"It's impossible," he replied, "you have to study; everyone studies, and you aren't a baby. . . . You'll be lonesome at first, but later you'll get used to it. . . . Be a good boy, and then your life will be good."

His father suddenly stopped speaking. He thought: "We all tell our children the same things, but it doesn't make them feel any better." His father sighed.

"Why did you send me here?"

His son began to cry.

"Are they mean to you?"

The son did not answer.

His father saw that something was wrong. Again he said tenderly:

"Are you having a bad time here?"

Not only children, but even adults, when sorrow comes to them, treat friends and loved ones unjustly, taking out their sorrow on them. His kind father began to irritate Carp.

"Why was I sent to this damned seminary?" he thought to himself, not saying a word to his father. "Why was I locked up here? My father doesn't love me, neither does my mother, my brothers and sisters can do without me . . . grown-ups always hurt children . . . if that's the case, I don't want to go home . . . let them . . . I don't care . . . why go home when everyone there hates me? They're glad I'm suffering. . . . They sent me here on purpose so I could be whipped, beaten, scolded. They let us go home on Saturday, but I won't go home."

Such were Carp's thoughts but all the same he passionately wanted to go home. Now was the time, it would seem, for him to bare his soul to his father, but Carp grumbled and thought to himself: "What for? It won't help!" He decided to say nothing to his father who never did learn of the moral and physical torture his son endured during his first days at school.

After his father left, fear was added to Carp's longing for home. He did not even suspect that he had begun his seminary career rather auspiciously in comparison with most green-horns. His classmates knew that he had come to the school with a cheerful expression on his face instead of tears in his eyes, and had responded to his first massage by kicking the bully in the stomach; he had been placed in a bottle, given a tousle, shown Moscow, and doused with water when Muscles beat him up—it never entered his mind to complain to the administration, and therefore he would not become a squealer; he had given Fatstuff a sound thrashing and had received a flogging on the very first day; when they teased him in the courtyard, he had grabbed some sticks and stones instead of running to the inspector; even during his *christening* he pulled a seminarian's hair—all these facts were the sort that commanded his classmates' respect. He would not have been regarded a greenhorn for very long, and that is the time when seminarians have the most trouble; but he had lost the ability to think things through: Lobov had temporarily destroyed that ability. If it had not been for Lobov, he would have gotten by somehow. But at this time of spiritual numbness the broad, bottomless, gaping abyss of seminary horrors opened before him, the force of which he had experienced with his own skin, flesh, and bones. Carp was now under the full, crushing influence of this force: a numb hopelessness, a dull despair lay on his heart, and if his classmates had continued to torment him, or if his superiors had continued to beat him mercilessly without allowing him to rest for the struggle, he would have become either a fool or a scoundrel. Remembering this terrible time, Carp says: "Many honest sons of honest fathers return home as scoundrels; many intelligent sons of intelligent parents return home as fools. Mothers and fathers cry when they send a son to the seminary, and they cry again when their son returns."

Carp avoided everyone and withdrew into himself. He was afraid of everyone.

This passive suffering, however, had to be resolved in some way, did it not? For the time being it could be resolved only internally. A feeling of terrible anger and hatred entered his heart, but he was afraid to let it out into the open. This feeling fired Carp's imagination, and bizarre scenes and ideas arose in his mind. He was carried away into a world of fantasy, the only place he could safely hide.

"Someone ought to burn down this hateful seminary!" he thought to himself. He liked the idea very much, and quickly he all but visualized his thoughts.

Carp imagines himself descending into the school's cellars with a flaming torch, building enormous fires there and, after making his exit, waiting for fiery tongues of flame to begin licking the damned chambers of the seminary. His anger sees the fire engulf the seminary . . . the walls crackle, buckle, and collapse . . . the odious classrooms are demolished . . . the repulsive books, texts, day-books, and registers are ablaze . . . administrators and teachers perish in the fire as do censors and auditors . . . Carp's vision stands before him in all its hallucinatory clarity. He hears the crackle and thunder of the crumbling building, the screams of dying administrators. . . . "Who's that groaning?" Carp asks. "Ah, that's Lobov writhing on the hot coals, he's been crushed by a beam, his eye has burst, his lips turn black, his bestial face splits apart. . . ." Carp finds sensual pleasure in admiring his images, and he feels a malicious, dreamy revenge. His nerves are overwrought; his pulse is beating at ninety per second; his head is burning. . . . When a boy with a vivid imagination is frustrated in real life, his hyperbolic revenge is expressed in abnormal images. Perfecting his evil dream, Carp repeats the same scene several times, delineating every detail, every trifle. Such psychological states, however, cannot continue for very long; the soul grows weary, and common sense gradually and imperceptibly begins to return. Lost in frenzied dreams, Carp for some reason remembers how he once accidentally injured a dove with a rock; afterwards, pangs of remorse kept him awake all night. . . . He begins to realize clearly that his visions are ugly and false, he chases them away, he feels an inner emptiness and disgust, and all that remains of his extravagant and fruitless dreams is a feeling of nausea.

The clear ring of a bell announced the hour for evening study.

Reality, to which he had closed his eyes and shut his ears, forced its way into his consciousness against his will, and revealed the utter childishness of his agitated imagination. He was sitting in class, in the back row, with his chin sadly on his chest. Conscience-stricken, he chased his dreams away and, as a result, he had no place, either within himself or in the world outside, where he could hide, but his body and soul demanded activity. In his pain Carp did not know what to do. He was very unhappy.

"Lord," he was thinking in unbearable anguish, "if only I could get sick!" This idea jolted his fantasies into a new direction. He had no other refuge but his imagination. And Carp is sick . . . he is at death's door . . . his family is crying near his bed and bids farewell "until the joyful morn . . ." Carp prepares to cross into eternity . . . the end is near . . . But from then on his dream changes course because he does not want to die. Nicholas the Wonder-Worker appears, cures Carp, and commands that he seek salvation in the wilderness . . . Carp pictures to himself a desolate, peaceful, angelic life, difficult feats, hymns, conversations with God. . . . He becomes a great saint. . . . He receives the gift of prophecy and wonder-working. . . . Local inhabitants gather to pay him homage. . . . He fasts for many years, prays, mortifies his flesh, does good deeds, and at last he sees himself summoned by the Lord, he sees his blessed remains, he sees . . .

"Carp!"

This was not a voice from heaven, but from the seminary.

"Are you *Big Nose*'s brother?"

Carp saw the terrible Muscles standing before him, and he instinctively drew back. . . .

"My God, he's come to beat me up again!" Carp thought.

"Is Big Nose your brother?" Muscles repeated.

"Yes," Carp answered without understanding what it was all about.

"It's alright, if he's your brother. Don't be afraid of anything now. I'm on your side because your brother is my best friend. Come to me if anyone hurts you. Understand?"

"I understand."

But, recalling the treacherous second-termer, Carp watched his new benefactor suspiciously. . . .

"Quiet!" Muscles shouted in a ringing voice.

More than one hundred students got ready to give Muscles their attention. This shows the influence he had in his form.

"Stand up," he said to Carp.

Carp got to his feet.

"No one dare hurt this fish," Muscles said to the form, pointing at Carp, "I'll break the neck of anyone who bothers him."

Carp felt relieved. . . .

"And, Carp, you report to me. . . . Tell me, who bothered you?"

"I don't know."

He really did not know whom to point out.

"Don't be afraid, tell me, who hurt you?"

"Nobody hurt me."

"That's impossible."

"They all hurt me."

This was more accurate.

"Who's your auditor?"

"Redtop."

"Good. I'll tell him not *to pick on* you" (to be strict in hearing recitations).

"Thanks, Muscles."

"If he asks for a roll, don't give him one."

"Alright, Muscles."

"So, listen to me," Muscles again addressed the form, "if anyone lays even one finger on Carp, he's in for trouble."

But this time a certain *Candelabra* replied:

"Well, some trouble!"

Muscles glanced in the direction of the voice. He did not reply, but he angrily clenched his fist.

"Don't be afraid," he told Carp, and began walking around the room.

Carp moved quickly and willingly from the world of fantasy to the world of reality. It was as though a mountain had fallen from his shoulders. Looking over his classmates, he saw that Muscles had made a very great impression. Carp felt relieved, cheerful, free. He began observing life in the study hall, and he was quickly fascinated by it.

But he did not even suspect he had become a bone of contention between Muscles and Candelabra. . . .

Who is Muscles?

Before he entered the seminary, Big Nose, Carp's brother, went to a private school where, over a pinch of snuff, he met Muscles, the son of a sexton's widow in town. They eventually became friends. Later they both entered the second form in the seminary. . . . Muscles was left behind in the second form; that is why we find this eighteen-year-old lad, Carp's classmate, declining nouns, memorizing "there is one God," studying *sums* and *differences*. Muscles was of medium height, ugly-looking but stoutly-made, and endowed with amazing strength. On one occasion he visited his friend Big Nose. They went to the river. Some peasants were fishing there. One of the fishermen was reeling in his line. "Uncle, let me reel it in," Muscles said, "and you stop the reel by grabbing a spoke." "Priestling, you must be out of your mind," the peasant answered. "Give it a good whirl," Muscles said. The peasant spun the reel so fast that its spokes seemed to fuse into one solid circle, and he kept spinning it faster and faster. Muscles stuck out his powerful palm, the thick spoke of the reel slammed into it, and the reel stopped still. The peasant merely stared at him in amazement. Muscles was not only strong; he was also very agile. On another occasion he again visited Big Nose. They went for a walk in a field, but no sooner did they come upon a fence when they heard behind them the voice of a peasant swearing at them for trampling his grass. The two friends climbed over a cemetery fence; the peasant was right behind them. Muscles boldly challenged him. "What do you want?" he asked the peasant. The latter was somewhat drunk and, flushed with wine, wanted to strike Muscles. His fist had already come halfway around, but just as the blow was about to land Muscles ducked quickly and slipped under the peasant's arm. After straightening up, he faced the peasant again and said with his arms folded: "Hit me again!" a second swing, and again in vain. Muscles faced him again and said: "Hit me again!" This time, too, the peasant's big fist could not find Muscles' face. Only then did Muscles say: "You missed three times, now grab the ground to keep from falling." As he said this he knocked the peasant off a grave. . . . This was the sort of fellow who together with Carp declined nouns, memorized "there is one God," and so forth. What is to be done? He was sent to the seminary late, previously he used to earn money for his mother by substituting for sextons: reading at wakes, singing carols, serving at church services and masses. He was a student, but his family and friends treated him as an adult. In general, Muscles was a kind person. He never used his powerful fists to exact a bribe or to elicit a base favor from anyone. If he hit someone in the face—for example, Carp when they first met—it did not necessarily mean anything: punches in the seminary were the same thing as small change in a shop. But to fall under the protection of such a person meant to shield oneself from all sorts of harm no matter where it came from. Muscles was not stupid, and it was not his fault that he began declining nouns so late.

Who is Candelabra?

Before we describe him, we first must tell you what *orts* are. In the seminary *orts* are pieces of bread left on the table after dinner or supper which have the marks of someone's teeth in them. There is a seminary superstition that eating an ort confers the strength of the person to whom it belongs. Many students ate orts all the time in hopes of becoming strongmen. Candelabra, an overager, had been eating them for several years. He was constantly bragging about his strength, which, in fact, was very great. He had fought with everyone in the form except Muscles. Muscles was a thorn in his side because he bore the palm of fistic superiority. He was also afraid of Muscles, and did not want to believe that Muscles could drub him. This question had been bothering Candelabra for a long time, and he decided to find out the answer to it today. . . .

Meanwhile, Carp had calmed down completely. He again made friends with Fatstuff, who turned out to be an utter fool. "So what!" Carp thought to himself and they began playing chimney sweep.

"Which hand?" he asked Fatstuff.

At that moment Candelabra walked up to him, grabbed him by the coat collar, laid him over a desk, and began bending him into runners.

"Stop it!" Carp yelled.

Candelabra pushed Carp's feet past his shoulders.

"Muscles!" Carp screamed.

"What?" he replied.

"Help me!"

Muscles appeared. Candelabra was waiting for him. He let Carp go.

Preliminary discussions began.

"Why did you bother him, you bastard?"

"What's it to you?"

"Did you hear what I said?"

"I'm deaf in that ear."

"You mean you want a fight?"

"Go ahead!"

"You think I won't?"

Muscles made a move towards Candelabra. . . .

"Touch me, just touch me!"

Candelabra made a move towards Muscles.

"Keep away, you hear!"

Muscles bumped Candelabra with his shoulder.

"Stop bumping."

The bump was returned.

This is the way seminarians throw down the gauntlet to one another when they want to fight.

The scuffle began.

Experts immediately concluded: "Candelabra is going to get killed." And, in fact, five minutes later Muscles sat on top of Candelabra, mashing him, and said:

"Give up or die!"

"Let me go! Damn you!"

"Are you going to bother Carp?"

"Get off me!"

"Watch your step!"

After wringing Candelabra's neck, Muscles released him.

Walking to his seat, Candelabra thought to himself: "Hell, those damn orts are no good at all. Still—maybe I ate too few of them." Afterwards he kept on eating orts and, perhaps, is eating them this very minute, although never again did he venture to tangle with Muscles. . .

Thus, the dark cloud of slaps, massages, and runners, of jabs, whacks, and spitballs, of punches, smacks, and knock-outs passed rather comfortably over Carp's head.

Again we repeat: the first days of seminary life do not pass as happily for everyone as they did for Carp . . . still, they leave their stamp on everyone, and they left their stamp on Carp.

Carp's first impressions at school were such that, as he himself says, he would have turned into a scoundrel or a fool if it had not been for Muscle's help. These impressions more or less determined the entire subsequent course of his seminary life.

In his attitude toward the administration Carp became a full-fledged seminarian, tough and unyielding. The basic principle of the brotherhood—hatred for the administration—took root and developed more fully in Carp than in anyone else. Before he came to school his upbringing had been fairly humane and decent, but the seminary was to place its stamp on him. The result of Lobov's flogging was that afterwards he could never again deal simply, naturally, and openly with his superiors. His trust in the administration had been destroyed once and for all. This showed itself mainly in the fact that he never could look a superior straight in the eye, but always askance; he never spoke in a natural tone of voice, it was always plaintive and affected, sepulchral and deep. He would always cower before superiors, and therefore he disliked meeting them. He felt a constant sense of guilt even though he had done nothing wrong. This strange feeling, causing him to behave as he did, was not born of fear because, as we shall see below, Carp was not very cowardly and frequently committed impertinences and pranks that few would have dared. The point is this. Carp clearly recognized he hated the seminary, its teachers, rules, textbooks, kasha, and cabbage soup, but at the same time he had to obey his superiors, smile at them, bow, and sometimes even flatter them. He found it impossible to be straightforward or to speak his mind because then he would be flogged, and so Carp always sulked in the presence of his superiors. It was not a question of fear, but rather of shame. If a human being is the least bit honest and self-respecting, and he has to cringe from fear that he will be slapped in the face, if he has to cringe involuntarily, unwillingly, inescapably, then he will do so like a man with a troubled conscience. This is what happened with Carp: either he was insolent toward superiors, or he behaved queerly. Many teachers probably sense they are bad teachers when they persecute students like Carp, when they harshly tell a student: "Look me straight in the eye, look cheerful and calm, recite the lesson firmly and clearly!" Such teachers maintain: "If a student can't look me straight in the eye, he doesn't have a clear conscience." There's no question that this is true. Indeed, a student knows he ought to spit in his teacher's face, but instead he must smile at him. He feels rotten inside, and he smiles in a peculiar way. Of course, Carp did not even understand why he spoke, smiled, and bowed in an unnatural way when he met one of his superiors; his analytical powers had not yet developed, and he could not ascertain that here it was a matter precisely of conscience; he sensed this instinctively, and only much later did he consciously understand the reason for his attitude toward authorities. But it in no way follows from all this that a student's timorousness before a teacher was always the result of secret hatred; it can be caused by simple shyness. But we are speaking only of Carp. Occasionally Carp's masked hatred was frankly expressed in an act of insolence, but its unveiled form was expressed very powerfully in the dirty tricks that he secretly played on the administration behind its back. It is true that during the first few years such dirty tricks were not Carp's specialty; nevertheless, as we will see in later sketches, once he grew a little older, he did them deliberately. In the beginning, and precisely during the period we are describing, he hated his teachers instinctively, but later on he became convinced that they deserved to be hated, absolutely deserved it. As he matured, his fear and shame turned into a deep, innate hatred for the administration. But of this second stage later. At present we find him still cowed and timorous before his mentors in the seminary.

Even at this stage of development, however, when his character was not yet fully formed, Carp's attitude toward his superiors was rather original in comparison with that of other seminarians who protested against the administration. Carp occupied an almost unique position in the seminary. At least half of the unhealthy conditions having an evil influence on other seminarians did not exist for him. His human dignity was protected by the sheer, raw muscle power of the strongest boy in the form, and this raw strength saved him. He did not have to fawn upon or flatter classmates, to tell them bedtime stories, give them money and rolls, pick various kinds of vermin out of their hair, scratch the soles of their feet, bring water to them, and so forth. He paid but three bribes while in the seminary, and each time under unusual circumstances. Protected by Muscles, and still a greenhorn, he soon obtained all the rights and privileges of a second-termer. The four years preceding Muscle's expulsion were sufficient for Carp to become accustomed to acting independently; he paid no attention to auditors, censors, or wardens. But despite his position he never used Muscles' fists to oppress others; he had almost lost his hearing permanently himself and he never forgot it, and henceforth he disliked domineering classmates and the use of physical force; moreover, Muscles did not like bullying and bribery either, and he would not have helped Carp with such things. Carp rarely asked for his help; when he had to, he fought most of his own battles, and if he was beaten up, he either called his opponent names or threw a rock, book or ruler at him; if he was fighting a stronger foe and did not have a weapon handy, he would use his teeth, fingernails, and feet, that is, he would bite, scratch, and kick. Carp was frequently beaten up, and he beat up others, but all this was in the order of seminary things—nothing more. Consequently, Muscles' protection, given Carp's own attitude, did not earn him the enmity of his classmates. Many students even liked him. Having felt at first hand the bitter fate of a helpless seminarian, he frequently used Muscles' fists, and sometimes his own teeth, fingernails, and feet, to help the oppressed. An auditor throughout his last four years at school, he was frequently punished for raising grades, and only once was he seduced by a bribe. His constant protest on behalf of abused individuals was expressed in the fact that he was particularly fond of fools. *Peters Teterins*, whom we mentioned in the preceding sketch, would have perished without him. Teterins was as strong as a bull, but his disposition was as meek as a lamb's. Everyone beat him up, spat upon him, and abused him. Carp defended him for six months and managed to put him back on his feet to the point where on one occasion he even struck Carp. Carp was not a fool himself, but he was fond of dunces and spent many hours with them, talking, playing, sharing his things, and helping them. This seemingly strange behavior was his way of protesting against certain aspects of seminary life.

Carp was attached to his home, but if he were to reveal his intimate feelings to intelligent seminarians, most of them would have invariably given him a massage since such intimacies are called *gushiness* in the seminary. Carp was more candid with fools than with anyone else; only with them did he speak of his family hearth, reminisce about home life, share family secrets; only with them was he openhearted in a human, unseminarian way. Carp, because of false shame and fear of ridicule, not only concealed the inner life that was so precious to him—he even affected a cynical attitude and made fun of gushiness so that a contradiction between outer form and inner content became almost second nature to him. His soul thirsted for human contact, however, and he surrounded himself with a special kind of fool. These fools were honest, good, kind, and openhearted. Thank God that there are many such fools on the face of the earth. It was only later on in the seminary that Carp made friends with intelligent people.[7] Is it possible, someone will ask, that Carp did not find a single intelligent human being with whom he could have a heart-to-heart talk? Such persons certainly existed, but in the beginning Carp did not make friends with them, and so it went for a long time.

Carp was most original, however, in his approach to seminary studies. When he entered school, he knew more than half of the material taught in his form. Studying was easy for him. The only exception was the *Rudiments,* which he had to memorize word for word, and which made him just as miserable as a certain ancient orator who would stuff his mouth with pebbles in order to perfect the art of eloquence, but even here Carp got by: he quite zealously stuffed his mouth with gravel from the badly gnawed *Rudiments.*[8] In other subjects he was at the head of his form, and he did not want to lose his prominent position because of one course. His classmates needed a whole study period to prepare what he did in a half-hour. On the other hand, this same ability damaged his seminary career later on. Studying in this way for two years, Carp had a lot of free time, and he got used to relaxing and doing nothing. When he passed to the next form, he found the work more demanding, for it was precisely the kind of seminary work that required those particular, special, indigenously seminarian abilities his classmates had developed during the two years Carp had wasted: but Carp still wanted to relax as before. The *grinds* soon overtook him, he fell lower and lower, and the day finally came when the register was defiled by Carp's zero. Whippings began. Carp thought: "Well, go ahead and whip me, you'll stop, you'll get tired!" He beat a relentless path to Kamchatka and, in spite of birch rods, he reached his destination. Here his laziness reached enormous proportions. During the first year he would at least bring books to class; in the second year he gave that up too; it was, in his opinion, a bad habit. His trunk contained an ugly mess of grammars, primers, and chrestomathies that he had torn to shreds; writing paper was used for scribbling, his pens were turned into whistles and blowguns, ammunition came from potatoes, turnips, and spitballs, his penknife was used to deface desks and for whittling. In the beginning Carp would go to his auditor every morning in order to record his learned zero; later, to make things easier, he would take a zero for the whole week; but he finally grew weary of this, too, and he told his auditor: *"Give me a permanent zero!"* Carp thus quite decisively rejected all seminary schooling, both sacred and profane. From time to time he became vaguely aware of the need to study and he picked up a book, but the book would drop from his hands. There was a time when Carp's cousin, a graduate of the seminary, began demanding to see his report card so he could follow his progress; Carp solved this problem, too: he forged a second report card, and he would send the document, with excellent grades next to his name, to his cousin who would then send him gifts in return. In the beginning Carp was lazy because, to tell the truth, he enjoyed being lazy, but later the point was reached where his *permanent zero* became a conscious principle. The teacher Krasnov turned his attention to him and made him study after class in his apartment; Carp could not hold out against Krasnov's system, and he began cramming his lessons, but after he had been coerced into second place in his form, his seminarian *permanent zero* became ingrained once and for all. He hated the education that was beaten into him, and it settled in his head like an uninvited guest; in essence, therefore, he continued to reject his education, the only difference being that earlier he did not understand what he was rejecting; now, having learned a lesson, he knew that this lesson, these pages, these words were precisely what he did not need. He then began examining and studying each lesson as if his bitterest enemy were trying to control his brain against his will, and gradually, with each new day, he discovered a great deal of nonsense and ugliness in his textbooks; this developed his ability to analyze and criticize, and later, while smartly reciting his lessons, he thought to himself: "Good Lord, what rubbish!" After long personal investigations Carp became completely convinced that a seminary education could ruin a human being if it was approached in a different way, and that only his method of treating it as something grotesque could possibly allow him to develop his intellectual abilities, his analytical powers, his wit, and even his knowledge of life without infecting him with nonsense. And our teachers in their divine wisdom never guessed that many good students approached their textbooks as a psychiatrist approaches the melancholy phenomenon of insanity. This explains the strange circumstance whereby so many capable and gifted people come out of the seminary in spite of the fact that they have absorbed an education that is the laughingstock of all educated people. The usual question is: how did they survive without being ruined, driven crazy, or made stupid? The answer is very simple: insofar as their education was concerned, a zero was deeply rooted in their soul. Long live the seminarian's "permanent zero!" It is a seminarian's salvation. And so, a zero, a zero forever, a zero forever and ever! Amen, which means: verily, or so be it!

This has been a more or less detailed account of what the seminary did to Carp. His attitude toward the administration was expressed in a constant timorousness, a sign of integrity that grew out of an awareness of his hatred for superiors; his attitude toward education was expressed by a permanent zero; among his classmates, with the exception of his last three years in the seminary, he found no sympathy for that side of his life which was most precious to him, and which comprised the main theme of his seminary existence, that is, he found no sympathy for his attachment to his home, and only fools were his intimate friends.

It was this theme that was the chief cause of the adventures and actions that we wish to describe below, and which took place during Carp's fourth year at the seminary.

The air of the third form is filled with strange melodies and voices.

"Brothers, do not rend your clothes, take thread and mend the holes," someone reads as if intoning the "Apostle."

"Cut it out," his neighbors tell him.

"Martha, Martha, are you anxious and troubled about many things?" the reader continues.

"Will you shut up, you bastard?"

"Sorrows and sickness have departed."

"Listen, pig, stop it."

"Tribute to whom tribute is due, honor to whom honor, but is honor so sweet if there's nothing to eat?"

"Fellows, give him a whack!"

"And lo, a voice from heaven, saying: kerboom!" [9]

Suddenly the reader bellowed. He had been given a most unappetizing massage. Today in class they were practicing church singing, and the reader was punished for preventing others from singing.

Noodles tells Barebelly (both are distinguished connoisseurs of church singing): "I'll sing the notes."

"And I," Barebelly replies, "will take the words."

"Begin!"

"Hit it!"

"Mi-re-mi-fa-sol-fa-mi-re," Noodles takes the lead.

"U-u-ni-i-ver-er-sa-al" Barebelly accompanies each of Noodles' notes with a syllable.

To take the notes while another singer simultaneously takes the words, and not make any mistakes, was considered the ultimate in church singing.

Fourteen-year-old Carp approaches the singers. He has a

worried look on his face; depressed and afraid, he is obviously awaiting the teacher.

"Fellows," he began.

"Move along, don't bother us," Barebelly answered.

Noodles was kinder.

"What do you want?" he asked.

"I can't get 'Lord, I cried unto Thee' in the seventh mode. Show me how, Noodles."

"Listen!" And Noodles sang: "I'm sad, so very sad, it's so long since I've seen my lad." This mode is sung in the same way, too. Now you give it a try."

Carp sang: "Lord, I cried unto Thee, hear me, hear me, O Lord."

"The melody's right, but you are way off-key."

"How does it go in the fifth mode?"

Noodles replied by singing: "If someone will treat, we'll have a drink."

"How does it go in the fourth mode?"

"Listen: 'The sheep went: baa, baa, baa.' Sing!"

Carp started "Lord, I cried unto Thee" in the new melody. Returning to the back row in Kamchatka, he kept repeating: "sad, so very sad," "if someone will treat," and "the sheep went baa." In church singing the text of "Lord, I cried into Thee" is sung in eight modes, or melodies; the words remain the same but the melodies change. Seminarians found this very difficult. The aborigines of the seminary thus invented various sayings that made it easy to remember how to sing in this or that mode. But Carp was not gifted with a musical ear, and for this reason he had been kicked out of the seminary choir long ago. In a few minutes he mixed up the melodies. Carp glanced at Noodles and Barebelly, wondering if he should approach them again, but, with a wave of his hand, he dropped the idea. "I wouldn't understand it anyway," he concluded, and sadly propped his head on his palms.

Church singing brought him much sorrow.

This singing is a bizarre phenomenon. It is hardly ever used in the actual liturgy. It consists of various religious songs. The music is strongly funereal and cacophonic; it is so drawn-out that one syllable of the text sometimes has seventy or more beats; and everything is sung in low, doleful, soul-rending, nauseating notes. What philharmonic mind introduced and sanctioned this liturgico-religio-musical monstrosity in the seminary? Church singing was compulsory *for everyone*, but not everyone had a voice or a good ear; there were students who lisped or talked through their nose, who stuttered or whistled when they spoke—what could they do? Nothing: sing like a nightingale and praise the Lord! This liturgical bleating appeared in all its splendor when the teacher ordered a whole form to sing together as a choir, when "singers and supplicants" were composed of good voices and bad, of gifted and ungifted students alike; when this happened, a musical horror filled the air, and a hymn to the Mother of God resembled a chorus from some wild Byzantine opera, a chorus, one would like to say, from the opera, *Shut Your Ears Tighter*. We are only surprised that this so-called plainchant did not split the seminarians' ears. But in describing church songs we should say that they also made the administration sick to its stomach; the administration realized that not everyone could sing and, therefore, since it paid no attention to church singing, ignorance of it was no obstacle to passing from form to form; grades were not even kept for this subject because lessons were sometimes suspended for a whole year. But the direction of seminary education depended upon the diocesan suprintendent, and school officials had to conform to his tastes; in the period we are describing the superintendent loved all kinds of *plainchanting;* hence, howling voices filled the seminary. Incidentally, the singing teacher was a certain Vsevelod Vasilyevich Razumnikov. By himself he taught church singing to several forms. Razumnikov possessed a good baritone, read music superbly, and played the violin respectably.

We should say a few words about Razumnikov since he was one of the best teachers in the seminary. In the first sketch we mentioned him as being an honest steward in the seminary. He established the post of *commissar,* who was chosen from older students, and his duty was to watch over the quality and quantity of the food. Food supplies were formerly managed by servants, each with several relatives, who had supported them at the expense of the seminarians' nourishment; but as soon as the commissar took over, he immediately exposed how the cook had stolen thirty pounds of meat and two sacks of buckwheat groats, for which the cook was dismissed from the seminary. At least one-third of the food previously stolen by servants was returned to the students.

Moreover, Razumnikov never punished anyone by depriving him of dinner or supper, apparently because he was afraid that someone might suspect him of making offenders go hungry for economic reasons.* He always opposed the

* In the seminary there were sometimes as many as one hundred offenders at the same time. To deprive such a group, one-fifth of the student body, of dinner or supper had obvious economic advantages. Almost all stewards realized this, and they tried to increase the use of hunger as a punishment. And, in fact, such deprivations were an important source of the so-called *surpluses* from which the administra-

pedagogical axiom: *Satur venter non studet libenter.** This was why students liked him.

In addition, he taught "Divine Law" and "Biblical History." And here he was more progressive than his colleagues. He forbade students to bring textbooks to class and to answer from them. Having explained the lesson plainly and clearly, he would make students repeat what he had said right in the classroom. When a student could not answer, he would make someone else explain the lesson to his ignorant classmate; if the second student was bad, too, he called on a third, a fourth, and so on. The whole form studied the lesson at the same time, and there were lively arguments about it. But even after this many students had a poor understanding of the lesson, particularly the weak ones, and Razumnikov wanted everyone without exception to be a good student. To reach this goal he decreed: *"Auditors will answer for the deficiencies of their charges."* Auditors were selected from the best students, they managed to master the lesson during class and, consequently, they were obliged to teach their charges during study periods. To avoid situations where a student would conspire with his auditor and come to class with a zero and say that the auditor did not want to help him, confirmation was required from the brotherhood; otherwise, the student was punished severely, and the auditor was in the right. Such procedures were too progressive for the seminary. Razumnikov eradicated sluggards. But the main virtue of his innovations was that in his class auditors and second-termers lost their power as a matter

---

tion received bonuses. When will teachers learn that a hungry student is just as unfit for studying as a glutton? We do not know. We can only say for certain that stewards of educational institutions will be the last to understand this simple truth.

* A full belly is deaf to learning.

of course and they had to turn from oppressors of their charges into their helpers, from masters into their friends. Razumnikov thus took a first step toward abolishing the vicious power of one classmate over another. He did not abolish punishments, and he even was very strict; nevertheless, such a teacher was rarely found in the seminary, particularly at this time when rank imbecility and swinishness reigned not only in the seminary but in other educational institutions as well.

Razumnikov had but one sin on his conscience: church singing. Granted, he left stutterers and monotones alone, but he held the pernicious conviction that anyone with any sort of voice could not fail to master the art of singing if he made an effort. Carp suffered more than anyone else at his hands, all the more since Razumnikov had an unusual disciplinary system: he would notice which punishment made the strongest impression on a student. He realized that for Carp nothing could be worse than being forbidden to go home. Despite the fact that Carp's expulsion from the choir proved he had no talent, Razumnikov would not listen to reason.

The singing teacher entered the classroom, joined the students in singing "Heavenly King," and he then turned directly to Carp:

"Sing it in the seventh mode."

Carp screeched.

The teacher told Noodles: "Show him how."

Noodles burst into song.

"Repeat it," Carp was told.

Carp screeched.

"Don't go home this week."

"Vsevolod Vasilevich, I haven't been home for three weeks."

"Now it'll be four."

"Forgive me . . ."

"I'll tell you this" the teacher answered in a firm, incontestable voice, "if you don't learn to sing, I'll keep you here over Easter."

The teacher walked away from him.

Carp turned pale and his whole body shook. Unlucky Carp! His remarkably wide throat, which nature had bestowed upon him, was the eternal source of his misfortunes. Even at home he had been punished for yelling so ferociously at a priest's daughter, who was teasing him, that his voice could be heard on the other side of the river. In the seminary he was christened Carp at the moment when, on the choirmaster's order, he let out a note that brought on convulsions in his listeners. Later his voice developed into a prodigious, deep bass; once again he was selected for the choir, and the choirmaster known as *Capella* (he was also known as *His Editorship, The Edifice,* and *Food Shop*) would use him as a breaching device, as the choir's battering-ram: when the moment came for a powerful note, the choirmaster would wink and Carp would scream, and he was ordered to keep silent on the soft notes—Carp found this insulting. Once Carp was exercising his voice in a room next to the seminary steward; since he almost deafened him with his thundering notes, the steward grabbed Carp by the collar, dragged him to the rector, and only out of kindness did he pardon him. The inspector hated him, saying that a man who could roar like a lion must have a bestial character: he was probably thinking about himself since he had an enormous bass voice that was incomparably stronger than Carp's, and he was a real brute by nature, which earned him not a piscine nickname like Carp, but a bestial one, *The Bear.* Even after he finished school, Carp, having downed a glass or two, let loose such a roulade in the street that a policeman had to admonish him that such roulades were definite violations of the public peace and quiet. One of the worst misfortunes caused by his voice visited him now. "With such an alto," Razumnikov thought, "it is impossible not to learn to sing." To be detained over Easter was a profound misfortune for Carp, and it drove him into many disgraceful adventures. . . .

He was crying quietly because of Razumnikov's words.

One person's sorrow is another's joy. The day of Razumnikov's arrival at the school was a day of triumph and good fortune for Noodles. Noodles was an eccentric fellow, crazy and kind. He had an ashen face with wide cheekbones, a head practically implanted in his shoulders, an unnaturally protuberant chest, and short legs that supported the rest of his torso; all this gave him an extremely bizarre appearance, in turn pitiful and ridiculous. An enigmatic, continually changing inner light shone on his face: it could be serious, even gloomy, but suddenly Noodles would blush for no reason and then burst out laughing, and all this would happen quickly and imperceptibly. Nevertheless, he was no fool. You see in his face a model of seminarian bashfulness which was particularly strong because of his unfortunate ugliness. If it had not been for this bashfulness, he probably would not have been sitting in Kamchatka. . . . Such was Noodles. But he became a completely different person when he sang something: he had talent. He had a rather pleasant voice and possessed a sensitive ear for music. His constant, dearest dream was to have his own violin and learn to play it, but the dream remained only a dream: he is now a cowherd at some monastery and, it is said, plays the horn superbly. . . .

Carp walked up to Noodles.

"What do you want?" Noodles said, cowering, shrugging his shoulders, and sticking out his strange face.

"Teach me how to sing."

Don't feed Noodles honey, just give him a song book.

"Let's go. First you have to learn the notes."

They made for Kamchatka and began singing "do, re, mi, fa."

"That's wrong: you want one pitch higher!"

Carp attempts to sing in the higher pitch.

"Too high, now you have to sing lower!"

Carp tries again.

They practiced church singing for a long time. Both were covered with sweat.

But then Noodles shuddered, crouched, straightened up, first frowned and then suddenly stuck a fico right under Carp's nose.

"What's that?"

"A fico!"

Then Noodles began laughing.

"What's wrong with you?"

"I won't teach you . . ."

"Please . . . Noodles . . ."

"You'll never get it."

Noodles ran away.

Carp fell into a rage. He bit his nails and, blinking his eyes, tried to hold back an angry, salty tear that rolled down his cheek.

"If that's how it is, then to hell with everything!"

He threw his song book on the floor.

"Damned school," he muttered.

Carp began misbehaving. If it were not for the damned punishments, Carp would have spent the time from Wednesday to Sunday resting peacefully on his laurels, but now he was irritated, and his life went awry.

Poor Katka, one of his favorite fools, came up to him.

"Do you have a piece of bread?"

"Would you like some of this?"

Carp offered hungry Katka a tightly clenched fico. Katka walked sadly away. . .

Carp went into the courtyard to amuse himself.

"Carpers, big eyes!" *Talyanets* greeted him; Talyanets was a boorish, bow-legged second-termer in the second form.

"Crooked legs, poker pegs!" Carp replied.

Talyanets began pestering him.

"On crooked legs it's five versts longer!" Carp answered, throwing a mudball at him, and returned to his classroom.

Another fool, *Shivers*, came up to him.

"Carpy," he said affectionately.

"What do you want, you brainless animal?"

"Carpy . . ."

"Go away, numskull!"

The numskull also walked sadly away from him.

Carp became obstinate and unfair. He sensed this, and his conscience began to trouble him. . . .

"Damn it, I feel miserable," he said in explaining his attacks of conscience.

Carp went to the fourth form, grabbed the door knocker, and began banging it; students in the lower forms did not have the privilege of entering the fourth form, and this was how they summoned students there. A student came out.

"Who do you want?"

"Tavlya."

"Sure."

Tavlya came out.

"What do you want?"

"I need a loan."

"How much?"

"Five kopecks."

"Seven by Sunday."

"No, not this Sunday, the next one. I can't leave. Where could I get it?"

"Then it'll be ten."

Carp thought for a moment.

"Alright," he said, waving his hand.

Tavlya counted out five kopecks. . . .

Carp went to the confectionery, ate three kopecks worth of rusks, and spent two on *sbiten*. The refreshment did not cheer him up. It only reminded him of tea and coffee at home. Carp became homesick.

"My God," he said, "will they really keep me here over Easter? I'll go and ask Noodles if he'll teach me again. No, to hell with them! . . . I can't learn . . ."

After this Carp started a fight over something, and even though he used his teeth, nails, and knees as usual, he still was beaten up.

Detention at school was the worst punishment Carp could receive. And even the decent seminary teacher Razumnikov did not realize that such punishments are vile, unjust, and pernicious. When teachers punish a human being by forbidding him to set foot in his home, they do not understand and do not want to understand the consequences: they instill boredom, depression, and apathy, they move him to do all kinds of outrageous things, they make him thoroughly disgusted with the schooling or moral principles in whose name he is penalized and put to shame, they elicit a hypocritical observance of the rules and a passion for breaking them. Do such results contribute to a sound education? Moreover, are the mother and father guilty of anything when, by order of a teacher, they do not see their son at home on a holiday, often a favorite son, often an only son? Why are brothers and sisters deprived of a brother's visit? Why are they punished by the teachers? In many families Sunday is the only free day they have—why is it darkened by the absence of a son or a brother? No one has the right to ruin someone else's holiday, it is unfair, it is unjust. And do a father and mother, if they love their son, have less influence over him than a callous teacher? Many teachers think so. There was, for example, a seminary inspector, the blockhead we called *The Bear*, who considered it a crime for a student to like his home; he reasoned that if a student wants to go home, he does not want to be in school, therefore he hates the education and morality dispensed there. It's a wonder that these celibate, childless monks did not punish children for loving their parents!

But you will never get through to such teachers by talking sense. Leave them be. Let's see, instead, what came over Carp when he thought disconsolately that he would not be allowed to go home over Easter. . . .

The arithmetic teacher in Carp's form was Pavel Alekseyevich Livanov; to be precise, there is not one Livanov but two or, if you will, Livanov is one person, but known in two *natures:* Livanov drunk and Livanov sober.[10]

The third session, which was after dinner, was devoted to arithmetic. . . . *Sentries* are standing at the entrance of the room, watching for Livanov. He enters the school gates . . .

"How's he look?" one of the sentries asks.

"He's swinging his arms, so . . ."

"That doesn't mean a thing."

"Don't you see him asking the gatekeeper for some snuff?"

"That's right. He's drunk as David's sow."

The sentries run into the room and rapturously announce: "Fellows, Livanov is in his drunken nature. . . ."

The form comes alive, books are hidden in desks. The room is full of laughter and noise. An overager known as *Cannon* puts on his fur-lined coat inside out. He stations himself by the door through which Livanov must pass. Livanov enters. Cannon rushes at him. . . .

"Lord, Thy will be done," Livanov says, stepping backward and crossing himself.

Cannon somersaults under a desk.

"We'll get to the bottom of this," Livanov says, going to his desk.

The classroom is noisy.

"Gentlemen," Livanov begins hesitantly.

"We are not gentlemen, not at all!" the students shout back.

Livanov thought for a moment and, gathering his thoughts, tried a new approach.

"Fellows . . ."

"We are not fellows!"

Livanov is taken aback.

"What?" he asks sternly.

"We are not gentlemen and we are not fellows."

"Right, that's right . . . I'll think it over. . . ."

"Think faster."

"Students," Livanov says.

"We are not students."

"What? Not students? Who are you? Ah! I know who you are."

"Who, Pavel Alekseyevich, who?"

"Who? Here's who: you are scamps!"

This scene is accompanied by the seminarians' constant laughter. Livanov becomes drunker and drunker. . . .

"Dear children," Livanov begins.

"Ha-ha-ha!" resounds the classroom.

"Dear children," Livanov continues. "I . . . I'm getting married . . . yes . . . I have a bride. . . ."

"Who? Who is she?"

"Oh, you imps! So that's what you want: I should tell you who it is. Do you want something else?"

Livanov shows them a fico.

"Eat it yourself!"

"No, you eat it!" he answered angrily.

Students in several rows pointed rather outrageous ficos at him. Inspired by their example, one student after another pointed a fico at their teacher. More than one hundred seminarian ficos were directed towards him.

"Devils! . . . Quiet! . . . Attention! . . . Obey your superior!"

"Lads, thumb your noses!" *Clown* commanded and, putting the thumb of one hand against his nose and locking the thumb of his other to his little finger, he thumbed his nose at the teacher. His classmates followed Clown's example.

At first the teacher was dumbfounded, then he became pensive, and, finally, he sadly lowered his head. He sat for a long time, for such a long time that the students stopped making ficos and thumbing their noses. . . .

"Friends," the teacher said, coming to his senses.

Gentlemen, fellows, students, scamps, dear children, imps, devils, and friends burst out laughing.

His face was covered with a drunken sadness. His eyes were moist. . . .

"Listen, listen! . . . Quiet!" the students said.

The room grew still.

"I am unhappy, fellows . . . I'm getting married . . . No, that's not right: I have a bride . . . that's not right either: I was refused . . . No, I wasn't . . . Yes, I was. . . . Oh, devils! . . . Oh, dogs! . . . Don't laugh!"

The students, of course, were laughing. A drunken tear moistened Livanov's drunken face. He began to cry. . . .

"Dear boys," he began, "no one will marry me, no one . . ."

Livanov began to sob.

"I have an ugly mug," he said, "a filthy mug. People toss such mugs out on the street. Spit at me, fellows. I'm rotten, fellows . . ."

"Rotten, rotten, rotten," echoed the seminarians.

"Yes," their teacher answered, "yes, yes, yes. . . . Spit at me . . . right in my mug."

Students begin spitting in his direction.

"I deserve it. . . . Thanks, fellows," Livanov says through his sobs.

Livanov had a face, not a mug, and it was, moreover, rather handsome; the girl he had meant to court never thought of rejecting him, on the contrary, he himself dropped her.

When drunk, Livanov feigned troubles he had never experienced. If an outsider had seen him, he would have felt sorry for Livanov, but seminarians thought of him as their *superior,* and they never missed a chance to harry him.

"Fellows," he continued, "I am departing to my Lord and my God . . . I shall enter . . ."

"Fellows, let's give him a massage!" Cannon shouted.

"What's that?" Livanov asked.

"A massage . . ."

"What is a massage?"

"I'll show you right now," Cannon answered, getting up from his seat.

"Don't do it! . . . I know what it is. . . . Be seated, pig. . . . I'll kill you! . . . Oh, you rascals! Making fun of the teacher! . . . is that it?" Livanov said, coming to his senses. "I'll give you all a flogging. . . . Birches!" he shouted, completely recovered. . . .

The room was silent.

"Birches!"

"I'll bring them immediately," the whip answered.

"Hurry up! . . Scoundrels, I'll give it to you! . . ."

Livanov no longer seemed drunk. "What the hell," thought the seminarians, "has he changed into his other nature?" This reflex of his intoxicated condition was only momentary, and afterwards the vodka had an even stronger effect; when the whip returned to the classroom, he saw that Livanov was completely out of his senses. Gritting his teeth and placing his fist on the table, Livanov stared wild-eyed at the students. . . .

"Birches," he said, for he had not forgotten his wish.

"What, Pavel Alekseich?" the whip answered, realizing how he should conduct himself.

"Birches . . ."

"All men are descended from Adam," the whip told him.

"Right," replied Livanov, again befuddled, "but the bir . . ."

"Exceedingly good, that is, pure, beautiful and safe."

183

"I don't understand," Livanov said, staring at the whip. "I was born in fifty-eleven, more or less, by the Kazan Cathedral."

"Honest to God, I don't understand." Livanov said resolutely.

It's easy to understand. It's written in the Book of Jeremiah."

"Where?"

"Under the ninth piling."

"I still don't understand."

"It's very simple: hence it turns out that the numerator multiplied by the denominator produces mortal sin."

"You say: sin?"

"Mortal sin."

"I don't understand a thing."

"Every breath praises . . ." [11]

"Praises what? . . . Pig! . . . There's no direct object in your sentence! . . . You devil. . . . What question indicates the accusative case?"

"The question 'whom or what' "

"So whom does it praise? What does it praise? Answer, you devil!"

"It praises the devil."

Livanov glanced angrily at him. . . .

"Are you serious?" he asked.

"I'll make thee the sign of the cross."

The student crossed himself.

"Did you say 'thee?' "

"I, thee, to me, by me, about everyone. . . ."

"Get out! I'll kill you!" answered the enraged Livanov, "I'm begging you, get out! I can't answer for myself when I'm drunk. . . ."

"He's gone," a student said.

"He is? What do I care about him? You get out! . . . Go to hell, you pig," the drunken teacher said, pounding his fist on the table. "You don't want to go? Then I'll go . . . I'm drunk . . . I'll go. . . ."

Saying this, the teacher suddenly stood up and walked toward the door. He was followed by laughter, shouts, shrieks, and yelps.

"None of this matters," he said, "in life nothing matters." And he walked out on the stairs.

As soon as Livanov reached the first step, the very whip who had been tracking him grabbed his leg. The drunken teacher flew headfirst down the stairs. He was lucky not to break his ribs.

"I tripped, damn it," the bedraggled teacher said, getting to his feet at the bottom of the stairs.

He was joined by the whip who had grabbed his leg.

"Did you get dirty?" he asked, "Allow me to brush you off."

"No need, my friend, no need at all. . . . Nothing matters. . . ."

The teacher finally went home.

This is what Pavel Alekseyevich Livanov was like when he was in his drunken nature. . . .

The scene we have described took place on Thursday. On Saturday Livanov came to class in his sober nature. The students behaved differently, and so did Livanov; they behaved decently, that is to say, decently in seminarian fashion. It was dangerous to joke with Livanov when his nature changed from drunk to sober. Livanov was not a bad man, generally, although he was no better than his colleagues as a teacher; on the other hand, at least he did not beat his students unconscious. . . . Lobov, Dolbezhin, and the Old Man represented the terrorist element among seminary teachers, Krasnov and Razumnikov represented the progressive element, and Livanov was a sort of mixture of both: he was sometimes as strict as Lobov, and sometimes inexplicably kind. In any event, no one liked to joke with Livanov when he was in his sober nature.

Carp did not appear on stage when Livanov was drunk, but today, when it was dangerous to joke with Livanov, he decided to cause trouble.

Although Carp was sitting in Kamchatka and had announced a "permanent zero" to his auditor, he was still a rather inquisitive fish. Here is an example. On one occasion Carp was passing time by tearing up Kuminsky's *Arithmetic;* he already had reached the section on division. Here his evildoings suddenly came to a halt. "Division?" he thought, "I can do division. . . . What comes after that? Concrete numbers. . . . What's that? First I'll find out, then I'll tear it up." With this idea in mind he began reading Kuminsky and mastered concrete numbers on his own. "Fractions are next, what are they?" he asked. He mastered fractions, too. He did all this in three sittings. Thus, if a person wants to study, he can get along without birches. "What's next? Decimals. I don't want to read it. . . . Enough." And he then tore Kuminsky to shreds. The day's assignment was "the reduction of fractions to a common denominator," and, although Carp had a zero in the register, he still knew the lesson, having prepared it without any urging or coercion long beforehand.

The teacher summoned *Poleax* to the board. Poleax, despite being an auditor, got mixed up.

"Fool," Livanov told him.

"He is a fool," Carp agreed from Kamchatka

"Who said that?" Livanov asked angrily. Carp's remark seemed insolent to him.

"I did," Carp answered. "Good heavens, Pavel Alekseyevich, he doesn't know how to find a common denominator: isn't he a fool?"

"You pig!" Livanov shouted.

"Good heavens, Pavel Alekseyevich. I'm in Kamchatka so I must be as dumb as they come, but I still know how to reduce denominators!"

"If you don't perform a 'reduction' for me, I'll flog you."

"Go ahead."

"To the board!"

Carp got up and answered perfectly.

"Well, didn't I tell the truth that he's a fool?" Carp said, pointing at Poleax. "Even I know how to do it."

Livanov walked up to Carp and Poleax.

"Give me the chalk," he said to Carp.

"Certainly . . ."

Taking the chalk in his hand, Livanov made a large cross on Poleax's face. Making the cross, he said:

"Lummox once, lummox twice, lummox thrice!"

"Well, he is a fool," Carp agreed.

Carp then returned to Kamchatka. Momentarily diverted by his answer, he soon became bored. He remembered the imminent danger of being detained over Easter. He got angry, and took it out on the slate board that happened to be before him. He took the wooden slats off the sides, and was about to smash them to bits when he put a finger to his forehead and said to himself: "Wait a second, friend, I have a violin here." He made a triangle with three slats, attached the fourth to the top, stretched some cords across it, fashioned a bow from one of the switches he found lying by the stove, and thus produced something resembling a fiddle. . . . This occupied him for a time, but once again his thoughts turn to Easter. "Damn it," he thought, "will they really keep me here over Easter? . . . I'd rather get whipped to pieces!" "They can whip me as much as they want, I don't care." "Is that true?" he reflected, "we'll try it." Carp picked up his fiddle and began drawing his bow, that is, a switch, across it.

Looking for trouble, Carp produced a horrendous screech that resounded throughout the classroom.

"Who did that?" the startled teacher asked.

"I did," Carp answered bravely.

The screech was so out of place and unexpected that the teacher was dumbfounded.

"What's the meaning of this?"

"Nothing."

"Pig . . ."

Carp calmly sat down. The incident astonished the teacher and for that reason alone he did not flog Carp.

"Rubbish," Carp thought in the meantime, "you'll give me a flogging!" And he picked up his fiddle.

This screech was even louder . . .

This time Livanov lost his temper. Infuriated, he rushed toward Carp. Carp knelt down on the edge of his desk.

"I've been punished," he said when Livanov came close to him.

"Kneel, you pig, until the class ends."

"I will."

The teacher could not understand what had gotten into Carp.

Gradually, however, he calmed down.

"No, you'll flog me yet!" Carp thought.

He picked up his fiddle, drew the switch across it, and produced the third and loudest screech of all. . . .

This time Livanov became absolutely enraged. He rushed at Carp with upraised fists.

"I'll kill you, you scoundrel!"

Carp was frightened, seeing the furious teacher, and when Livanov ran up to him, he jumped to his feet, dashed across rows of desks above his classmates' heads, and disappeared through the door.

For a long time the teacher could not regain his composure. The teacher paced about the classroom for a long time. He was in a terrible rage, and at the same time he was astonished. "I can't understand it," he thought, "what got into that scoundrel?" The event's originality separated it from the ordinary run of things, and this circumstance probably explains why Livanov did not report Carp's acts to the inspector. If he had, Carp would have been pulling splinters from his body for a week: in the seminary such insolence as Carp's was severely punished, so severely that afterwards the student had to be carried to the infirmary on a *piece of matting*. Carp was lucky. . . .

Carp was flogged that day, nevertheless. In a rage he went and broke some windows in the school, he was caught, and even though he called the entire host of heaven to bear witness that he had broken the windows accidentally, he was *smacked*, as he expresses it, about fifty times.

Such were the beneficent consequences of Razumnikov's punishment: it only infuriated a human being, but in no way directed him to the path of truth.

Let's see what happened next.

Students going home from the seminary received written passes good from noon Saturday until five o'clock Sunday. On Saturday students went their separate ways, most of them to their homes. The school became deserted.

Carp remained in the seminary.

Students usually spent their free time in their bedrooms. Carp was in *The Boot*. He was unbearably sad. He fell on his bed, put a pillow over his head, and began to sob. We adults take a child's misfortunes very lightly. Can a child experience true suffering? A majority of my readers, of course, will answer: no. And yet some sorrows in childhood are profound and painful, such sorrows as a human being cannot forgive even when he becomes an adult. Lying on his bed, Carp hated everyone. Can a child harbor deep hatreds? He can. If a human being did not learn to hate as a child, he would not be able to hate as an adult. The seminary gave Carp impressive lessons in hatred, anger, and revenge—the seminary is a marvellous training ground for hell!

For a townie who is used to spending holidays at home nothing could be worse than a holiday spent in the seminary.

Carp somehow survived until the vigil service.[12]

Students were divided into two groups: one group went to the church in the monastery, the other remained at the seminary. The first group consisted of students who had clothes that were the least bit decent; the second group consisted of tatterdemalions and ragamuffins whom even the seminary administration was ashamed to allow out in public. Since he had been forbidden to go to town, Carp stayed with the ragamuffins who also had been forbidden to go to church in the monastery.

At six o'clock the bell rang, and the tatterdemalions went to a private vigil service in the so-called *fifth room*, that is, in classroom No. 5. This was a large, long room with rows of desks. A huge icon of Christ sitting on his throne hung on the front wall; one of the monks from the monastery conducted the vigil service before this icon. Students moved the desks to one side, against the wall. A rather large area was created where students could stand. The analogium was placed to the right of the icon, and nearby stood the *mixed fellowship*, an amateur choir consisting of ragamuffins and tatterdemalions who remained in the seminary.

Carp was a very religious boy when he was a child. In addition, a great deal of sorrow was stored up in his heart. As soon as the vigil service began, he fell to his knees and began praying fervently. As often happens in childhood, the substance of his prayer was aimless and vague. He asked nothing from God, he complained of no one; forsaking the world around him, he soared somewhere with all his soul. His prayer was ardent and it was intense. . . . A half-hour passed in this way, and with each bow Carp became more and more impassioned. A very nasty incident, however, suddenly put an end to his bliss.

As Carp was finishing a fervent bow, his neighbor, the fool Teterins, gave him a friendly massage. Carp was startled, and Teterins looked at the palms that had just held Carp's face and saw they were wet.

"You're crying," he said to Carp.

Carp's religious ecstasy was over.

"Are you crying?" Teterins repeated.

Carp became angry, all the more so since he was ashamed of his tears.

"Bonehead," he answered and gave Teterins a kick.

"What were you crying about?" the dull-witted Teterins asked.

"Leave me alone, you ass."

"Tell me!" persisted the good-natured dolt.

"Here you are!"

Carp gave him a very painful kick.

"Mean Carp," the fool paid his compliments. . . .

Thus was Carp's prayerful mood destroyed. [Carp simply became bored. He began studying the religiosity of his fellow worshippers. Students liked their seminary temple better than the monastery's because they could worship only in the temple where they were also flogged. The private service was shorter and gayer: it was abridged and enlivened as much as possible. The sexton, a student, intoned the words so quickly when he read the psalms that all you could hear was the smacking of his tongue and lips, but the sense . . . students did not insist that it make sense. . . . "Leave it be," they used to say. To characterize church services in the seminary we must tell the reader the following anecdote, Two merchants, one very fat, the other so-so, were sitting in a steaming bathhouse and discussing spiritual matters. "No, you tell me," the so-so merchant says, "what is a sexton?" "It's obvious, he's a servant of God," the fat one answered. "That's nonsense." "What is a sexton, you tell me!" "I'll tell you right away," answered the one who had asked the question. "A sexton," he says, "is a pipe through which the voice of God passes, but . . . it doesn't touch it, that's what!" "Right," the fat one agreed, "you hitted the nail right on the head." [13] After such a definition the reader will understand us when we say that seminarians were not celebrants during the vigil service, they were simply pipes. . . . In addition to the sexton's unintelligible reading there was also some grotesque singing. The *mixed fellowship* liked to blast, roar, bellow, and shriek— these terms describe the thunderous singing in the seminary.

Singers and supplicants would stand and egg on those seminarians whose bellows and windpipes are well constructed. When the seminary prays, it roars. . . . But if only this were the end of it: in the Russian land nonsensical reading and aneurismal singing accompany most Orthodox services, but a devout Russian has long grown accustomed to it, and the service still nourishes his religious feeling; no doubt, this long-suffering, devout human being would become indignant if he went to a vigil service in the seminary. We saw that Carp received a massage during the service. Such incidents were very frequent during a vigil service. Worshippers would shove each other, laugh, and spit again and again. . . . Only ragamuffins standing in the front rows behaved decently, but students in the middle were screened by other classmates, and they played cards and dice. Polecat was picking pockets, *Sneezer*, a second-termer, was asleep on his coat, *Pavka*, a townie who had been detained at school because of laziness, was studying a lesson. . . . Massages, pinches, spitballs, and slaps were only *somewhat* less frequent and more restrained in comparison with the usual study hour.

In the seminary all this was called going to church. . . .

But we cannot hold back our angry thoughts. And we will not hold them back. We will speak our mind—fortunately, times are such that one *may* speak out and *must* speak out. . . .

Seminarians have their own kind of religiosity. In the seminary you will always find a mixture of wild fanaticism and complete personal indifference to religion. The fanaticism of seminarians, like every fanaticism, contains not a drop, shadow or hint of that feeling of Christian love which forgives, reconciles, and equalizes everything. A fanatical seminarian considers Catholics, and especially Lutherans, to be such villains that for them fires have been stoked and hooks forged in hell from time immemorial. In addition, every seminary fanatic is invariably something of an ignoramus, as are all fanatics. Ask him the difference between Catholic and Orthodox, Orthodox and Lutheran, and he will spout more nonsense than any peasant woman from the most out-of-the-way village, and yet, he will consider it his duty, indeed his calling, to hate Catholics and Protestants. But such students are to be pitied, to be pitied: if you prepare their religious attitude for dissection, if you remove the sheet that adorns its essential nature and conceals it from the non-specialist or the imperceptive observer, if you unravel the scholastic and dialectical snares preventing a bold, accurate analysis of the facts, do you know what you will find in most instances of seminary religiosity? You will find complete, absolute *atheism*, not a conscious atheism, but rather the animal atheism of an uneducated man, the atheism of a cat or dog. They call themselves believers, and they lie: they neither believe in nor rely upon that God to whom woman, children, idealists, and people in misfortune like to turn. And what could develop a religious feeling in them? Certainly not the *sacred* subjects which they memorize while cursing and gritting their teeth! These subjects, covered by their *authors* with muck and buffets, corrupt human beings. Seminary texts are written in such an atrocious language and are paved with such impassable rocks that they can produce, at best, a kind of spiritual whey, but they cannot awaken a religious feeling in a student. Reading a seminary textbook is like biting through a thick rope. But try biting this rope, try memorizing all this seminary nonsense word for word, letter for letter, and at the same time see if you can bring yourself to believe it and turn it into a conviction, to make it part of your "flesh and blood," as one seminary teacher enjoined his students; if you do, I assure you that you will take leave of your senses forever. But the main cause, the real heart of all this, is not the rocky, stoney, thorny content of these courses.[14] Although religion is not disseminated in the seminary with fire and sword, as with the followers of Mohammed, it is disseminated with birches, hungry stomachs, the pulling of hair from the head, punches, and slaps. For example, Lobov would give an order *to elevate* a student *into the clouds* and to put the "Divine Law" right under his nose, and in the meantime he would shout wildly: "Study, study the lesson right now!" We believe that such actions on the part of the seminary administration gradually and imperceptibly, but nevertheless quite radically, turn students into complete athcists.

When children enter adolescence, only idiots remain stubborn fanatics, and all they take from the seminary is a fear of the devil and hell, and a hatred for infidels and scholars, but they do not receive from the seminary that love for man preached by Christ, those feelings and principles that today are called humanitarian, because the seminary is always a hotbed of Askochensky's doctrines, its convictions always bear the unfortunate stamp of *Family Talk*, the spittoon of Russian religious literature.[15] But most seminarians, as they grow older, sense that there was something wrong with their schooling, and they became totally indifferent to the faith for which they had been so cruelly whipped for so many years. Most students are shaped in this way; nevertheless, there remains a minority composed of the most intelligent seminarians, the flower of seminary youth. These intelligent seminarians fall into three types. The first type tends to be idealistic, spiritualistic, and mystical, but at the same time it consists of people who are innately honest and decent, of good people. In the course of their independent development they use their own individual minds and experiences to purge the seminary faith flogged into their souls of all its horrors, and they then create a new faith of their own, a human faith which, after donning their cassocks and becoming priests, they preach to their parishes under the name of the Orthodox faith. The people love such priests, and the so-called *nihilists* respect them, because these priests are fine people.

Seminarians with a materialistic bent make up the second type. A time comes when their ideas are in a state of ferment, basic questions arise which demand categorical answers, their convictions began to waver, and then these people, by dint of their own dialectic and guided by observations of life and nature, break the chain of contradictions and doubts seizing their souls and begin reading writers like Feuerbach, for example, whose prohibited book is even dedicated to seminarians in the Russian translation; [16] after this they become profoundly atheistic and abandon their religious vocation consciously, freely, and honestly, considering it dishonorable to preach something they themselves do not understand and for which they are fed at their parishioners' expense. These are fine people, too. At first these seminarians regret that they must renounce eternal life, as their materialism demands, but later they find strength within themselves to live with their renunciation, they achieve peace of mind, and then there is no turning back in the development of a seminarian atheist. They are invariably honest people and, if they do not become sensualists, active people whom everyone values. Having become atheists, they would never think of preaching a violent godlessness. Their definition of atheism itself is completely different from our usual definition of the term. Here is how they summarize their nihilism: "In matters of conscience and basic convictions it is unlawful and pernicious for anyone to forcibly intrude upon another's beliefs; therefore, because I am a man of rational convictions, I will not go out and demolish churches, drown monks, or rip down icons from my friends' walls because in so doing I will not spread my convictions; human beings must be educated, not coerced, I am not the enemy, I am not the tyrant of the conscience of true believers. I do not employ sarcasm, not to mention insults, when I talk with a believer, and I do not joke about things he holds sacred unless he permits it; otherwise, I will not speak with him concerning matters of faith. But, since I do not constrain my fellow man's freedom of conscience, I do not wish mine to be constricted. Can you teach me? If not, move on. Do you want me to teach you? If not, I won't argue, for it's none of my business. Under such conditions we can get along because an honest atheist and an honest deist will always find points of mutual agreement. What is atheism? Godlessness, unbelief, a conspiracy and rebellion against religion? No, it is not that. Atheism is nothing more or less than a certain level of consciousness that any respectable person may adopt without fearing he will turn into a wild beast, and whose business is it if I am on this or that level of consciousness? And if you find this galling, come and instruct me in another line of thought. If, however, you try to coerce me, I will pretend to believe, I will dissemble and do you mischief on the sly, so you'd better leave me alone. That's all!" Some seminarians are like this. Everyone loves and respects them, and an honest priest, having met an atheistic comrade, will gladly shake his hand if he is in fact a decent man. That's how it should be. But the seminary fashions another type of person out of its intelligent students: these are atheists who conceal their unbelief behind priestly cassocks. These gentlemen are repulsive individuals—they are thoroughly permeated with a stinking lie that destroys their honor and all sense of shame. Hoping to hide their own unbelief, these cassock-wearing atheists scream louder than anyone about morality and religion, usually advocating the most extreme and insane intolerance. If these ordained atheists become seminary teachers, look out. Convinced that unbelief is inherent in every human being and nevertheless faced with the necessity of teaching religion, they immediately introduce both Jesuitry and principles of the Turkish faith into their teaching. In their opinion the best guardian angels of the seminary are squealers, informers, tattletales, sycophants, and traitors, and the most effective means of inducing religiosity is to slap, birch, and starve the students. They cannot abide Christ's lesson to his apostles: "In a house where they do not believe you, shake off the dust that is on your feet, and that's that"; [17] they want to inject Turkism into the Christian faith: "We will flog man for his mortal sins and then drag him to heaven by his hair if we have to—and our work is done!" These ordained atheists cultivate their egoism, the source of every atheist's activity, but they defile it and it becomes repulsive whereas the egoism of good atheists is a beautiful principle. They preach raging sermons not because they fear for the eternal damnation of their *fold*, but because they fear for the eternal damnation of their *gold*; before every sermon they feel their pockets to see if there's a hole, and if there is, they mend it with a sermon instead of a patch. These ecclesiastics are the chief lackeys of young ladies and merchants' wives whom the Russian land knows for their perpetual sanctimoniousness and pious prostrations: they fleece these stupid women; moreover, from their number come the most avid thieves and blasphemers in the clergy. Although their capacious pockets contain the money of believing, devout parishioners, it is not often that they would move a finger to help some starving widow in their district—all the more so since their bellies have been stuffed full of currency for a long time. If they get their hands on any authority, they make disgraceful use of it: if they feel they have power, they use it for evil. For example, a writer we know published two very sensible, honest essays on the religious question, and what happened? He received an anonymous letter saying that if he did not stop writing such essays his widowed mother would be evicted from her pensioner's apartment and deprived of her last piece of bread, whereas he, the writer, would be sent to jail. I am certain that an ordained atheist must have written this letter because, when you speak frankly to such a person, he takes up the cudgels against you. These are the sort of gentlemen trained by the seminary! Such gentlemen are despised by honest seminarians who do not believe that they themselves have the right to don a cassock, and by believers within the clergy, its educated element—a good priest will always shake the hand of a good atheist, and he will always turn his back in disgust on a colleague who does not believe in his vocation. That is as it should be. But enough for now. The church service in the seminary brought all these thoughts to mind; it began so reverently for Carp, then it was interrupted by a massage, and it ended with Carp playing odds-even at the close of vespers. . . .]

Carp's rotten holiday in the seminary came to an end.

"Would they really detain me over Easter too?" he thought. He was terrified. He knew what Easter was like in the seminary. It would have been better if Easter did not exist at all on the seminary calendar. Students looked forward impatiently to the holiday, and everyone expected something unusual and extraordinary to happen on that holy day; faces are merry, bright, and kind; classmates are considerate of each other and affectionate; not a single blow is struck in the whole seminary. Choirs go to church after rehearsal, sing resonantly and enthusiastically, gaily exchange paschal kisses, and after the service return to the seminary where they break their fast.[18] This is all quite pleasant, but when the fast-breaking is over, so is the holiday in the seminary. If students had simply been given a day or two off, they would have celebrated in the usual way, but Easter is a special holiday and one should spend it differently. And so the young seminarians scurry from one corner to another in search of their holiday, and they cannot find it. Where is it? It got lost somewhere or, more precisely, it was left at home, on native soil. The young seminarians involuntarily recall Easter Sunday under their own roof, they all sense that this is the wrong way to celebrate it, and Easter evening is unbearably dull; everyone is homesick and listless. To spend a whole week in such a state is very hard. That is why Carp's sentence was an Easter holiday in the seminary and not a whipping: the latter served no useful purpose whatsoever.

Carp, however, vowed he would escape this punishment at any cost. . . . But what will he do?

"I'll run away," entered his mind more and more frequently.

That evening he fell asleep with this happy thought.

"I'll run away," Carp thought again when he woke up the following morning.

Carp was beginning to like the idea, and an incident involving a young runaway finally made up his mind. Here's what happened. A village lad called *Fortunka* was brought to school; barely seven years old, he was homesick for a long time. One night, when seminary life had made him particularly miserable, Fortunka decided to make his escape. He undertook this venture without any money and without knowing where he might find shelter, putting his hope in the words of a popular school song that tells how a poor boy, soaked to the skin and shivering from the cold, was taking a walk one day and thinking: "God feeds the bird in the field and sprinkles the flowers with dew, and he won't abandon me, either." And, in fact, the boy did meet up with an old woman who took him into her home. . . . Although this song was Fortunka's only hope, he nevertheless rose from his bed late one night, pulled on his clothes, tied something in a bundle, and went outside. "It was evening and stars were twinkling," as the aforementioned song has it. Fortunka started to climb over the fence, he sat down under a clear sky, and worried about which way to go. "It's alright: God also feeds the bird in the field." This seminary bird wanted to flap his wings and fly from the fence. . .

"Halt!" Fortunka heard someone's threatening voice. Someone's powerful hand pulled him from the fence and set him on the ground. The soldier *Fetter*, the school baker, stood before Fortunka; he had caught him at the scene of the crime.

"What were you up to?"

"Nothing, honest to God."

"Please come along with me, mate."

"Fetter, forgive me."

"Come along, come along."

The soldier pulled Fortunka after him. He took him into his bakery. We mentioned earlier that this soldier was basically a kind person in spite of his boorish, brutal character.

"What were you planning to do, ah?"

"I just wanted to take a walk . . ."

"You mean you wanted to run away. . . . Why?"

"It's no fun here, Fetter . . ."

"No fun? And will it be fun after the inspector flogs you? And where would a little boy like you go?"

"I'd go home."

"You rascal! How would you get home?"

Still, the soldier liked Fortunka.

"Sit down here instead," he told the boy, "and eat some flapjacks and butter."

These kind words cheered Fortunka, and he began eating the flapjacks he was given. The soldier talked with him about his home, and was as kind as could be.

"Well, you've had a bite, now off to bed with you. And forget about leaving school, I'll catch you."

Fortunka went to his bedroom, and God's little bird fell fast asleep.

But the next day, despite his kindness, Fetter felt obliged to report the attempted desertion. . . . "I'll flog him," the inspector said. But when Fortunka was brought before him and he saw a mere child who was too small even to be whipped, the inspector spared him.

Nevertheless, running away was one of the most serious crimes in the seminary. Therefore, Fortunka's plan, even though it came to nothing, started the school talking.

"They caught a runaway," Kamchatkites were saying.

"What did they do to him?" Carp asked, full of curiosity.

"Nothing."

"Really?"

"The inspector forgave him."

"I'll run away too," Carp's secret plan became more and more fixed, "they won't give me a whipping even if they catch me."

He began discussing runaways with his classmates.

"Are there a lot of runaways?"

"Yes, there are."

"I bet they really get it."

"They sure do."

"Is it true," someone asked, "that our *survivors* hide in a firewood yard?"

"It's true, only keep it to yourself."

"Do you think I'd squeal?"

"You'd better not. I've been their guest."

"How do they live?"

"Very well. The survivors have made themselves a cell in the firewood pile and they hide there."

"What do they eat?"

"They steal. They've been living like that for more than a month. Sometimes they beg alms. . . . Sometimes they come here, to school, and our lads give them some bread. . . .

"We won't betray our own," the listeners answered proudly.

"I'll run away too," Carp thought to himself, and with each passing moment he became more excited. . . .

"And how's our *suitor* getting along?" someone asked about the student mentioned in the previous sketch. "It must be the fifth time he's run away. How many times has he been flogged for running away?"

"Four times, but he doesn't give up. They flog him, he covers eighty versts, and on foot, too. He gets home, his father begins beating him, he runs from his father back to the seminary. He gets a whipping here, and he goes home again: the birches keep driving him back and forth."

"At least the *suitor* wasn't flogged to death," Carp reassured himself, listening avidly to his classmates' conversation, "I'll stay alive too."

"You think the *suitor* is something? No, you take some real runaways: the Danilovs."

"And they're townies besides, aren't they?"

"Right; they forge letters from their parents saying they have to stay home because of illness, the administration doesn't worry, their family knows nothing, and the Danilovs roam about town. Once they roamed about for a whole term."

"Is it true that once they were caught with a gang of thieves?"

"Absolutely. But some other thieves ransomed them from the police. They kept on selling stolen nankeen for a long time, and were making big money. When they ran out of places to rob, they would hire out as laborers."

"That is something! Any news of *Menshinsky?*

"I don't think so. . . . And it's been a long time since he ran away."

"He'll be the slipperiest of them all. Remember how he once stole the inspector's watch chain and attacked him with a penknife? Someday he'll slit his throat. And that's not the only thing he's done: he once tried to knife his father."

"And he gets away with it. All they do is flog him."

"Anyone else would have been given a wolf passport long ago, but he has protectors."

What they said about Menshinsky was true. He was an example of what a brutal education can do to a human being. It turned Menshinsky into a wild animal who would not hesitate to stab a man to death when he was angry. They talked about him for a long time, wondering how his last escape would turn out. The time before, at his father's behest, he received such a beating that he was carried all but lifeless to the infirmary on a *piece of matting*.

The idea of leaving the seminary lodged like a nail in Carp's brain. "Even if they punish me, I still won't get what Menshinsky got: I won't steal anything and I won't attack anyone with a knife. Let them whip me afterwards; as for now, at least I'll have some fun." He began planning his escape. In taking so bold a step he was a little smarter than Fortunka. He wandered about the gates and looked for a way to sneak past them; this was not easy since the gatekeeper kept a sharp eye on seminarians and allowed no one to go through the gates without a pass from the inspector.

"If only I can get out, then I'll go and find the cell in the firewood and join the survivors. If they don't take me in, I'll go somewhere else. It doesn't matter."

These were Carp's thoughts as he stood at the school gates with the firm intention of carrying out his scheme.

Suddenly the school doors opened wide and a cart appeared. A priest followed behind. The cart stopped at the inspector's house, and the priest, too, made his way there. Out of curiosity Carp peeked through the matting covering the cart and involuntarily jumped back. Two terrible eyes glared at him from under the matting. . .

"They've brought Menshinsky!" he shouted.

Menshinsky really was lying in the cart, tied hand and foot. Having fled to his village several versts away, he was discovered by his father during the night, bound with ropes, and sent back to the seminary. They were afraid to transport him untied—he would have run away for sure. . . .

A crowd of students gathered around the cart.

"Menshinsky!" the students repeated.

He only glanced angrily at his classmates; he hated all of them at this moment.

"How did they catch you?"

"Were you tied up all the way?"

"For all forty versts?"

"Go to hell," he answered, and closed his eyes.

The inspector appeared, and the crowd broke up.

A half-hour later students were ordered to assemble in the fifth room. Menshinsky was dragged into the room, tied up, tossed on the floor, and undressed; two servants sat on his shoulders, two on his legs, two stood at his sides with birch rods, and the whipping began.

The famous runaway was given a vicious beating. He took about *three hundred* blows and was carried unconscious to the infirmary on a piece of matting. . . .

This flogging made a strong impression.

"It's terrible," Carp thought, "he's foolish, and so is running away!" "I'd better stay here over Easter."

From then on Carp lost all desire to run away.

"On the other hand, do I have to stay here for Easter? No, I'll break out of the seminary somehow. Tomorrow we have church singing," Carp thought, "and the matter will be settled: do I go home for Easter or don't I."

This is when he became scared. As the ominous day of confinement approached, he felt sicker and sicker. A new kind of feeling joined his hate and homesickness: nothing seemed to matter, and he fell victim to that morose view of the world known as misanthropy. When he tried to amuse himself in some way, nothing came of it. He bought some dice and started playing with them. "What a stupid game!" he said a few minutes later and tossed the dice across the floor. He took a cookie from his pocket and began munching it, but soon the cookie flew toward the stove. He joined his fools, but the fools only infuriated him. Questions began to arise in Carp's mind that no fool could hope to answer. "Why is everything in the world arranged in such a rotten way? Why are people mean? Why is a weak man always crushed and oppressed? What's the reason for all this? They say the devil is the cause of it all, that he led people astray, but who led the devil astray? Once there was a paradise on earth but now everything on earth is rotten. Why is this so? How did it happen?" Fools, of course, were not interested in such questions. Carp scurried from corner to corner and was very upset; finally, he crawled under a desk in his beloved Kamchatka, pulled an overcoat over his wretched head and wept bitter tears. Crying, however, brought him little relief. Gradually, however, he lost consciousness and, exhausted by the day's events, somehow fell asleep. He woke up with a headache, and his first question was about Easter.

Carp thought his grief would drive him mad. But suddenly his face began to brighten, a certain hope crept into his heart, as if he saw a solution to his situation. He was not sure if he should do it or not. But the conflict was quickly resolved.

"I won't die, God willing!" he muttered, and began doing such strange things that a man unfamiliar with the mysteries of seminary life could have thought he had lost his mind.

Evening. Classes were over. Suppertime was near.

Carp went outside, found a large puddle, sat down next to it, and began taking off his boots. Then he began wading through the water in his socks just as if he had actually turned into a fish. After this operation he put his boots on over his wet socks and walked around the courtyard for a long time. Even though the spring ice had melted and the weather was relatively warm, during the evening there still were light frosts in the courtyard. Carp was staking his health; but when his socks dried out, he waded through the puddle again, and once more he repeated his trick. It was all quite absurd. But

Carp did not let up. He deliberately ate nothing at supper even though he could not complain of a poor appetite. After supper he took another walk in his wet socks. When he returned to the bedroom, he soaked his tie in cold water and wrapped it around his neck. Everyone fell asleep, but he kept tossing and turning in bed. When he no longer could keep his eyes open, Carp got up from bed, took his suspenders and used them to tie his leg to the head of the bed, a position in which it was impossible to fall asleep. He refused to fall asleep. Carp was torturing himself of his own free will.

What was the meaning of all this?

"I wonder if I'll get sick?" Carp thought, "They'll take me to the infirmary tomorrow, church singing will go on without me, and I'll be allowed home for Easter. I won't die. Even if they take me home sick, it'll still be better!"

This explains Carp's crazy behavior. . . .

When a seminarian entered the infirmary to avoid trouble, or hid in outhouses, or built a cell in a firewood yard, or fled into the forest or to his home, this was called in the local dialect: to survive.

There were many *survivors* in the infirmary. We saw what Carp did to land there. With the same goal in mind students cultivated rashes and deliberately refused to treat them, they gazed at the sun for a long time to develop night blindness, they rubbed their necks with canvas or stuck pins in them to make them swell, they picked open their noses, they aggravated wounds on their legs, and so forth.

To hell with a seminary that makes students resort to the same means of escape that recruits use to escape being drafted, that is, cutting off fingers and yanking out teeth. Splendid!

The next morning a *guard* took Carp—pale, bedraggled, barely able to stand up—to the seminary infirmary.

Carp paid very dearly for his way of *surviving:* first, he had to risk his health; second, the infirmary was one of the most dreadful places in the seminary.

It was divided into two sections: the *sanitary* section and the *contagious* section.

The *sanitary* section was located in a room beneath the pharmacy; it adjoined the sickrooms. The iron beds in these rooms were furnished with mattresses as solid and hard as stone, and they were infested with swarms of bedbugs and other vermin. The walls of the rooms were fading, stained, moldy, and overgrown with moss; rats and mice had gnawed holes in the floor. The *contagious* section was one huge room across the corridor from the *sanitary* section, and it was even more inviting: it was something like a leprous pit seething with festering sores, scabs, and all sorts of infections. Next to this pit was the kitchen with its putrid, stomach-turning stench and rot. The adjacent waterclosets made matters worse. Patients received very poor care. The air was musty because of poor ventilation, the food was scanty and vile: the *haver meal*, which seminarians nicknamed *braver-meal*, and the two-kopeck rolls, while they rinsed out stomachs, provided little nourishment; the linen was dirty and torn; outer garments were no better; especially remarkable, however, was the so-called *sakkos* (an ancient word meaning tatters, rags, penitential clothing), that is, a coarse, grey robe made from camel's hair; [19] in addition, there was a strict regulation that every patient must wear a dirty nightcap on his head, which made the patients look exactly like beggars and fools. The medicines, it goes without saying, were worthless: cantharides, balsams, mustard, camomille, *oleum ricini,** fish oil, salves for rashes, and various plasters; apparently, there was nothing

* *Oleum ricini* (Lat.), castor oil.

else. Only in extreme cases did they resort to something a little more expensive.

In addition to all this the attendant was a certain Mokeich. He was deaf in his left ear, deaf in his right, and stupid from head to toe, but he did have a good heart. He was firmly convinced that doctors, especially young ones, were always stupider than their attendants. Mokeich liked to boast of his felicitous touch, which probably induced him to trade the pharmacy's scales for drink, and henceforth he always measured everything by hand—he would shake some powder into his palm, say "half an ounce," and sprinkle it into a jar. He usually treated school employees and a few local inhabitants, heaping abuse on his doctor in the process.

Dobrovolin, the seminary doctor in the infirmary, saved the lives of students. If it had not been for him, seminarians would have died like flies. Students who remember him speak of this man with deep respect and love. He had an excellent store of knowledge, he constantly followed the progress of science, and in three years or so he earned himself a tremendous reputation. He was always ready to lend a helping hand; moreover, his kind expression, his tender, earnest voice, and his bedside manner inspired hope in his patient. Poor folk found him ready to help at any time of the day or night: when he visited a poor man's shack, he would bring him medicine, food, and money. Although he had a rich private practice, his kindness knew no bounds and, when he died, Dobrovolin left an inheritance of only *fifteen kopecks*. When newspapers published his obituary, a great many admirers joined together to help his family in their misfortune.

Dobrovolin, a priest's son himself, had a deep love for seminarians. He conducted an active and intense war against the school administration. But despite all his energy he could not change a thing in this wretched nest. The infirmary remained a horrible place.

And yet a seminarian would go to this stinking, filthy, diseased place for the same reason that people in earlier times went to a place of worship, seeking protection and deliverance. A seminarian sought his deliverance in the horrid infirmary. And do you realize that even here a student did not always avoid the evils of the seminary: there were occasions, albeit quite rare, when *sick students were whipped*. It's true.

But Carp endured everything, bore everything lest the administration rob him of Easter at home.

Carp spent Easter at home. He paid dearly for it. . . .

This, gentlemen, is how our young seminarians run away and survive.

1863

The Seminary in Transition

FIFTH SKETCH

Several young seminarians were playing blind man's bluff in the dormitory corridor. One of them, with eyes blindfolded and arms outstretched, was trying to catch his classmates. The players, joking and laughing gaily, tugged at his coat, hid from him in the corners, or quietly tiptoed around him. The boy in the blindfold, nicknamed *Hawk*, ran after the voices. Suddenly everything became quiet and Hawk met an unexpected obstacle in his path, having hit his head against a soft something that felt like a pillow stuffed with fine down. He grabbed this strange object. By all indications he had hold of somebody, but who was it? None of the players was so soft, potbellied, and rotund. Hawk, however, without investigating the matter further, cried out with delight:

"Aha, I've got you, dearie!"

He began examining the round object with his hands because in blind man's bluff you not only have to catch someone, you also have to guess who it is. . . . Suddenly Hawk heard a threatening voice above him:

"It's you I've got, you scoundrel!"

The voice was unfamiliar.

"Who is it?"

"It's me!"

It seemed to Hawk that a wild animal had dug into his hair, and now it was pulling him ferociously around. He quickly tore off the blindfold and stood agape: he saw before him a very fat, rotund, red-faced man whose belly comprised more than two-thirds of his body.

"Father, what do you want?" Hawk asked in amazement.

"Here's what!"

The stranger let go of Hawk's hair and began slapping his cheeks with gray suede gloves. . . .

"Didn't you recognize your superior, you rascal? Didn't you recognize him? Is this how you show respect for authority?"

He continued slapping Hawk with his gloves.

"Caps off!" he told the other students.

They automatically bared their heads.

"To class! . . Get a move on! . . .

The seminarians vanished immediately. The new superintendent had gone to see the inspector.

"A new one, a new one!" rang through the whole school. . . .

The greatest excitement was in the fourth form, the most influential form in the seminary.

"He's already managed to thrash Hawk," students told one another.

"Fat devil!"

"Bald!"

"Rounder than a balloon!"

"Fatter than lard!"

"Softer than wax!"

"Lighter than down!"

"Shinier than crystal!"

"He's a paunch, not a priest!"

The angry seminarians showered him with abuse and ridicule.

"Another devil on our backs!"

"Fellows, didn't I tell you," one seminarian began, "that we'd never see a better superintendent than *Stargazer!*"

"Honest to God, Stargazer was a good man!"

Stargazer was the nickname of the retiring superintendent. We have rarely mentioned him in our sketches. The force restraining the menacing current of seminary life was always embodied in the inspector. And this was actually the case. The superintendent rarely appeared in the classrooms, dormitory, or dining hall; he did not even go out into the courtyard very often, and he tried to leave the premises during school hours. He was something of a myth to seminarians, a superior being who mysteriously directed the fate of the seminary; his personal appearances were limited almost exclusively to examinations, and for the most part he appeared to students in the person of the inspector. Students harbored many preconceptions and superstitions concerning this mysterious power. He was considered an extremely learned astronomer and mathematician. The reason was that Stargazer once had informed his pupils of a lunar eclipse several days before it took place, invited the best students to observe this interesting natural phenomenon with him, and explained it to his companions who, of course, did not understand anything he said; indeed, it was mainly because they understood nothing that they became convinced of the superintendent's enormous erudition.

Subsequently students noticed that the superintendent trained a telescope on the heavens at night and, hidden by a curtain, on classroom windows during the day. . . . "Our superintendent," students said, "is a stargazer," associating that word with erudition beyond the reach of ordinary mortals. The telescope trained on the classrooms made students nervous. Many seriously believed that Stargazer could see everything that happened in class, even through stone walls. "Such telescopes exist," they said. There were even some who thought there were instruments that made it possible to hear who was talking and what he was saying. Of course, liberals in the seminary made fun of devices that could see and hear everything, having outgrown a belief in ghosts, goblins, and devils (there were quite a few of these in the seminary), but nevertheless they, too, believed in Stargazer's infinite erudition and, moreover, they involuntarily fell under the influence of that mysterious fear with which he surrounded himself and which he apparently tried to encourage. He would come to class unexpectedly, and he never failed to baffle students with his extraordinary ways. For example, on one occasion the classroom door opened, servants appeared carrying a blackboard, and on the blackboard was a blank map of Europe, that is, a map without the names of mountains, rivers, cities, and the like, which were indicated by copper pins. The students had never seen anything like it. Then Stargazer himself arrived. He began questioning the best students about the blank map. The students, as they say in the seminary, couldn't make head or tail of it. Stargazer then began explaining the geography of Russia *with annotations*, that is, he told them the notable features of certain mountains, lakes, and places, whereas seminarians were used to memorizing the nomenclature alone; but what amazed them the most was that he knew the name of every town marked by a pin, the name of every river marked by a wavy line, and so on. "How does he remember all this? Why doesn't he make a mistake?" After such performances Stargazer would vanish once again into his mysterious residence for a long time. . . .

Everyone trembled when he came to class. Students cannot

remember an instance when he, administering a punishment himself (a rare event), exceeded ten blows (cruel floggings were the inspector's business), but students were incomparably more afraid of Stargazer than of the inspector. Impenetrable mystery usually accompanied the blows. He would inform the student of his crime even though no one knew about it except the culprit himself, and, in addition, the crime was always a serious one, for which the inspector would have beaten the student until his blood flowed freely; the important thing here, however, was not the physical pain but the very fact that the superintendent himself had administered the whipping. How did he know everything? Seminarians were well aware that he kept a terrible black book (mentioned in the first sketch) in which were recorded all student crimes and upon which were based the evaluations of their conduct, but how did information get into this demonic book which, in turn, clouded Stargazer's face with darkness and gloom? Fools blamed telescopes and listening devices. Simpletons with the least brains asserted that long ago Stargazer had sold his soul to the devil, which enabled him to learn everything from the stars, and they considered him a sorcerer. The brighter students suspected that someone was squealing; but no matter how closely they watched Stargazer, no matter what pastes * they used, they could discover no hint or trace of squealing; like birchings, squealers were the inspector's responsibility.

* A squealer usually brought all the rotten filth of the seminary to the attention of the chief *at night* so as to conceal his despicable service from the brotherhood. When seminarians investigated a squealer, they used, among many other means, *gummose paste* which was always available in the dispensary. The paste is placed on the staircase leading to the chief's apartment and around his door. The next day they inspect students' boots, and if they find the evidence on someone's sole, they usually treat him as a certain squealer.

Everyone was puzzled by this circumstance. Everything tended to surround Stargazer's personality with mystery, obscurity, and, perhaps, even sorcery. He lived alone, quietly and modestly, and women never visited him. During examinations seminarians saw him surrounded by their other superiors, all of whom treated him with deep esteem and also, for the most part, with something akin to fear. . . . There were rumors that the higher authorities respected him and appreciated his work. It was rumored that he had proposed to lift the theological academy into the air and that he no doubt would have succeeded if only he had been given a very large sum of money; that the English had invented a boat that sailed under water, and after things went wrong and they learned of Stargazer's great erudition, they summoned him and the boat did travel under water. Such was Stargazer in the eyes of students.

Stargazer was always enigmatic, mysterious, and his tenure at the seminary ended rather strangely; a potbellied man arrived, thrashed a student, and called himself not superin-tendent but rector—up to this time there had been no rectors in the school. But what was he really like, this man who embodied the supreme and mysterious power of the seminary administration? Was he really an astrologer or alchemist, a sorcerer, or even a demon? Only after completing the course did students learn that Stargazer was actually a very ordinary mortal. He had had a good education, even though he never thought of inventing submarines or listening devices. It seems to us that the mysterious quality of his personality can be explained very easily and completely. During the period under discussion, given the absurd practices that go on over most of Russia, it was difficult and often impossible to be a completely honest and humane public servant. We have explained more than once that education and morality in the seminary were so abnormal that they could not be maintained without brutality. Stargazer, however, was a kind man, and he could not stand the horrors of the seminary; consequently, he isolated himself in his apartment there and left everything to the inspector. Seminarians, of course, could not understand this. The whole secret of his power, therefore, was that Stargazer was not in his proper place, he was a man without a calling, certainly no sorcerer or demon. He tried to have as little contact as possible with the seminary. This is why he rarely appeared in our sketches, while it was always the inspector who decided everything.

But the inspector, Stargazer's colleague, also retired long ago, even earlier than he did. Times changed, seminary mores changed. When the old inspector left, spartan punishments in the school decreased at least by one-half, whipping students *under the bell* was abandoned, students were not forced to hold bricks in upraised hands while kneeling in the courtyard, frequently in the mud; they were not forced to kneel on the edges of desks; victims of vicious whippings were not carried away on a piece of matting; the administration smashed the teeth and broke the ribs of its pupils less frequently, and the seminary itself declined and deteriorated: in the past at least fifty percent of the students were overage, now they made up no more than ten percent. The seminary was progressing in its own way. . . .

1863

Notes

First Sketch. A Winter Evening in the Seminary

1. Nikolay Aleksandrovich Blagoveshchensky (1837–1889) was Pomyalovsky's classmate in the seminary and one of his closest friends. An editor, journalist, and minor novelist during the 1860s and 1870s, he wrote the first biography of Pomyalovsky in 1864, and it remains a basic source of information about his life and work.

2. Pomyalovsky is making ironic use of an Orthodox funeral prayer: "Do Thou, the same Lord, give rest to the soul of thy servant in a place of brightness, a place of repose, whence all sickness, sorrow and sighing have fled away (*The Service Book of the Holy Orthodox-Catholic Apostolic* [*Greco-Roman*] *Church*, translated by Isabel Hapgood [Houghton, Mifflin and Company, 1906], 370). In Russian "a place of verdure" (*v meste zlačnem*) can also mean a place of evil and debauchery, that is, a den of iniquity. The point here is that the seminarians are buried, as it were, in a place where "sickness, sorrow and sighing" have not "fled away."

3. Pomyalovsky may have in mind two edicts of the Holy Synod in his reference to the period of compulsory education and the law of overage. The first edict, promulgated in 1850, abolished an earlier regulation that compelled sons of clergymen

to attend religious schools. The second, in 1851, established limits on the enrollment of religious schools, which were becoming overcrowded.

4. An allusion to Pushkin's poem "The Robbers" (1825).

5. I have translated those nicknames that clearly mean something: Carp, Spitter, Nonsense, Mumbles, Satan, Toadfish, Fir, and so on. I have transliterated the rest, although these, too, deserve some comment. Certain nicknames reflect the seminarians' study of Latin: Supina, Comedo, Azinus, Idol. Others like Vasenda, Mitakha, Sashkets, and Grishkets are playful diminutives of the students' given names. And there are several nicknames, for example, Tavlya and Six-eared Chabrya, that seem peculiar to the seminary. Finally, there is the poor lad called Katka: his nickname is a diminutive of Ekaterina (Catherine).

6. Brotherhood (*tovariščestvo*), as Pomyalovsky uses it, is roughly equivalent to student body, but the Russian term connotes a solidarity among students that the English term lacks.

7. Wolf passports were documents given to expelled students that made it impossible for them to enroll in any other Russian educational institution.

8. A dogmatic (*dogmatik*) is one of the eight short hymns to the Mother of God, each of which expresses a certain dogma about her. Dogmatics are memorized as paradigms to be used in modal singing. "Glory of all the world" (*Vsemirnaja slava*) is the first dogmatic.

9. The seminarians liked to lace their speech with words and phrases which reproduced or imitated the solemn, archaic language known as Church Slavonic in which the Bible and Divine Liturgy were written. One of the main characteristics of Pomyalovsky's style is the clash between the elevated language of the Church and the vulgar colloquialisms of schoolboys. In this case, the last two expressions are from the Theme-song (*Irmos*) of the Seventh Canticle of the Great Canon of Saint Andrew of Crete, a penitential canon read during Lent: "We have sinned, we have

transgressed, we have lied before you, nor have we observed, nor have we done what you have commanded us, but do not condemn us at the end, God of our fathers." The first phrase, "We have tricked him," is the seminarians' own invention, a combination of a colloquial verb meaning "to dupe" and a Church Slavonic suffix.

10. Kamchatka is the traditional Russian schoolboy expression for the back rows of class where sluggards and dunces are seated. Kamchatka itself is a large peninsula on Russia's furthermost Eastern frontier, a favorite place of exile both with the Czarist government and the Soviet regime.

11. A "mode" (*glas*) is, in effect, a chant composed of several distinct melody lines. Each of the eight modes in Orthodox church singing has its own liturgical hymns, and a canon, which are chanted according to the musical structure of the mode. The eight modes comprise the so-called *Oktoikh*, a liturgical cycle lasting eight weeks. The mode changes every week for eight weeks, as do its hymns and canon, and then the cycle begins anew. The *Oktoikh* is an earlier Eastern version of the Gregorian Chant, and was in use as early as the fourth century. It was systematized in the eighth century by Saint John Damascene. The primary musical system of the *Oktoikh* is called the *Obikhod*, which I have translated as church singing.

12. A parody of two well-known Russian verses, Zhukovsky's "Night Watch" (1836) and Lermontov's "Air Ship" (1840).

13. From Pushkin's verse "The Devils" (1830).

14. The beginning of the prayer "Many Years" (*Mnogaja leta*). When it is said for the Czar, it reads: "Unto our most God-fearing Sovereign, the Emperor of All the Russias, grant, O Lord, length of days, a peaceful life, health, salvation and prosperity in all things; as also, conquest and victory over his enemies; and preserve him for many years" (Hapgood, 556). The seminarians' variation turns the prayer into a joke in praise of laziness.

15. "The Apostle" refers to the Acts of the Apostles and the Epistles, a selection from which is read at every service.

16. "By the waters of Babylon," Psalm 136, is sung during matins in the five weeks preceding Lent.

17. A line from Koltsov's verse "The Mower" (1835).

18. Student "whips" punished classmates for minor infractions. Soldiers employed at the school were called upon to flog students for major offenses.

19. The *pfimfa* was used in many seminaries and schools to deal with students like Semyonov, and the same can be said for the other barbarous tortures and tricks that Pomyalovsky describes.

Second Sketch. Seminary Types

1. Peter of Amiens (1050–1115), also known as Peter the Hermit, was a French monk who was a popular preacher during the First Crusade. In 1096 he led thousands of peasants across Europe to Constantinople. His followers, lacking adequate leadership and supplies, plundered the countryside during their journey.

2. Pancakes are one of the traditional Russian dishes during Shrovetide.

3. These words invoke *Sivka-burka,* a magic steed in the popular Russian fairy tale of the same name. A literal translation of the Russian would read: "Stand before me like a leaf before the grass." The phrase is used to mean: come immediately.

4. This is another example of the seminarians' fondness for Biblical-sounding phrases. A similar wording can be found, among other places, in Psalm 34, and in various sections of the Divine Liturgy.

5. *Shiten'* is a hot drink made from fruit, berries, spices, and honey.

6. In this parody of the Divine Liturgy, Aksyutka combines expressions from two hymns sung at Easter. The first is from Canticle IV: "David, the ancestor of our God, danced with leaping before the symbolical Ark of the Covenant. Let us also, the

holy people of God, beholding the fulfillment of the symbol, rejoice in godly wise: for Christ is risen, in that he is almighty." The second is from Canticle V: "When they who were led captive in the bonds of Hell beheld thy loving-kindness infinite, O Christ, they hastened to the light with joyful feet, exalting the Passover Everlasting" (Hapgood, 229). The expression "with joyful feet" has lost its religious coloration and is used now in the sense of doing something joyfully or in a slightly tipsy condition.

7. During the Orthodox funeral service a candle is placed in the hands of the deceased.

8. Barsuk is using an expression from the Easter Canticles: "Let the ungodly perish at the presence of God. But let the righteous rejoice (Hapgood, 234).

9. Students were whipped "under the bell" only for the most serious offenses. The whole school would assemble in the courtyard, a guard would begin slowly and solemnly ringing a bell, the culprits would then be led to the middle of the yard, and the flogging would begin.

10. I. S. Mazepa (1644–1709) was a Ukrainian Cossack leader who, on behalf of Ukrainian independence, betrayed Peter the Great and deserted to Charles XII of Sweden during the Northern War. He was excommunicated by the Church in 1708, and routed by Peter at Poltava in 1709. "Mazepa" became a colloquial term for "traitor."

11. "Heavenly King" (*Carju Nebesnyj*) is said at the beginning of classes in the seminary, and it also begins the Orthodox prayer service (*Moleben*): "O heavenly King, the Comforter, Spirit of Truth, who art in all places and fillest all things; Treasury of good things and Giver of life: come, and take up thine abode in us, and cleanse us from every stain, and save our souls, O Good One" (Hapgood, 559). The seminarians' prayer, it would seem, was not heard.

12. A possible source of the expression "on the clouds" (*na

vozdusjax) is the Glorification (*Veličanie*) in the Matins of the Protection of the Holy Virgin: "We glorify you, most holy Virgin, and we honor your venerable protection, for you were seen on the cloud (*na vozduse*) by Saint Andrew, praying for us." If this is, indeed, the source, then the irony could not be more bitter.

13. The icon is taken from the wall to bless people on solemn occasions. Aksyutka's meaning here is that even if the icon worked a miracle, he still could not study.

14. "Redouble the beating" (*Suguboe raza*) may be a brutal pun on the "Redoubled Litany" (*Sugubaja ektenija*), so called because each response is repeated three times.

15. This prayer is also said during the Orthodox prayer service and sometimes at the completion of a difficult task or project: "Meet is it of a truth to bless thee, O Birth-giver of God, ever blessed, and all undefiled, and Mother of our God. More honorable than the Cherubin, and beyond compare more glorious than the Seraphim, Birth-giver of God, we magnify thee" (Hapgood, 562).

Third Sketch. Suitors from the Seminary

1. Seminarians were served two meals, dinner at noontime and supper in the evening. By implying here that they received only one meal a day, Pomyalovsky may be falsifying for effect.

2. The bride-showing (*smotriny*) was the official meeting between the bride, bridegroom, matchmakers, and families. At this meeting a final decision was made whether or not the boy and girl would marry.

3. Fourteen years, that is, four years in the parish school, four in the district school, and six in the seminary proper.

4. I am not sure what Pomyalovsky has in mind here, but I'll suggest two possibilities. The first and more plausible one can be found in the *Book of Degrees (Stepennaja kniga)* (1563), which

contains an apocryphal story about Igor's marriage to Olga. When they first meet, Olga sees that Igor is lusting after her, and so she says, among other things: "Give up your thoughts; control yourself while you are young, and then madness will not seize you and evil will not touch you; foresake crime and falsehood. If you yourself are tainted by any shameful acts, then how can you punish falsehood, and be a just judge of your people." Igor heeds her advice, leaves her in peace, and later they marry. The less likely source is in the *Primary Chronicle* under the year 945: "In this year Igor's retinue said to him: 'The servants of Sveinald are adorned with weapons and clothes, but we are naked. Go with us, Prince, after tribute, and you will profit and so will we.' " Igor agreed, and met his death during the campaign.

5. Teachers were obliged to keep a day-book in which they recorded a student's academic progress, his behavior, his best subjects, his most frequent offenses, and so on.

6. A *bogatyr'* is the heroic knight of the Russian historical epos known as the *bylina*. The comparison of a knight's head to a beer caldron or barrel occurs frequently in these poems. It also appears in the popular folk tale "Bova Korolevich" which Pomyalovsky mentions later in the sketches.

7. Divine law (*zakon božij*) includes the basic history of the Old and New Testament, Church history, the prayer service, and the short catechism.

8. "Bova," more exactly, "The Tale of Bova Korolevich," was a popular chapbook in the eighteenth and nineteenth centuries. Its origin is a thirteenth-century Carolingian romance about Bueves d'Anston which traveled all over Europe. It was translated into Russian by the beginning of the seventeenth century and thoroughly Russianized to conform to the conventions of Russian folk literature.

9. Pomyalovsky is referring to the chain of command in the school system of the Orthodox Church. The superintendent of the parish school was subordinate to his counterpart in the dis-

trict school, the superintendent of the district school answered to the head of the seminary, and the latter reported to the head of the theological academy.

10. In Pomyalovsky's time a paper ruble, the so-called assignat, was worth approximately one-third of a silver ruble.

11. The seminary referred to here is not the elementary boarding school described in the sketches but rather the seminary proper which boys entered after completing their primary education.

12. Another example of the seminarians' use of Biblical citations, which can be found in Matthew 6 : 26.

13. Pomyalovsky has in mind the chapter "Escape" in Dostoevsky's description of the Siberian penal colony, *Notes from the House of the Dead* (1862). This chapter and "A Winter Evening in the Seminary" appeared in the same issue of Dostoevsky's journal *Time* in May 1862.

14. "Rejoice, O Isaiah" is a short hymn sung during the rite of holy matrimony. Goroblagodatsky's chant is also part of the ceremony, and can be found in Ephesians 5 : 33.

Fourth Sketch. Runaways and Survivors

1. Using words like "baptism" and "anointing," Pomyalovsky turns Carp's flogging into a parody of a Christian ritual.

2. Pomyalovsky and Carp are the same person, hence the author's *very* intimate friendship with Carp.

3. *Ispolatchiki* are three choristers who greet the bishop when he conducts services. Their name derives from the phrase they sing in Greek: *Eis polla, Despota* (For many years, O Master).

4. In his *Lives of the Caesars*, Suetonius tells how Nero castrated the boy Sporus, dressed him like a woman, married him, and treated him as his wife. Pomyalovsky's sense, apparently, is that the choristers were treated as concubines.

5. A reference to a satirical story of the seventeenth century,

"The Tale of Yersh Yershovich." Yersh, or Ruff, asks to spend a little time in Rostov Lake. He settles there, raises a family, takes control of the lake, and begins beating and robbing his neighbors. The other fish eventually bring him to trial, and he is punished. This story has become a popular Russian fairy tale in which the ruff lands in a fisherman's net, and then in the fisherman's stomach.

6. Pomyalovsky's phrase is "black teachers deprived of having children." He is speaking about the Black Clergy, or monks, who were sworn to celibacy, as opposed to the White Clergy, parish priests who were married. The Black Clergy occupied the highest and most influential positions in the Church.

7. Again, the seminary here is not the boarding school, but the seminary proper.

8. *The Rudiments* (*Načatki*) is the partial title of a seminary textbook. Its full title: *The Rudiments of Christian Teaching, or A Short Sacred History and A Short Catechism.*

9. "Brothers, do not rend your clothes. . . ." This is another example of how seminarians would improvise on the Bible and the liturgy for their own amusement. "Martha, Martha . . ." is from Luke 10 : 41. "Tribute to whom tribute is due . . ." is from Romans 13 : 7, although the conclusion is the seminarians' own invention. "And lo, a voice from heaven, saying: kerboom!" is from Matthew 3 : 17, but without "kerboom."

10. The seminarians are mocking a central doctrine of Christianity, namely, that Jesus Christ was one person, but with two natures, divine and human.

11. This is from the Gradual (*Prokimen*), which is said before the Gospel during matins: "Let every breath praise the Lord."

12. Pomyalovsky is describing a *Vigil Service* (*Vsenoščnaja*). The service is held on Saturday evenings and on the eve of great feasts. It consists of vespers, matins, and the first hour. Much of the service is conducted in darkness, with the only light coming from red vigil lamps.

13. This anecdote satirizes the belief that a priest is an instrument of God, through which the Holy Spirit works.

14. An allusion to Christ's parable about seeds falling among rocks and thorns in Matthew 13 : 1–9, Luke 8 : 4–9, and Mark 4 : 1–9.

15. *Family Talk* was a weekly magazine published in Petersburg from 1858 to 1877. Its aim was to teach the Russian people "the rules of morality." Both the magazine and its editor, V. I. Askochensky (1813–1879), were synonymous with a most fanatical obscurantism, bigotry, and reaction.

16. Ludwig Feuerbach's *Essence of Christianity* (1841) had a strong influence on radically-minded young men and women in the 1860s. It became the bible of their atheistic humanism. The folklorist P. N. Rybnikov published a Russian translation of it in London in 1861.

17. Pomyalovsky's variation of a phrase to be found in Luke 9 : 5, Matthew 10 : 14, and Mark 6 : 11.

18. On Easter the Orthodox faithful greet one another by kissing three times on the cheeks.

19. A *sakkos* is also the dalmatic that the bishop wears in place of a chasuble during the Divine Liturgy.